The Daughters of Jim Farrell

The Daughters of Jim Farrell

Sylvia Bambola

Heritage Publishing House

Also by Sylvia Bambola

The Salt Covenants
Rebekah's Treasure
Return to Appleton
Waters of Marah
Tears in a Bottle
Refiner's Fire
A Vessel of Honor

The story and main characters in this novel are fictitious. Any resemblance to actual persons or events is strictly coincidental. However, all historical novels must, of necessity, be based on fact, and I have tried to accurately describe the times and historical events that provide the novel's backdrop. A glossary has been inserted in back to aid the reader in not only separating the historical characters from the fictitious, but to clarify some unfamiliar words.

ACKNOWLEDGMENTS

A big heartfelt thanks to my family and friends who encouraged me even in the difficult times; to my daughter, Gina, especially, for reading and editing the manuscript, and finding all those pesky words that didn't show up in "spell-check".

And last of all to the many authors that provided the historical information I needed in order to write this book, some of which I include below:

- *Anthracite Roots* by Joseph W. Leonard III
- *Growing Up in Coal Country* by Susan Campbell Bartoletti
- *Early Coal Mining in the Anthracite Region* by John Stuart Richards
- *Allan Pinkerton The First Private Eye* by James MacKay
- *Thirty Years a Detective* by Allan Pinkerton
- *A Patriot's History of the United States* by Larry Schweikart and Michael Allen
- *Making Sense of the Molly Maguires* by Kevin Kenny
- *Manners and Morals of Victorian America* by Wayne Erbsen
- *The Essential Handbook of Victorian Entertaining* Adapted by Autumn Stephens
- *What Jane Austen Ate and Charles Dickens Knew* by Daniel Pool

- *AT HOME The American Family 1750-1870* by Elisabeth Donaghy Garrett

I'm also grateful for the vast wealth of information on the internet that often helped clarify things for me. What an amazing information age we live in!

Dedicated to

Lauren and Matthew
I love you more

CHAPTER 1

Pennsylvania, Spring 1873

"Do you want to live with shame all your life?"
Kate Farrell stood rigid in front of the small crackling fire and watched her sisters sink deeper into their damask-covered chairs. She was determined to win the argument this time. "Can't you see? If we don't do this, our name will be tarnished forever."

Virginia looked up from her sewing. "Will you give us no rest, Kate?"

"Do you think it's easy being the eldest and always having to do the hard things? Do you think I like having to push and goad you?" Didn't they understand how much she hated being harsh? Especially here, in their cozy back parlor, their sanctuary, where no boarder ever entered unless invited.

"We've pleaded with you a dozen times to drop this. Why won't you?" Virginia pressed.

"Because it's too important. We need to settle this once and for all." Kate ignored the moth-like embers that landed on the woolen baize near her feet and walked over to where her sisters sat. "Well! What do you say? Will you do it or not?"

Her sisters avoided her gaze; one studied the fire; the other, the sewing on her lap.

"It won't bring Father back," Virginia finally said, placing her mending on top of a small side table. "And Mother has already told you to let it go. Besides, we don't have the money to hire a detective. You've already inquired, remember? Must I remind you that a Pinkerton gets three and a half dollars a day, plus expenses? We just can't afford it."

"That's unworthy of you. You never consider money when it's one of *your* causes." Kate tugged at her bustle, then began pacing. The small heels of her black-laced boots skimmed the floor cloth, nearly snagging a barely discernible lump. "And I won't even ask how much you spent going to Massachusetts last year to picket with Susan What's-her-name." It was low to pretend she didn't remember Susan's last name when that's all Virginia had talked about for months. But Kate was desperate. She needed Virginia on her side. Once she was, Charlotte would surely follow. "You know we can afford to do this if we pool our money."

"Anthony. Her name is Anthony. Susan B. Anthony." Virginia's voice was icy.

"You're behaving like a vigilante, Kate." Charlotte finally removed her gaze from the hearth. "You insult us, bully us, in hopes of forcing us to do this, when even Mother doesn't want you to. You know how I feel, how we both feel. Virginia and I want to get on with our lives while you are only interested in revenge."

"*Get on with your lives?* What kind of lives will they be as long as the world thinks our father is a murderer? Surely you understand this shame will follow us wherever we go. It may not worry you, Charlotte, but I guarantee it troubles that stuffy fiancée of yours."

"You go too far." Charlotte's long slender fingers, which had all the while been lying idly on her lap, now moved in nervous jerks along the upholstered arm of her chair. "I know what you think of Benjamin; that he's unfeeling and shallow, but I assure you he's quite the opposite, and is, in fact, the very portrait of kindness and profundity."

"And his mother? Mrs. Gaylord? Is she such a picture?" Kate snapped.

"I suppose *you* would call one shallow who believes the severest test of a lady is giving a formal dinner party and having to serve bread sliced less than an inch and a half thick." Charlotte picked her thumb. "Mrs. Gaylord claims thin bread is so *plebeian*. But Benjamin is not at all like that. Even you, Kate, would have been impressed with him last night. The perfect gentleman in both dress and manners; never once hesitating to introduce me to his most important guests—the visiting Winthrops and Hancocks. He even made sure to include me in a lengthy conversation with Franklin B. Gowen himself."

"You never did tell us about the party," Virginia said, appearing eager to keep the conversation from falling back into Kate's control.

"We've been so busy this morning with chores, and . . . well, quite frankly I wasn't sure you'd care. Both yours and Kate's interests are so far removed from mine, and sometimes you make me feel silly for liking the things I do, but if you really want me to . . . ." Charlotte paused and looked at Kate.

"Can't you talk about this later?" Kate turned and walked to the corner desk where she picked up a small, black leather notebook.

"Well . . . ." Charlotte's face took on a defiant look. "Virginia wants to know, and I'm just dying to tell someone and so I *shall*. It was oh, so fabulous! The tables, three in all, were covered in long white damask cloths that hung to the floor and shimmered in the candlelight. Oh, they must have taken hours to press! And large Dresden baskets, filled with flowers, sat in the center of each table amid place settings of fine English china and long-stem crystal goblets. And pressed cloth napkins were folded beside each plate. Imagine! A napkin for everyone! And in the room, standing at perfect attention, were two footmen and a butler. I mean *real* footmen and a *real* butler, not like that clumsy groom and gardener snooty Mrs. Roach had serving at her dinner party last month. And the food! How can I describe it?

There was lobster with Dutch sauce, and oyster pate and lamb cutlets and venison and . . . ."

"Stop! Not another word about damask cloths and butlers and oyster pate! If you're such a silly creature, Charlotte, that that's all you care about, then so be it. But I for one am doing this, with or without the two of you. I've saved a few dollars and I'll earn more from my quilt. It would be easier if we pooled our money, but I can do it without you. And I *will*."

A sound, like a mouse's squeak, escaped Charlotte's lips as she dropped her face into her hands and began to sob.

"Oh, honestly, Kate! Now look what you've done. You can be such a brute!"

"I won't apologize, Virginia. We must face facts, even you, Charlotte. The truth is we are lepers. Social lepers. No one in Sweet Air wants anything to do with us. And Benjamin Gaylord might love you, Charlotte. He may even want to marry you still, but that mother of his would be happy to see him break your engagement. Don't think she doesn't talk to him about it either! We can hardly be her idea of a socially acceptable family."

"Don't listen to her, Charlotte. I'm sure Mrs. Gaylord has no such thoughts."

Charlotte dabbed her eyes and said in a near whisper, "I have ten dollars, Kate. I've been saving it for my trousseau, but you can have it."

"You mean you'll undertake this venture with me?" Kate could hardly believe her ears. She was sure Virginia would be the first to cave.

When Charlotte nodded, Virginia threw up her arms. "I hope you're satisfied, Kate. After months of my telling her women should stand up for themselves, you have, in a matter of minutes, reduced her to this!"

"Virginia, it's not that. Truly," Charlotte stammered. "It's just, well it's just . . . ."

"Just what?" Virginia said softly, as she glared at Kate.

"It's just that Mrs. Gaylord wants to take Benjamin to London this May in time for the Derby, and then Ascot. Of course they'll stay through July for cricket, especially the contests between Eton and Harrow, as well as Oxford and Cambridge."

"What does that have to do with anything?" Kate said, trying to stuff her impatience where it wouldn't do any damage. She could always talk to Virginia. Virginia made sense. Virginia talked about things Kate understood and cared about. But Charlotte lived in a different world, or at least wanted to. A world of finery and polite society. A world they had all known a bit about when Father was alive. But things were different now. In order to avoid financial ruin, they had been forced to turn their large, stately home into a boardinghouse; forced to see to the comfort of strangers while ignoring their own. Everything had changed except Charlotte's peculiar logic, a logic that often sounded muddled. "Just take your time and tell us what you mean."

"You know London's social season begins in May. There'll be no end of parties and balls and dinners and breakfasts—fifty or sixty at least!"

"Make sense, dear," Virginia said, now sounding a bit impatient, too.

"Don't you see! All the debutants will be coming out then. The balls, the dinners, the parties are given so they can meet eligible men. And get *married*! And that's just what Mrs. Gaylord is counting on. She's hoping Benjamin will meet someone more suitable, and when he does he'll break our engagement." Charlotte lowered her eyes. "That's what I was told by an unimpeachable source last night. I've tried to convince myself that Benjamin is strong enough to withstand both his mother and temptation, but suppose he . . . . Oh, I think it's horrid of her to try to break us up! I'm still the same person I was before Father died. Doesn't she see that?"

Virginia's lips pursed. "I'll give you the fifteen dollars I've been saving, Kate."

"I . . . I know you wanted it for your newspaper. And I know how long you've been saving. But I think you're making the right decision." Kate suddenly felt guilty. Virginia had been planning to return to Massachusetts in order to learn how to start a liberal weekly here in Sweet Air, a newspaper fashioned after *The Revolution*, a now defunct periodical that Susan Anthony and Elizabeth Stanton once published. She had even hoped that Anthony and Stanton would sponsor her efforts. "I'm . . . sorry. Truly sorry."

"It can wait." Virginia tented her fingers. "We'll do this first. I suppose you're right. We owe it to Father and ourselves. But bear in mind, Kate, even if we get a Pinkerton agent to take our case, there's no guarantee he'll find anything. There's no guarantee he'll be able to clear Father's name."

Kate waved the small leather notebook in the air. "I've scoured Father's notations a dozen times and still can't make sense of them. But I believe the answer lies here and that a Pinkerton is just the one to find it."

"So, it's settled." Charlotte's gaze drifted back to the fire, her beautiful porcelain-like face, glum. "Forgive me, Kate, for being such a goose and giving you so much trouble."

The sight of both sisters so downcast pricked Kate's heart. *Love is patient, love is kind, love doesn't seek its own way,* she heard her mother's voice drone in her head. Oh, why was she always trying to get her way? Why was she so headstrong? Her sisters were right, she was a bully. That would explain why it was so easy for her to overlook their feelings: Charlotte's broken heart and Virginia's dashed dreams. *Oh what a wretch I am.* And was Mother right too? In saying Kate had allowed a root of bitterness to take hold? What did bitterness look like, exactly? Did it look like tall gallows, and the bound and hooded body of her father dangling at the end of a rope? She closed her eyes. Was it so wrong to seek justice?

"I'm sorry about Mrs. Gaylord," Kate said, opening her eyes and looking at Charlotte. "And I'm sorry about your newspaper," she added, turning to Virginia.

Life had been much simpler when Father was alive.

Kate nearly dropped her mixing bowl when the explosion rattled windows and doors and made the whole house groan. She ran from the kitchen, followed by her mother and Virginia, and headed toward the large windows in the front parlor, the "best parlor" Mother called it. The boarders had already abandoned their comfortable chairs and were gathered by the windows that Mother only partially shaded "for cheeriness sake."

"I'll get that for you, Mrs. Clayton," Kate said when she saw the stooped, elderly woman wrestling the shades for a better view.

Mrs. Clayton stepped aside then ran her hand over her neatly secured bun. "Oh dear. Do you think it's the Sherman Colliery? It sounds so near. So . . . terrible."

Kate rolled the canvas as high as possible, revealing a panoramic view of Sweet Air and the distant countryside. From this perch on "their" hill Kate saw a billowing cloud of sooty-looking smoke that made her heart plummet. The last time she saw something this large the William Penn mine had exploded, killing five. Many claimed that Pennsylvania coal country took one anthracite worker a day, through injury or death. But here, in Schuylkill County, home of the most dangerous anthracite mines in the world, she knew the number was often higher. When she opened the window the deafening shriek of the breaker whistle filled the room.

"Is it the Sherman?" Mrs. Clayton repeated.

Kate put her arm around the trembling woman. Only yesterday, Widow Clayton told everyone how her grandson was promoted to fire boss at the Sherman Colliery. "No. The smoke is further west. It's got to be the Mattson."

"I think you're right," Virginia said, wiping her wet hands on a rag. "The *Miner's Journal* has been predicting trouble for weeks, ever since the railroad took over the Mattson. And a few days ago some of their coal cars were derailed and the mine boss got a 'coffin notice'."

"Could just be fire damp," said Colonel Smyth, a retired Union officer who had distinguished himself at Vicksburg. "The miners are always grumbling about the marsh gas at the Mattson."

"Or maybe it's a cave in," said Miss Rodgers, the spinster piano teacher who, some say, was once a famous stage personality. "Aren't most mining accidents caused by falling roofs?"

"It's no cave-in. And not fire damp, either," said Clarence Thumbolt, a retired railroad man. "It's the Mollies. Who else would send a coffin notice? It was a warning there'd be trouble. And no one can conjure up more trouble than that bunch. This is their doing, mark my words."

"If it is, perhaps they have a reason," returned Jasper Wright, the new dentist from Philadelphia who seldom left the boardinghouse before ten to open his office.

"And what would you know about these troublemakers? Being an out-of-towner and all," demanded Thumbolt. "I've been associated with these parts for more than thirty years and could tell you stories that would curl your hair. Why, just a few years back didn't the Mollies assassinate Patrick Burns, foreman of the Silver Creek Colliery? A good man, too. Killed him because he caught them stealing from the company. And two years ago it was poor Morgan Powell. The Mollies killed him just for being a Welshman! You don't want to get on the wrong side of that bunch. Believe me, they could bring down a whole mine if it suited them."

Jasper Wright jutted his chin as he secured one of the small pearl buttons of his gray waistcoat. "Sometimes bad conditions produce bad men, sometimes . . . ."

"Whatever the cause, it's sure to be serious." Mother said, ending the conversation. "Kate, get my ointments and some clean rags. We need to go."

"I'll come, too," Virginia said.

"No, just Kate. Her stomach isn't as queasy as yours. No telling what we'll see. You stay and finish scrubbing the knives with brick dust, then make that sassafras solution for Charlotte." She lowered her voice. "And see that Charlotte washes down *all* of Mrs. Clayton's furniture."

Kate followed Virginia back to the kitchen, relieved that Mother had not asked her to oversee Charlotte, who, as the youngest, often needed monitoring whenever she was asked to do a chore she despised, which encompassed housework in general, and eradicating vermin in particular. But Kate didn't want to go to the colliery either. What would she see? Certainly an army of tearful wives and mothers, and an angry mine boss cursing the injured. That always got her, seeing a mine boss yelling and swearing at the wounded, bleeding men, blaming *them* for the accident. But there was no getting out of it. She couldn't let her mother go alone.

She rummaged through the pantry until she found the large leather pouch containing medicinal herbs for teas and poultices, as well as a generous supply of glycerin and arnica for wounds, and pulled it from the shelf. Then grabbing a handful of clean rags, she stuffed them into the bag. For as long as she could remember, Mother had been going to the mines after an accident. There were no hospitals in the lower anthracite region, and the collieries assumed neither care nor responsibility for their injured or dead. Wounded men, even those losing limbs, were simply put on a plank and carried home. When Kate was younger she never understood why Mother went. Father was a railroad man. But gradually she came to realize Mother's ties to coal country ran deep. She had grown up here, and many friends and relatives had lost their lives in these mines.

"Hurry, Kate!" her mother shouted.

Kate placed the pouch on the table, then removed her apron. Her cotton day dress was frayed around the high square neckline and as faded as a rag. It hung awkwardly, too, since she refused to wear a crinolette while doing housework, pinning back, instead, the outer skirt to form a rather limp imitation of a bustle.

Even so, it was fine for going to the mine. The never ending plumes from the breaker would coat her with coal dust in no time. Miner's wives regularly complained how their laundry, if left too long on the line, would turn black. Coal dust covered everything in the patches. It was one reason Father, along with many affluent people in these parts, chose Sweet Air to build their houses, a place where the prevailing southwesterly winds tended to blow the dust away. So, no, she needn't change her clothes, not for the mine.

But it was the telegraph office that worried her. Would she cause a scandal? She needed to send her telegram to the Pinkerton office in Philadelphia. All together, she and her sisters had thirty dollars. Kate's quilt should bring in another five. Enough for a Pinkerton's train fare from Philadelphia to Pottsville, then a week to investigate. She expected there'd be few expenses with free room and board at their house. But a week? Would it be enough? Could the Pinkerton clear her father in a week? If not, what then? Well . . . there was always the jewelry Father had bought her. Good jewelry that would fetch a good price. She wouldn't mind parting with it for his sake.

Kate draped the strap of the pouch over her shoulder. "Do I look all right?"

"You're worried about how you look? You're not usually vain, Kate, especially in the midst of tragedy."

"I'm sending the telegram today."

"Oh . . . I see." Virginia's eyebrows arched.

"If we're lucky, Mr. Pinkerton will have one of his men here by week's end."

"Have you told Mother?"

"I'll tell her before we get to the telegraph office."

Virginia puckered her lips, "I wouldn't want to be you."

"And I wouldn't want to be you. *You* have to get Charlotte to scrub down Mrs. Clayton's room." With that, Kate scurried out the kitchen, past the milling boarders and toward the front door where her mother stood waiting.

⌒

Charlotte hovered by the stove watching Virginia drop a handful of sassafras bark into a pot of water. "I don't know why I have to be the one to wash down all of Mrs. Clayton's furniture just because she saw one little bug. How do we know she wasn't just seeing things? After all, she's getting on in years and her eyes can't be that good."

"Her eyes are just fine. And you know how fast bedbugs can spread. No decent boardinghouse would remain operational for long if they allowed their rooms to become infested."

Charlotte watched the water turn brown. "Well, I hate bugs! I hate anything that creeps or crawls. Everyone knows that, and still I always get this job. And the smell of that brew! It makes me ill."

"Stop being childish. It has a delightful aroma, and you know it. Almost like licorice. And it will be most effective on Widow Clayton's bugs."

"If she has any." Charlotte folded her arms across her chest. "When I marry I shall never wash another piece of furniture. It will be a most pleasant life, being married to Benjamin and having servants enough to do all these tedious chores."

"I wish Mother didn't go every time there was a mishap," Virginia said, stirring the bark with a wooden spoon. "She always looks so tired when she gets home."

"When I become Mrs. Benjamin Gaylord, I shall see to it that Mother is well cared for. I will insist she come regularly to our house and sit in our garden while I take my oils and fill canvas after canvas with lovely flowers, especially tulips, for they are my favorite. And then at Christmas I will make presents of all my paintings."

"That plume of smoke is *so* large." Virginia removed the pan from the heat. "I don't think I've ever seen one as big. If only women could vote, things would change around here. When I have my newspaper, I'll make women's suffrage a household word."

Charlotte retrieved the bucket from the corner, all the while hoping Virginia would change her mind and wash down Widow Clayton's room herself and give Charlotte a less odious chore, as Virginia sometimes did. But by the time she brought the bucket to the stove and Virginia filled it with the steaming sassafras solution, Charlotte knew there would be no getting out of her chore today.

"The water is *so* hot. I suppose no one would care if I scalded myself as long as I made Widow Clayton happy."

"By the time you gather your supplies and prepare the room with drop-cloths, it should be cool enough."

Without a word, Charlotte picked up the bucket and left, all the while feeling a bit put out that while Mother and Kate were traipsing off to the mine, she was left to chase Widow Clayton's phantom bugs. Well, she and Benjamin were to be married in eight months. Just eight more months and this drudgery would end. These days, this thought was the only thing that made life bearable.

Just tell her and get it over with.

Kate followed her mother along the dirt path. *Tell her, tell her,* Kate's mind nagged as she tried not to breathe in grit and smoke.

People rushed past, kicking up more grit as they headed for the Mattson. The sound of an odd-hour breaker whistle always brought out anxious friends and relatives. Most of those clogging the path were women with small children, but there were a few men, too.

Someone had finally silenced the whistle, but even from this distance, Kate could hear men's panicked voices and coal cars clacking on steel tracks.

When they reached Higgins Patch, Kate saw women holding babies and standing around in worried little circles. If she waited much longer her mother would be pulled in by all this, and she'd lose her chance.

"Mother, we . . . that is, Virginia, Charlotte and I, have decided to hire a Pinkerton to help clear Father's name."

"I know," came the unexpected response. "And before returning home you want to go to Pottsville to send the telegram."

"How . . . did you know?"

"Because I know *you*, Kate." Mrs. Farrell trudged ahead, not breaking her stride. "And I knew you wouldn't let this go."

"I have to clear Father's name or at least try. You understand, don't you? Please don't be angry."

"If it's my blessing you're after, I can't give it. Look around, Kate. Look at these women with their gaunt faces, wondering if their husbands will be coming home tonight. Wondering if the babies they cradle will have a father to see them grow up. And amid theses worries they try hard to make a decent life for their kin, stretching both their pennies and their faith. Can't you see there are better uses of your time and money? God will vindicate us when He wills. So no, I can't give you my blessing. But I'm not angry. I'm not angry because I understand your pain, too."

It was worse than Kate expected. Seven men, all arranged in a line, lay dead beneath dirty tan-colored canvasses. A smoky haze permeated the air, making the scene appear dreamlike. Only the weeping and wailing around her told her it was real. She watched, through burning eyes, as men ran in all directions while the mine boss barked orders. From the chatter around her she was able to piece together what had happened. Someone had used blasting power on both the mound of shoring timber and on the culm bank—the mine's waste dump—causing a fire. While a dozen men fought the flames that raged in the timber mound, seven others concentrated on the nearby bank. Burning fragments of timber had landed on the bank, and as the men tried to remove them, the slag shifted beneath their feet and buried them alive. The Molly Maguires were sure to be blamed. They always were in matters of mine sabotage, just as the laborers or miners were blamed for all mine mishaps.

Her mother was already comforting one of the weeping women. Other women soon gathered.

"Mrs. Farrell, thank you for comin'," said Mary O'Brien, the known leader of the group. And then they all began talking at once.

"Mrs. Farrell, kind of you to bring your bag but it won't do no good."

"Oh what a black day for Higgins Patch!"

"Mrs. Farrell, it was Margaret Duffy who lost her James, God rest his soul."

"And aren't the Carroll brothers lyin' right next to him?"

"Not to mention Jack Kelly and one of the Dooley boys."

"And James O'Shea, and just when poor Colleen was gettin' over losing her son, Thomas."

"But 'tis none sadder than Patrick Doyle—him leavin' four wee ones and a sick pregnant wife. 'Tis sure as sunrise the company's gonna turn them out of their house, forcin' them onto the street by week's end. And what will poor Irene do then?"

Kate watched her mother dispense hugs, and kiss tear streaked cheeks. Mother was well loved in Higgins Patch for the many kindnesses she had shown to its inhabitants over the years. If only Kate could be more like her. Maybe then she could trust God for justice instead of trying to bring it about on her own. A vigilante, that's what Charlotte had called her. *Vigilante.* Such a harsh name, when all Kate wanted was to protect them, protect their futures.

As Mother spoke in soft tones to the newly widowed Margaret Duffy, and as the other women slowly drifted away, Kate's attention was drawn to a group of breaker boys who had gathered nearby to watch the dozen men now trying to put out a fire almost impossible to extinguish. The timber mound was nearly under control, but it was the culm bank that posed the problem. A culm bank could burn for years, polluting not only the air with sulfurous smoke but the ground beneath it for miles around. With Pottsville so near, the Mattson Colliery—now owned by the Philadelphia & Reading Coal & Iron Company—would be pressured into smothering the tip with an eight to ten-foot earthen cap. An added expense no colliery wanted. If such a large sum had to be laid out, an investigation into the Molly Maguires was sure to follow, and that usually stirred up anger in the patches.

From where Kate stood, the breaker boys were barely visible through the smoke. There were four in all, and so young—the littlest looking no more than six. She moved closer. It vexed her that children this young worked at the breaker. It was a dangerous place where boys sat on backless wooden benches, straddling long moving iron chutes while picking slate and rock from the coal passing between their legs. And this for up to twelve hours a day while dust and smoke and steam clogged their lungs, and coal crushing machinery severed limbs. No laws protected these children. The one law regarding age required boys to be twelve before working, but that was inside the mine. Outside, it wasn't unusual to see boys as young as five carrying tin lunch pails.

When Kate got closer she saw that the littlest one, who wore a dirty overcoat, a cloth cap drawn low over his forehead, and laced hobnail boots, had bleeding fingers. And though he seemed as interested in the burning culm bank as the others, from time to time he'd get distracted and rub his hands together as though trying to gain relief. Kate had seen "red tips" before. Obviously he was new on the job and not used to the "muck," the irritating sulfur on the coal that caused fingers to swell, crack, and bleed. And since he wasn't allowed to wear gloves, he would have to wait for his fingers to harden, as all fingers did after awhile. But now they were surely painful.

Without a word, she walked up to the boy, bent down, and opening her leather pouch pulled out a rag and the arnica salve. Working quickly, she began cleaning his blackened and bleeding finger tips. But instead of pulling away, as she expected, he just smiled, revealing small uneven teeth. Then she applied the salve and bandaged his fingers.

"How do you expect him to pick out the culm from the chute, now?" growled a large, coal-dust covered man standing over her.

At the sound of his voice the boys bolted and headed toward the dark, hulking breaker with its grinding machines, deafening noise and billowing black soot. Kate rose to face the angry breaker boss who carried a big stick and smelled of whiskey.

"He's so little," Kate said, hoping to assuage his anger so he wouldn't abuse the boy when he got back to the breaker. Breaker bosses were notorious for their cruelty, and this boss seemed in a foul enough mood to lay his stick across that small boy's back. "He's so little," she repeated.

"No littler than some."

"He'll work better now, because his fingers won't hurt so much."

"We'll see."

Kate touched the dirty sleeve of the boss's overcoat. "Please don't punish him for what I did."

The man jerked his arm away. "Did you make him come out here to gawk at the fire? Did you make him leave his chute? Do you think he should get paid for slacking, while others are in there doing their job?"

"It costs you nothing to be kind. He's just a little boy."

The man pushed his soot-covered face closer to Kate's. "Look, Miss High and Mighty, I saw your father hanging at the end of that rope. I saw how he squirmed and kicked like a girl, so don't be putting on any airs here. I don't need no killer's daughter tellin' me how to do my job."

As the man walked away, Kate swore to herself that the tears in her eyes were from the smoke and nothing more. But the only thing she wanted now was to go to Pottsville and send her telegram.

After spending two days scrubbing down every piece of Widow Clayton's furniture as well as washing her bedding, walls and floor, Charlotte was glad for the chance to escape the boardinghouse and spend a few hours in the lovely Gaylord mansion. And she didn't feel guilty, either. It was, after all, for charity. And hadn't Mrs. Gaylord made it clear, long ago, that Charlotte was expected to attend *every* time the society ladies, or at least the most important ones, met on behalf of the Women's Benevolent Society of Greater Pottsville? With Mrs. Gaylord at the helm, they spent the time sewing nightgowns, and knitting blankets and scarves and sweaters for the ladies in the Home for Indigent and Infirm Females, called the "Women's Home" for short.

And wasn't it Mrs. Gaylord, herself, who, soon after Charlotte's engagement to Benjamin, explained that the purpose of having her join the group was so she could "understand her responsibilities as a future Gaylord"? According to Mrs. Gaylord, it was the obligation of those more fortunate to look out for the welfare of those less so.

Though Charlotte disliked knitting and sewing, she enjoyed being in this exalted company. And she had learned much: how to participate in the casual banter of the privileged, how to speak to a servant, what the well-dressed woman wore in the morning, the afternoon and evening, and how women of privilege helped their husbands through social contacts, teas and dinner parties, and of course their philanthropy.

Now, sitting in Mrs. Gaylord's best parlor, surrounded by the type of ambiance only the rich could afford, she didn't even care that she kept poking herself with her knitting needles. More than a dozen prominent women filled the room, but the quartet, the same four women dominated the conversation as usual: Mrs. Gaylord; Elmira Crump, whose husband owned the large furniture store in Pottsville and another in Philadelphia; Lucinda Wells, a widow and beneficiary of her husband's vast holdings, which, among other things, included two of the largest collieries in the Pottsville area. And finally, Hester Roach, whose husband owned Martin's Dry Goods Store in Sweet Air, and who wasn't quite in the same league as the others, but always managed to insert herself into the conversation, nevertheless.

"I understand the Women's Home had to squeeze in another five ladies last week," Lucinda Wells said, her knitting needles clicking feverishly as she knitted-and-pearled multiple rows on her afghan.

"It's an epidemic, that's what it is," responded Elmira Crump. "I still blame it on the War for leaving so many women to fend for themselves. Didn't thousands of wives lose their men on the battlefield?"

Hester Roach clucked her tongue. "The War's been over for eight years. I don't see how you can keep blaming it on that. These women must have been of low character to begin with or they wouldn't have fallen. There's simply no substitute for good breeding."

"You are so right, Hester." Mrs. Gaylord looked up from her sewing and glanced at Charlotte. "Adversity is the true test of a woman's character. If she falls, then it's due to some inner deficiency."

Charlotte dropped another stitch and frowned. Why was Mrs. Gaylord looking at her so strangely? She wasn't a "fallen woman." The fact that her father had been convicted of murder shouldn't impinge on her character or reputation. And she resented Mrs. Gaylord's suggestion, albeit only by her look, that it was otherwise.

"A woman of real character would never fall," persisted Mrs. Gaylord.

"Oh, pshaw." Lucinda Wells rested her knitting on her lap and pursed her lips. "Why do you think there's been an epidemic of prostitutes since the War ended? Because these war widows can't find jobs to support themselves, that's why! And many have children they're unable to feed so they go into the only business they can. As you well know, there are few opportunities for a woman in most occupations.

Not all widows are as fortunate as I. William left me well cared for, God rest his soul."

Hester shook her head. "There's enough honest work to be had, even for desperate widows. I say it's a matter of character. Poor character will always be exposed."

Mrs. Gaylord nodded. "Yes, and once a woman loses her reputation it can never be regained. I'll even go further and say it also applies to her family. Find a rotten apple and you'll discover that the whole bunch is liable to be rotten, too. A bad tree is sure to produce bad fruit."

Charlotte's cheeks burned under Mrs. Gaylord's gaze. If she had been unsure about Mrs. Gaylord's insinuation before, she was no longer. Clearly, Mrs. Gaylord was making a point. But what? That Charlotte was no longer acceptable? That she was a "fallen woman" because of her father, and no longer belonged among their members? Whatever Mrs. Gaylord's full intent, at the very least she meant to insult. It made Charlotte realize that her unimpeachable source had been right all along, though she still didn't want to believe it. But it really must be true. It seemed that Mrs. Gaylord had come to view Charlotte as an unacceptable daughter-in-law.

"Yes, hard times will reveal the quality of a tree," Mrs. Gaylord repeated.

Lucinda Wells chuckled. "Well, let's hope you ladies never fall on hard times because I'd hate to see what that would expose on your trees. And quite frankly, you are all too old and homely to become prostitutes. All except our dear Charlotte, here."

At once the conversation ended. And as Charlotte resumed her work, she remembered Kate's words: "this shame will follow us wherever we go." For the first time Charlotte clearly felt its weight. And it felt ugly and dirty, and so very very unjust.

Oh how unkind the world could be to those who fall.

Charlotte didn't know how she ended up here. She had been walking for hours, trying to compose herself, and here she was in front of the Women's Home. She studied it now: a large three-story Victorian covered in grey stonework and sporting long narrow windows, most of which were shaded by what looked like soiled beige canvas. It had been donated to Pottsville by a wealthy, now deceased, widow expressly for homeless women. Some say it was because the widow's daughter had run away years ago and was reported to have lived a ruinous life, a life that ended tragically on the streets of a big city.

But whatever the truth, the home had sheltered many women over the past fifteen years, especially after the War.

As Charlotte stared up at the stately structure she wondered what a "fallen woman" looked like. To her knowledge she had never seen one. Did they look like her? Had they once had a happy home before disaster struck? And what of their families? Why didn't they help? She thought of her family now, her mother and Kate and Virginia. How fortunate she was to have people who loved her, who cared for her. And what a selfish ninny to complain about chores as she was so prone to do!

She took a step closer. Dare she go in? What would she see? Her future? What if Mrs. Gaylord was able to convince Benjamin to break off their engagement? And what if she suddenly lost her family? It could happen. She had heard of such things. Hester Roach was full of these stories. What would she do then? If fate was unkind, she could . . . yes, she could become one of the fallen.

She heard a chilling shriek coming from one of the second floor windows and jerked backward. No. This was foolishness. What was she thinking? She wiped her clammy hands over her skirt. Surely, she was mistaken. Surely, Mrs. Gaylord hadn't meant anything unkind by her remarks. Whatever her private thoughts concerning Charlotte,

Mrs. Gaylord was a genteel woman. Too well mannered to offend deliberately. It was all a mistake. Charlotte was just being overly sensitive. After one last look at the house she turned and headed home, all the while wondering why her heart was still pounding and why she could barely keep from crying.

Virginia sat on her bed holding the empty mahogany box in her hand. Over and over she traced the mother of pearl inlay on the hinged cover. How long had it taken her to fill this box? Two years at least. That's how long she had been saving for a printing press. Two years, and now nothing to show for it. She had given all fifteen dollars to Kate for the Pinkerton.

She tossed the empty box aside. *Oh, what was the use?* If all she could save in two years was fifteen dollars it would take thirty years to save the two hundred she needed. That's how much it would cost to buy that 1842 Stanhope "in need of refurbishing" which she saw advertised in the *Pottsville Evening Chronicle*, though surely it was gone by now. Bargains like that didn't last long. But it had shown her it was possible to get a press for a reasonable price and, well, she had hoped that some in the women's suffrage movement would be induced to bankroll her effort to open a liberal paper here in coal country. Still, she had to have some money of her own to invest. To show those in the movement she was willing to risk her own capital, and not just theirs, in order to further the cause.

With a sigh, Virginia rested her head on the large down pillow that smelled faintly of lavender. She was kidding herself. By the time she earned enough money for a respectable deposit on another press, even one as moderately priced as the Stanhope, she would be an old woman.

So was that it? Was that the end of her dream? She was never one to give up easily, so why was she doing it now? Was it because of Kate's insistence on hiring that detective and stirring up the past? Virginia had yet to recover from her father's death, and now Kate was pulling the scab off that wound and making her and Charlotte and Mother relive the nightmare all over again. And what if the investigation led in a direction no one was prepared to go? She supposed there was nothing she could do about that. Whatever the truth, they would have to live with it.

Suddenly, she bolted upright. This wouldn't do. She couldn't quit this easily. She had no control over what the Pinkerton would or wouldn't uncover, but there was something she could do about her own life, about her dreams, her ambition, and it wouldn't get done lounging on her bed feeling sorry for herself.

She would get a job. It was the only reasonable solution. It was the only way she could refill her box again. But it could only be part-time. She was needed here at the boardinghouse and wouldn't leave her mother or sisters in a lurch. That meant longer hours. Still, she was young and strong. She could manage. And the time spent on her outside job could be made up at home by getting up earlier or working later. It was possible. Yes. It was definitely possible. She *wouldn't* let her dream die. And wasn't this the best time to start a newspaper? After all, it was the era of the "Penny Press" when most people read two or more newspapers a day.

Virginia sprang to her feet. Now where did she put the latest addition of the *Chronicle*? She would look under "New Advertisements" where jobs were sometimes posted. She had seen an advertisement for a part-time female packer at the Pottsville mill. She knew full timers got paid sixty cents a day. For six days work, that meant three dollars and sixty cents a week! A part timer should get half that, which meant she could buy a press before her hair turned gray.

CHAPTER 2

───── ⌒ ─────

*Y*ou *must exhibit the heart of Christ.*
    Mother's familiar admonition replayed like a stubborn tune in Kate's head.

Remember God loves them, too.

She tightened her grip on the large quilt draped across one arm and tried to pretend she didn't see Mr. and Mrs. Samuel Baxter leave the planked sidewalk and cross the cobblestone street in order to avoid her; the very sidewalk financed by her father and other wealthy members of the community he had managed to enlist, "so that the ladies wouldn't soil their dresses." Had the Baxters forgotten that? She had seen their sneers, seen how they had put their heads together and whispered, then laughed. And she had seen them tilt their head back in a superior manner before leaving the sidewalk.

Remember God loves them, too.

Well maybe God did love them. He could afford to be magnanimous. He didn't have to live in a small town full of hypocrites; people who were friendly enough when they had wanted favors from her father but now . . . . Kate sighed. She wished she could look beyond the prejudice they had encountered since Father's death, as Mother was always encouraging her to do. But it was a hard thing to love a hypocrite. It was even harder to live beneath a shadow of shame. One had to put up with so much. Even the contempt of people like the

Baxters who, not so long ago, would have given their prize rooster to get an invitation to a Farrell dinner party.

The heels of her black-laced boots clicked against the wooden planks of the sidewalk. For-give, for-give, for-give, they seemed to sound out. She changed her cadence. Forg-ive, forg-ive, forg-ive. This was maddening. She quickened her pace, but when something squished beneath her boot, she stopped. Looking down, she saw she had stepped on the contents of someone's chamber pot, thrown from one of the upper windows. Like all the shops along this street, owners and their families lived in quarters above their stores.

Serves you right for taking yourself so seriously.

She scrapped her shoe against the edge of a plank, wondering if the town was ever going to hire a water wagon to wash the streets and sidewalks. Then she checked her hem and was relieved to find it un-soiled. This was one of her best day dresses—a pale green delaine with a tiered and ruffled skirt-back supported by a perky bustle. A white satin bow decorated the bustle and a matching white satin ribbon, hanging from her small bonnet, brushed the middle of her back. Kate had carefully chosen her outfit. She knew that the backward sweep of the dress complimented her shapely figure and the color complimented her dark chestnut-colored hair.

Charlotte had praised her lavishly. Mother just shook her head. But was it wrong to not want to be mocked? Or looked down upon? Or shunned as if she had a contagious disease? But there was a practical side, too. It wouldn't do to appear seedy or threadbare when selling her quilt. Any hint of financial hardship and the implacable Martin Roach would make bargaining more difficult. He was a master at converting the desperation of others into his gain.

She quickly checked her reflection in the four-foot high bay window of the hardware store, and adjusted her bonnet with her free hand before scanning the display of cutlery, tin-ware, toys, and hand tools. Her eyes lingered on a man's razor and shaving cup before continuing on her way.

She ignored the clicking of her boots as she passed the coppersmith; the large Tavern and Inn; the hatter that sold bonnets and straw hats for women as well as bowlers and derbies for men; the apothecary and bookshop that shared a small building; the new clothing store that was a thorn in Martin Roach's side since it sold gent's ready-made clothing as well as ladies' gloves, hosiery and dress buttons, and "cut into his profits."

When she reached Martin's Dry Goods Store she suddenly felt queasy. The quilt had taken months to make with its cream and pink and rust-colored small print fabric sewn into five large star-blocks and four alternating blocks with a pieced border. It was the best quilt she had ever made. She needed to be firm no matter what Martin said. Five dollars. That's what the quilt was worth and that's what she wanted.

The money was more important than ever since yesterday she received a telegram from the Pinkerton office in Philadelphia accepting her father's case and saying that one, Joshua Adams, would be arriving at Pottsville tomorrow and would appreciate being met at the train. So her business needed to be concluded today. If only she could deal with Hester, Martin's wife. Hester was far more reasonable. Maybe if . . . .

She felt the impact even before she heard his voice; felt herself reel backwards; felt the quilt slip from her arm.

"I'm . . . terribly sorry."

Kate couldn't see who spoke. She was sprawled across the planked sidewalk; her bonnet flopped forward covering her eyes. She felt a hand slip under her arm then pull her upward. Once on her feet she pushed her bonnet backward and stared into the smiling eyes of a young man who, Charlotte would have immediately declared, had no fashion sense whatsoever. He carried a bulging scruffy carpetbag and wore a brown, wide-brimmed felt hat that only countrymen or farmers wore. His black, double-breasted frock coat had sloping shoulders and opened to reveal a rumpled, beige waistcoat with notched collar. Around his neck was a black silk cravat, loosely tied. His beige trousers flared at the bottom and only partially covered his boots. Flared trousers had gone out of style years ago; so had sloping shoulders; and a *farmer's* hat . . . well, it would have made Charlotte laugh. But Kate wasn't laughing. She was staring at his mud-caked boots—boots that were now firmly planted on her beautiful star quilt!

She shrieked like an owl then shoved him aside, but too late. Her once beautiful quilt now hosted two large footprints. "Look what you've done!" she shouted, not caring that people had turned to stare. "How am I ever going to sell this now?"

The man's face reddened. "It was clumsy of me. I apologize Miss . . . Miss . . . ."

"Farrell! Kate Farrell!" she snapped, forsaking proper etiquette that frowned upon respectable ladies introducing themselves to strangers. But such formalities seemed unimportant as she tried gathering the quilt before it suffered greater indignities. "If you were any kind of a gentleman, you'd assist me!" she said as her bonnet flopped forward again.

"Did you say *Farrell*? Your father wasn't James Farrell, was he?"

Kate let the quilt drop, then shoved her bonnet backward and glared into the sky-blue eyes of the stranger. "Yes, Jim Farrell was his name. What is that to you?"

The man grinned as he pulled a paper from his pocket then waved it in front of her. "Your telegram, Miss Farrell. To Mr. Pinkerton. I'm Joshua Adams, the detective assigned to your case. Surely you got our telegram from the Office Manager telling you I was coming?"

"You were supposed to arrive tomorrow! At Pottsville!"

"Ah, so that's why no one met me, and why I have all this mud on my boots. Your footpaths are rather primitive. But never mind. Obviously, a clerical error has been made, and once again I must apologize. Please forgive the mix-up." Joshua Adams put down his bag, then picked up the quilt, folded it and draped it over his right arm. "Please tell me how I can make it up to you." With his free hand he took up the carpet bag.

Kate stared at the quilt for a minute then at the handsome man whose face seemed all apology and remorse. "I was planning to sell that quilt for five dollars and the money was going toward paying your fee. I will deduct that amount from your final bill."

Joshua chuckled. "I'm impressed. I see I'm dealing with a shrewd woman who will keep me on my toes."

Kate took the quilt-draped arm Joshua offered, not impressed by him at all, and wondered, as they headed toward her lovely house on the hill, if Mr. Pinkerton hadn't made a mistake, and rather than sending one of his many legendary operatives, had erroneously sent his office clerk instead.

Virginia tented her fingers as she sat in the parlor studying the man in front of her. Young—early twenties, good looking, animated and eager, perhaps a little nervous, too, judging by the way he kept clearing his throat. Not at all what she expected. Her vision of a Pinkerton agent was of an older man: quiet, reflective, dignified and a bit intimidating. Certainly this operative never served with Alan Pinkerton when he headed the Union Intelligence Service during the Civil War or when he foiled the plot to assassinate Abraham Lincoln. Just what experience did he have anyway? Surely this wasn't his first case?

"I'm sorry your Mother can't join us." Joshua Adams cleared his throat yet again. "Her insight is necessary to the investigation, but I can get that another time. So . . . let us begin. I'd like a statement from each of you."

He removed a note pad and square English pencil from his coat pocket, walked to the corner desk, pulled out the chair, and after turning it to face the room, proceeded to sit down as if he owned the place. But his position made using the desk uncomfortable as it forced him to lean sideways when he wrote, and made Virginia add "foolish" to her mental description of him.

As Joshua Adams scribbled on his pad, Virginia noticed how he kept glancing at Kate as though taking a reading of her attitude. She had seen this before. Kate had that effect. People always seemed to want her approval. Kate, the headstrong one; capable, provincial, solid but sometimes rash, like Father. Perhaps that's why Father had always been partial to her, though he tried to hide it. So unlike his feelings for Virginia which tended to be ones of anxiety and perplexity, though he tried to hide that, too. But Father had always been a bit unnerved by the daughter whose dreams had been too large for him; the daughter who wanted to push the boundaries of conventional womanly endeavors.

"Miss Kate, would you start by giving me the details of this case?"

Virginia sank lower in her chair as she watched Kate's face contort. *Now he was in for it.*

"This *case* happens to be the unjust execution of our *father*. Kindly remember that." Kate's violet eyes flashed beneath thick, black lashes. "You'll be dealing with four women who have endured a great loss and I do hope we can count on your tact and sensitivity."

"I . . . beg your pardon. I meant no disrespect. But a good detective can't afford to muddle facts with emotions. I'll endeavor to be as sensitive as possible, but if you want results, I must, above all, be accurate and thorough."

Virginia quelled a smile. *Ah, a man who can hold his own.* She braced herself for Kate's reaction. To her surprise, her sister remained calm.

"Point taken. I can recommend no one better to outline the facts than my sister, Virginia. Let her be the first to speak."

Joshua nodded then turned to Virginia and readied his pencil.

"For you to understand what happened," Virginia said, coming directly to the point as usual, "I must go back a few years and talk about the man who changed everything, and brought us to this end. The man: Franklin B. Gowen; a lawyer who eleven years ago was elected district attorney for Schuylkill County. By the following year he was making eight thousand dollars annually, a tidy sum considering most mine workers made less than three hundred. From there he went on to head the legal department of the Philadelphia & Reading Railroad. Within five years he became acting president. He was only thirty-two. As president he quickly took over the Schuylkill Canal and the county's feeder railroad lines. This gave him control over all transportation both in and out of Pennsylvania's lower anthracite region. But Mr. Gowen was ambitious. Not content with his victories, he set his sights on the local collieries. One problem: the charter of the Philadelphia and Reading Railroad prohibited the company from owning mines. An obstacle Mr. Gowen was willing, and eventually able, to overcome. It took a bit of trickery, but the charter was ultimately changed."

"Virginia!" Charlotte's back was as rigid as a knitting needle. "That is imprudent. Mr. Gowen is very influential in these parts, and nothing escapes his notice. It would not do if he heard you talk that way."

"Well, unless you plan on telling him, dear, I don't see how he'll find out." Out of the corner of her eye, Virginia saw a strange look come over the Pinkerton's face, as though he was offended by what she had said. Surely, he didn't know Mr. Gowen? Or did he?

"About two years ago Mr. Gowen began buying up mines from small independent operators. Before the railroad started mining coal it made its money hauling it. Even here Mr. Gowen exerted pressure, and manipulated the market. He believed cheaper coal would create a larger market thereby increasing the tonnage his railroad transported. Through a series of maneuvers he was able to bring down coal prices from three dollars a ton to two-fifty, breaking the backs of many independent miners. As you can imagine, it caused quite a stir around here, not to mention undue hardship for the families who owed their subsistence to the mines. This led some collieries to oppose the further purchase of mines by the railroad. They feared if Mr. Gowen obtained a monopoly he'd manipulate the cost of coal as he had done before, and bleed the mine workers dry. My father, who was the Superintendent of the Schuylkill Division of the Reading Railroad, was well known and respected in these parts. That's why Mr. Gowen enlisted him as land agent, one of many, to help persuade those resistant independent operators to sell their mines. Roger Blakely, the man my father was accused of killing, was one of them."

Joshua Adams was clearly agitated as he put down his pencil and rose. "I appreciate the history lesson Miss Virginia, but I think it would be more beneficial to focus on those details pertaining directly to your father." He walked to the fireplace, now used only in the evenings or on chilly mornings, and stood with his back to the women. "More relevant facts would serve us better."

"Well, the *fact* is, Mr. Blakely didn't want to sell. And on that premise alone the prosecutor based his case, claiming my father tried to change Mr. Blakely's mind, not willing for his 'lucrative commission' to be forfeited, and that during this effort they argued and fought and my father killed him."

"Mr. Adams, you took copious notes during the 'history lesson'," Kate said a bit tersely. "Do not these more pertinent facts deserve to be entered into your notebook?"

Joshua turned from the fireplace, his forehead looking like plowed furrows. "Of course," he said, walking to the desk and scribbling something on his pad. "Please continue, Miss Virginia."

"My father told us that Roger Blakely had sent him a note asking to meet him at his colliery after sunset; that he had important information to share. Father insisted his visit had nothing to do with the sale of the colliery, and that Mr. Blakely was already dead when he got there; killed by his own knife. Unfortunately, my father discarded the note before the meeting and was unable to find it again."

"Any evidence of theft? Something to indicate a robbery?"

Virginia shook her head. "The only thing missing was a worthless paperweight."

"Which was curious," Kate added, "since a stack of paper money remained untouched on his desk. So obviously the motive wasn't robbery." She glanced at Virginia. "Now, tell him about the notebook."

"The notebook . . . yes, Father's notebook. It's on the desk by your right hand, Mr. Adams." Virginia watched the detective pick it up and flip through the pages. "In it are lists of names. Most are independent colliery owners, but not all. Kate thinks there may be clues in the way the names are listed and grouped, and why some are underlined and others not. Kate thinks it can help you with the case."

"Kate thinks! Kate thinks! Virginia, you make it sound like I'm the only one who sees value in Father's notebook, when we've all agreed there could be something in it."

"Well . . . yes, Mr. Adams . . . we . . . think there will be something useful in there." *Poor, expectant Kate.* So hopeful that this young, nervous Joshua Adams could be the instrument of justice she so desperately wanted. *And poor downcast Charlotte.* Who only prayed for this whole dreadful affair to be over so she could get on with her life.

But Virginia knew her own feelings—which ran in an entirely different direction—were just as strong as those of her sisters. For what Virginia had never discussed with either Kate or Charlotte, what she had never allowed to fully enter the foyer of her mind until now was . . . suppose Father really *was* guilty?

⌒

"Have we wasted our money, do you think?" Charlotte removed the quilted bonnet from an ornately scrolled silver teapot. She had been fretting about this for hours, ever since laying eyes on that ridiculous Mr. Adams. She may not have the keen mind of her sisters but she knew deficiencies when she saw them, and she saw plenty in this Pinkerton agent. Could someone unable to properly dress really deduce clues and bring their family's unfortunate matter to a happy conclusion? She doubted it.

"Well, have we wasted our money?" she repeated. When no one answered, she poured her perfectly steeped tea, which she had been carefully timing for the past seven minutes, into one of the three cups positioned neatly on the round tea table by her side. "I mean, this Mr. Adams . . . well . . . just look at him. How can he be credible? Aside from not even knowing how to dress, consider his face! Even that defies fashion. Instead of sporting a proper mustache or beard, he has scraped himself to the skin."

She glanced at her sisters who sat in nearby chairs, illuminated by the small crackling fire in the hearth and two green astral oil lamps on side tables. She had wanted to voice her concerns earlier but the business of running a boardinghouse had prevented her. Now she would have her say. If they were going to dredge up this whole unpleasant matter, they should at least have someone capable of doing it properly. Otherwise, even more scandal could ensue. And . . . that would be intolerable.

"And consider his questions!" Charlotte handed a steaming cup to Kate. "The same ones over and over again: 'Why did your father discard the note? What were the first words he said when you saw him that night? Why was there blood on his hands and coat?' I tell you I was ready to scream! I mean . . . how many times did he want us to repeat our recollections? And what presumption! Suggesting that he pose as our country cousin while investigating Father's case!" Charlotte picked up a small plate of buttered bread and handed it to Kate.

"Imagine that any of us would actually claim kinship with that man! For my part, I'd be mortified." She raised a fresh cloud of steam as she poured Virginia's tea, then her own. "And he's impertinent, too. I think he forgets he's in *our* employ. He certainly took you down a peg, Kate." Charlotte peered at Kate over her cup as she drank, feeling a bit guilty that she had been pleased by the take down. "So no, I absolutely will *not* claim any kinship with him."

"You'll claim it. We all will," Kate said. "We'll do exactly as he says. We must give him every assistance if we expect him to succeed."

Charlotte returned her cup to the muslin covered table—a table which, much to her embarrassment, was vastly inferior to Mrs. Gaylord's who served tea wearing white gloves, and whose buttered bread was so carefully rolled it never soiled her gloved fingers. She disliked confronting Kate, the sister who always seemed so sure of herself and intimidated Charlotte. She took a moment to compose herself, then placed her hands on her lap. "You may wish us to participate in this ridiculous lie but are you prepared to tell Mother of the deception? You know it will grieve her that you have chosen this path, especially since she's been opposed to your plan from the beginning."

Charlotte's breath caught when she saw the pained expression on Kate's face. She didn't want to be cruel. Or shallow. Though she knew she was sometimes both. But she wasn't loved and admired like Kate. Nor did she possess the brains and ambition of Virginia. All she had were her fine looks and a man of high position who wanted to marry her. For her, life was never going to get better than this. But already Benjamin Gaylord was struggling beneath the cloud of her shame. Must he endure more by now having to make the acquaintance of an unseemly relative; a relative, by all appearances, the Gaylords would assume had crawled out of some back country cow pasture?

She wanted to clear Father's name. Truly she did. But she had never spoken of any country relatives. Would Benjamin think her false? Think she had been misleading him? Think that perhaps she had even more embarrassing relatives she was keeping from him? Would she slip even more in his or his mother's estimation?

She stiffened in her chair. "Surely there must be another way? Surely this Joshua Adams can come up with a more acceptable pretense? Why can't he just say he's one of our boarders or . . . something . . . else?"

Surprisingly, Kate smiled. "Charlotte, dear, is it the dishonesty that concerns you or having to admit to the Gaylords you have an unbecoming relative?"

Charlotte felt her cheeks burn, and looked away.

"I despise using deception," Kate continued, "and Mother will not approve. But let me bear the consequences. I'll tell her myself. I think we must allow Mr. Adams his lead."

Virginia, who had been gazing at the fire while drinking her tea, leaned forward and placed her cup on the table. "Charlotte I understand your concern. I know the association Mr. Adams proposes will not sit well with the Gaylords, but it will hardly be the severest test of your mettle, and you must be brave, dear, and prepare for it."

"Why, whatever do you mean?"

"I don't mean to be blunt, but here it is, we must assume that whoever killed Mr. Blakely is still in the area. And he will hardly sit still while our *cousin* stirs things up. Beating bushes and overturning rocks always bring out the snakes."

"You're not suggesting that any of us could be harmed, are you?" Charlotte's heart pounded.

"Virginia, I don't think we need to . . . ."

"No, Kate. You wanted to pursue this, we all did. But we must be prepared for the consequences. And all I'm saying is that this investigation could produce some danger not only to Mr. Adams, but to us all."

"That's . . . ridiculous. Who would want to hurt us?" But even as Charlotte said it, she felt her heart sink. Once, when she had been on a hunt with the Gaylords, she and her horse became separated from the group and happened upon a fox ensnared in a trap that had been carelessly left out and meant for some pesky raccoon. One of its legs was nearly severed from the force of the snapping steel, and she had watched in horror as the fox chewed the rest of it off, then hobbled away. It was eventually cornered by the dogs but she never told anyone what she had seen. Nor had she forgotten it. Now she wondered if a person could become that desperate. Desperate enough to hurt himself and others in order to avoid entrapment. And with the fresh vision of that fox in her mind's eye, she knew the answer was "yes".

Kate tapped lightly on the thick mahogany door. "Mother, may I come in?" When a soft voice answered "yes," she opened it and entered. Her mother, dressed in a cotton nightgown, sat on the edge of her four-poster bed brushing her long hair that was always kept beneath a net by day. Kate marveled at how lovely and young her mother looked with her hair down. A deep auburn, it showed little sign of graying.

Her mother rested the silver trimmed brush on her lap and smiled. But Kate saw the worry in her eyes as though she knew this visit would not be a joyous one.

"I fear you will be unhappy with me." Kate sat down beside her. "But Joshua Adams, the Pinkerton agent you met earlier, is going to protect his cover by claiming he is our country cousin, and I have convinced my sisters to go along. Please do not blame them. I take full responsibility. But he must have a pretext that is reasonable. If he claimed to be one of our boarders would it make sense for him to ask questions about Mr. Blakely's death? Why would a perfect stranger care? But if he's a relative who has come to help clear Father's name, well . . . you can see how that is more believable."

Her mother put down the brush and began braiding her hair. "Do you think God works through lies and deception? Do you really think His will can be done in this manner? Just what do you expect to gain?"

Kate rose to her feet. "I don't know. The truth, I hope. And justice."

"You already know the truth. And as for justice, you know how elusive that can be, as the many proofs in the collieries and surrounding patches testify. Oh, Dearest, do not look for justice in this world, but rather look to God. In the end, He will right every wrong."

"I'm determined to do this, Mother. I need peace. But how can I find it without answering this puzzle? This thing gnaws at me so. I've tried telling myself it doesn't matter, that I can live with the shame, but I can't. How do you do it, Mother? How?"

Her mother took Kate's hand and held it a moment before releasing it. "I am sad over our loss. And in many ways I even feel cheated. But I don't feel shame because I know your father, the kind of man he was. And so do you. And all the false accusations in the world can't change that."

"I accept that here." Kate tapped her forehead. "But not in here." She placed her hand over her heart. "Hating is wrong, I know, but I can't help it, Mother. I hate all those jurors who found Father guilty, and the judge, and the prison officials, and all the vultures who came out to watch the hanging. Sometimes . . . sometimes I feel as if I hate the whole world."

"I know you don't mean that, Kate. Even so, you must guard your heart. It's easy to hate. It's the easiest thing in the world. But hate is torment. Like a worm, it is never satisfied. It will eat at you, consuming you more and more as time goes on. You'll never have the peace you seek if you allow bitterness to grow. I beg you, Kate, don't compound one sin with another."

"I can't let it go. I wish I could, but I'm not like you." Without another word she left the room. But as Kate closed the door she heard her mother praying and knew the prayers were for her.

⌐⌐

Kate hadn't meant to snoop. Not at first, anyway. Like her sisters, she was assigned the task of changing the straw-filled tick that covered the bed slats in all the bedchambers, and had volunteered to do Joshua Adams' bed, which raised eyebrows, including Mother's. But Kate wanted to see how Mr. Adams lived. It would tell her much; perhaps even revive her dwindling confidence in him. His first impression had been most unsatisfying. Even her sisters questioned his abilities.

At first glance his room appeared in good order, a great contrast to the condition of his clothing. Well, that was something in his favor. Perhaps he possessed some measure of discipline after all. As she opened the top seam of the tick on his bed, she spotted an ornate leather case on the corner of his small desk. Next to it was a sharpening bone, a leather strop and a small brush of badger hair. All shaving implements. Did the ornate case contain his razor? It seemed rather large. Father had maintained a full beard which he trimmed with scissors, so the only razors she had ever seen were those in the hardware store window.

Sidestepping the two large bundles of straw on the floor, she moved toward the desk. This was unlike her. She never violated a boarder's privacy. On the other hand, didn't she have the right to know more about the man she had hired? In spite of her nagging conscience, she picked up the case, opened it, and was surprised to see not one but seven ivory-handle razors, all arranged in a neat row, and each held in place by a thin leather strap. She had heard it said that seven was the number of razors a prudent gentleman owned. *A razor for every day of the week?* She pulled one out. It had a nice balance, and the gleaming blade and highly polished ivory handle testified to the care given these instruments. It also revealed something about their owner. Apparently, Joshua Adams was careful, fastidious and perhaps a bit vain.

She reinserted the razor and was about to close the case when she saw a tattered edge of paper poking from the torn lining along the bottom. She stood a moment, fighting the urge to pull it out, then temptation got the better of her. The paper proved to be not one but five carefully folded news clippings. She scanned them quickly. One she recognized as Benjamin Banner's piece on the killing of the Welshman, Morgan Powell, nearly two years ago, which he had credited to the Molly Maguires. Kate had always thought that as editor of the *Miner's Journal*, Banner had done more than anyone, as this piece reflected, to tag the Mollies as villains, and often without proof. But what troubled her most was that his article had been written long before her telegram to Mr. Pinkerton.

She didn't recognize the author of the next clipping but as she read it, it seemed vaguely familiar. "The brutality of that secret organization known as the Molly Maguires cannot be understood by rational minds. If these criminals are allowed . . . ."

"Find something interesting?"

The sudden sharp voice made her jump. She turned to find Joshua Adams standing in the doorway, his handsome face taut, his eyes clouded by anger. At once she crumpled the clippings and tried to stuff them back into their place but the wad was too thick. Without a word Joshua walked over and took both clippings and case from her hands.

"I . . . know how this looks. I didn't mean to violate your privacy. I . . . ."

"No? What then?" He piled the clippings on top of the razors, closed the case, and placed it on the desk. But his hand remained, and his fingers tapped against the leather.

Kate felt her cheeks burn, felt perspiration dot her forehead. "Well . . . obviously I *did* violate your privacy, and I'm sorry. And nothing I say can justify it. You would be correct in calling me any number of unflattering names. But since the deed is done I'll not pretend I'm unconcerned by what I found. You had several clippings concealed in your case, a case not designed to carry papers, and all of them about Molly Maguire activity in this region, and all dated well before I contacted your agency."

"And your point is?" Joshua's blue eyes looked as hard as one of Mother's metal pots.

"It raises the question of you having divided interests. It forces me to ask whether you are here to solve my father's case or for some other purpose. And I will not leave this room, sir, until you have given me a satisfactory answer."

"I suppose you have the grit and stubbornness to carry out your threat, but I cannot give you that answer. There's more at stake here than you realize."

"And that is answer enough. It tells me I was correct in my assumption. And my response to you, Mr. Adams, is that you are discharged! Your services will no longer be required. You will please leave this house at once."

Kate stood with hands on her hips expecting him to heed her command, but to her surprise he just stood there, defiantly. "You are discharged, Mr. Adams!" she repeated.

"That is impossible since I've already told everyone in town I'm your cousin."

"What is that to me? Relatives come and go. No one will think twice about you leaving."

"You . . . don't understand. It's my cover. I cannot change it now."

"Speak plainly, sir."

"You are asking me to reveal information I am not authorized to reveal."

"Then we are at an impasse. Someone must yield. And since you are standing in *my* house, it will not be me."

Joshua Adams turned and walked to the bedroom door then closed it.

"Mr. Adams! That is highly improper! Please open . . . ."

"You have nothing to fear from me, Miss Kate. But no one must overhear. And what I'm about to say must be kept in strictest confidence. Not even your mother or sisters can know."

"I hardly think . . . ."

"Give me your pledge or I will be unable to continue."

"It . . . seems highly irregular but I suppose . . . if it's necessary . . . all right, you have it. Now tell me what this is about."

"Recently, the Philadelphia and Reading Railroad hired Alan Pinkerton to investigate the activities of the Molly Maguires due to the increased incidences of sabotage at their mines."

"What! Are you telling me you work for *Franklin B. Gowen*!"

"Yes."

"Does that mean the reason you took my father's case was to provide a cover for your true purpose?"

"Yes . . . but that doesn't mean I didn't intend to help you. Because I did. I do. I'll investigate your father's case as well as fulfill my primary assignment."

"And what if that's not good enough? What if I don't want someone who will spend but a few spare moments of his time on my case? What if I just send you away and tell everyone who you really are?" To her surprise, the detective grabbed her shoulders and leaned so close Kate was able to clearly see the tiny freckle at the corner of his mouth.

"You mustn't do that. The Mollies can't know they're being investigated. We have . . . we have a man inside, someone who has infiltrated their organization. If they get wind of Mr. Gowen's investigation they could scrutinize all those new in their ranks and uncover our mole. A life could be lost."

Kate shook off his hold. "That's a harsh dilemma you offer, and I resent it, Mr. Adams!"

"Let's not be foolish. Let calm reason prevail. We can help each other. You need assistance in clearing your father's name, and I need a cover that will enable me to move about freely. What do you say?"

"You try my patience, sir, but no, I will not reveal your secret. And perhaps you can do some good regarding my father. However, as of today, I will no longer pay you a wage, and you will be charged room and board. Even so, one question remains. How do I know I can trust you?"

Joshua Adams glanced at his razor case. "I think the better question is, how do I know I can trust *you*?"

CHAPTER 3

C harlotte reached for the brass knocker on the massive glass and mahogany door. She was grateful Mother had let her come. And surprised. Perhaps Mother had seen how much it meant to her. And though their boardinghouse was upside down from spring cleaning, Mother had even helped fix her hair. Charlotte felt a sudden pang of guilt for leaving her sisters to the arduous task of whitewashing walls and dry rubbing wooden floors, but the feeling was quickly over-shadowed by her excitement at having been invited to the Gaylord mansion for tea.

Her hand lifted the knocker, and with more force than necessary, struck it against the brass plate. Though the invitation was for low tea at four o'clock and not the more prestigious high tea that took place an hour later and was often accompanied by a meal, Charlotte was gratified nonetheless. She was sure this invitation proved that all her suspicions concerning Mrs. Gaylord were unfounded, and that she had quite misunderstood Mrs. Gaylord's feelings toward her.

The door was opened by a man Charlotte had never seen. He ush-ered her into the spacious best parlor, where Mrs. Gaylord was seated on a red velvet chair. Positioned nearby was a tea table covered with a lace cloth and arrayed with a sterling silver tea set and two exquisite gold rimmed tea cups. Nestled in-between was a gold rimmed plate mounded with buttered bread.

Mrs. Gaylord gestured for Charlotte to take the chair beside her. "You look lovely, my dear."

Charlotte glided her hand across the pearls around her neck seeking to direct Mrs. Gaylord's attention to the fact she was wearing Benjamin's recent gift. "Thank you. And thank you for your gracious invitation."

"I did want us to visit before the preparations for my trip to England entangled me." Mrs. Gaylord poured tea with white-gloved hands then handed the cup to Charlotte.

A feeling of guilt overcame Charlotte again, this time for thinking so ill of Mrs. Gaylord. *Oh, how one's imagination can become as rabid as a dog!* She smiled a warm, penitent smile as she helped herself to one of the rolled slices of bread Mrs. Gaylord offered her. "I see you have a new doorman."

"Good help is so hard to find these days. I've put up with Alfred for far too long. I hope this new man will not be a disappointment. These constant problems with the servants weary me so. Why, only yesterday I found the upstairs maid applying some of my perfume behind her ears. Imagine! I fear I'll have to deal with her, too, once I return from England. I don't suppose you know of anyone suitable?" Mrs. Gaylord shook her head. "No, you wouldn't. Still . . . I suppose neither one of your sisters is available or looking for work?"

Charlotte nearly dropped her cup. "Mrs. Gaylord, I hardly think . . . ."

"I'm looking forward to our trip. I think it will be good to get away. For Benjamin, especially. We're rarely able to socialize with truly cultured people. And dear Benjamin is so bored with the plebeian society here. It will be so gratifying to see our English cousins again. Fourth cousins, actually, but utterly charming, especially Abigail who is only a year younger than my son. They've insisted we stay with them while we are abroad."

"Oh? I . . . don't believe he ever mentioned his cousin to me."

"I can't imagine why. Abigail is not only a young woman of means, but of breeding, too. And from a family of breeding. Not like some distant relatives one finds crawling around on his family tree. And so accomplished! As well as beautiful." Mrs. Gaylord placed her half-eaten bread on the tea saucer. "Actually, she's *quite* beautiful. I understand she has planned a plethora of parties and outings for Benjamin. And he will be a most eager participant, I assure you."

Charlotte drained her cup, placed it on the tea table, then rose, grateful that the long skirt of her dress concealed her trembling legs. "It was most gracious of you to take time from your busy schedule and show such hospitality."

"A pleasure, my dear. I wanted to say 'good-bye' before our trip. I do hope you won't spend the time we are away moping about. You are young, and . . . somewhat attractive. We shall be gone quite some time and I suggest you find enjoyment where you can. I'm sure very soon you'll forget about us completely. I find that is common among women in certain circles—their ability to transition from one alliance to another, seizing upon whatever promising opportunities come along. At any rate, I'm glad for this visit. I hope it has brought about a better understanding between us."

Charlotte jutted her chin. "I believe I understand you quite well. But I wonder if Benjamin does."

When she saw Mrs. Gaylord's face go white, Charlotte turned and, without being escorted to the door, exited the mansion.

⌒

Virginia hadn't expected the position of packer to be filled. She had gone to the Pottsville mill to talk to the foreman soon after deciding to apply for the job and was met with the crushing news that a woman had been hired only an hour before. And though Virginia had been scouring the *Chronicle* for the past several days, she had found nothing remotely suitable. Then, during the flurry of spring cleaning, just as she was washing down all the bedsteads with brown soap, a new idea emerged. The answer had been there all along. She knew how to run a house, the appropriate time to strip a room of furniture or take down bedsteads, how to removed tacks and carpeting before dry rubbing a floor, how to fold and pack curtains with camphor or tobacco, how to mix white sap and wax for polishing a table and so much more. In short, she was more than a competent domestic. She could hire herself out, and with her skills, receive a decent wage. And despite her name, maybe there were still those who would be willing to enlist her services. But one couldn't just go knocking on doors. She'd have to approach this properly.

She removed her soiled apron and climbed the steps to the second floor, then entered the converted sitting room which now served as bedroom for both her and Charlotte.

She filled the basin then washed her hands and face. It had been a long day. Still, the three of them, she and Mother and Kate, had managed to finish all the floors even without Charlotte's help. Now, there only remained the dinner to prepare, and of course the dishes afterward. But tonight, while she and her family sat in their back parlor, she would broach the subject of her wanting to seek employment. She imagined Charlotte would object, but Virginia would have to change that somehow since she needed her sister's help. And as Virginia dried her face and began thinking about the best argument to use, she heard Charlotte's footsteps behind her.

"Did you have a pleasant time at tea?" Virginia said, turning toward the door.

"Yes, quite."

Virginia frowned when she saw Charlotte's strained face and how she removed her gloves and tossed them on the nearby table.

Charlotte normally wrapped them carefully in paper immediately after each use. "We were able to finish all the floors, so tomorrow we'll wax furniture—one of the few chores you don't seem to mind.

"And speaking of chores . . . I . . . was going to wait and discuss this with you later, but maybe it's best I tell you now so you can get used to the idea and not be so shocked when I tell the others. The thing is . . . I need a job. How else am I ever to have enough money for my newspaper? I applied for the opening at the mill but was too late. And judging by the *Chronicle* there's no other work to be had for miles. Not for a woman, anyway."

Virginia slipped on a clean apron then sat on the bed. As Charlotte pulled a day dress over her head, Virginia noticed her sister's tea gown sprawled across the other bed. Not like Charlotte, who was usually so fussy with her things, to be so careless with one of her good dresses. "Is something wrong? You seem distracted. Would you prefer I wait until we are all together and . . . ."

"No. I'm fine. Just . . . tired. Finish what you were saying."

"Well . . . as I mentioned, jobs are scarce. But with your help, I think I can solve my dilemma. You still have connections with many of the more affluent families in our area. I'm considering . . . no, what I'm planning on doing is hire myself out as a domestic, and . . . ."

"You *cannot* be serious!" Charlotte's hands trembled as she secured the little horn-buttons of her high collar. "Have you no pride? Do you want to disgrace us all?"

"It's an honest trade! And I'm not ashamed to do honest work. I have dreams . . . plans . . . and I'm willing to work hard to make them happen."

"You cannot do this! *Please*, Virginia." Charlotte walked over to the small side table and picked up her pearl necklace. "Take these." She stretched out her hand. "Take anything of mine you want. Use it and whatever else you think is worth something to buy that press you've been talking about, but please, *please* don't hire yourself out."

"I . . . could never take your pearls or anything else of yours. But why does this upset you so? I know you feel you have a position to maintain because of your engagement to Benjamin but . . . ."

"I could never face the Gaylords if you did this!" Charlotte's hand remained outstretched. "Never! For my sake, for my future happiness sake, *please* don't do this."

Virginia rose and walked over to Charlotte. With her handkerchief, she gently blotted the tears that were sliding down her sister's cheeks. "All right, dear. It's all right. Don't cry. If it means that much to you I'll find another way to earn money."

"Mr. Adams has information concerning Father's case," Kate said, addressing her sisters and hoping that what he had to share would vindicate him in their eyes. She directed him to the high back chair near the fireplace where a single log, the last of the season, crackled softly.

He was bareheaded; his blond, wavy hair looking as though he had been caught in a windstorm. His clothes were also untidy: a wrinkled single-breasted jacket of coarse brown flannel sported several chipped horn-buttons; and matching trousers, that were woefully too short, skirted the top of his scuffed black ankle boots.

Though the outfit was a masquerade, it made Kate cringe as she glanced at Charlotte. "Mr. Adams asked me earlier if he could meet with us after dinner."

At once, Virginia put aside her sewing while Charlotte looked pained, as though Kate had just said Jasper Wright, the dentist, was coming to extract one of her teeth.

"May I proceed, Miss Kate, or should I wait for your mother?"

"Mother will not be joining us."

"Very well, but please convey my information. Let her know that I've received a note from one of the workers at the Mattson Colliery; someone who claims to have useful information. For the past several days I've been visiting the collieries around Pottsville asking about the night Roger Blakely was killed." He turned to Kate. "I told them I'd make it worth their while if they shared any information they had."

At once Kate felt annoyed. What right did he have to offer anything without consulting her? "Just what did you promise?"

"A day's wages."

"Oh, Mr. Adams, we hardly have money for that!" wailed Charlotte. "We had to pool all our resources just to hire you."

"Don't worry, I have enough." Kate knew this statement would satisfy Charlotte, who was ever eager to insulate herself from their financial woes. But what of Virginia? Her nature was to be curious; to inquire until satisfied. And Kate could hardly tell Virginia that she still had almost all the funds they had pooled; and that in addition to collecting money for his room and board, which she planned to give Mother after this whole unpleasant business was over, she wouldn't be paying Mr. Adams another cent for his services. But she couldn't stomach another lie. *Not another lie.*

"You really have enough to cover this added expense?" Virginia sounded unconvinced. "How is that possible?"

"Well . . . ."

"I'm only taking half pay," Joshua blurted.

"And why is that?" Virginia seemed more skeptical than ever.

The detective raked his hair and grinned sheepishly. "To be honest, this is my first case. And since I'm learning on the job, I felt it only fair to discount my fee."

He looked boyishly handsome and so utterly believable that even Kate was fooled. But only for an instant. It hardly seemed credible that Alan Pinkerton would send an inexperienced operative on behalf of such an important client as Franklin B. Gowen.

"So, this is your first case. I thought as much." Charlotte frowned. "You did seem to lack . . . well, sir, forgive me for saying it, but you did . . . you *do* seem to lack the bearing and manner of a great detective." Charlotte fingered the string of pearls nestled against her throat; Benjamin's gift, which, she had confided to Kate, she was careful never to wear in the morning ever since Mrs. Gaylord told her that a proper lady didn't wear pearls before noon. "Your inexperience is most unfortunate, but I suppose we have no choice but to accept the services of a novice. Still . . . how can we be sure you are capable of . . . ?"

"Have you made arrangements to see this man?" Kate interrupted, surprised that Joshua Adams appeared unruffled by Charlotte's censure.

"I sent a note suggesting we meet tomorrow after the mine closes, and this morning received an answer. The meeting is on."

"Well that *is* good news. Of course I'll be going with you." Kate sat on the edge of her chair. She would have gone to Higgins Patch that instant if she could.

"And I'll be going, too," Virginia added.

"Don't look at me!" Charlotte said, looking horrified. "I wouldn't think of going to that foul, grimy place. I'd hardly feel safe in daylight, but at night? In the dark? Oh, my. I don't even want to think of the danger. You know what they say about Higgins Patch. That it's a stronghold of the Molly Maguires. Oh, no! You go if you must, but I'm content to be left out of it altogether."

"No one is going, except me," Joshua said.

Kate clenched her jaw as she squinted at him. *Higgins Patch. Molly Maguires.* The words swirled in her mind like the powdered chalk they used to clean their pewter. Was this another lie? Was Joshua

Adams really going to Higgins Patch to seek information about her father's case? Or was he going on his own errand? And making Kate pay for the privilege? *A day's wages?* All right, she'd pay. But not unless she was there to hear this man for herself. "I *am* going," Kate said, springing to her feet. "And no amount of arguing will change my mind."

"And I'm going, too." Virginia also stood now. And by the look on her face, Kate knew no amount of arguing would change Virginia's mind either.

"Ladies, this is foolishness. I can't allow it. I can't be responsible for your safety. Listen to Miss Charlotte. She's right. It could be dangerous. It could . . . ."

"We're going!" Kate said. "And we'll take responsibility for our own safety."

Her words seemed to end the matter, for Joshua Adams nodded as though realizing he couldn't fight them both. But in the weeks ahead, Kate would remember these words and wish she had not been so headstrong.

⌒

Kate was on her knees rubbing one of the freshly scrubbed brass andirons with mutton suet when Joshua Adams burst through the door of their back parlor.

"Forgive the intrusion, but your Mother said I would find you here, and that it would not breach proper etiquette if I came since it was she who insisted I do so."

Kate placed the andiron on the drop cloth protecting the floor and rose. Absently, she brushed a wisp of hair from her forehead. She had spent the past hour cleaning the hearth and andirons, and was covered with the telltale evidence of her efforts. Her hands and arms, and most of her apron were blacked. She stood staring at him wondering what her mother could have been thinking by sending him to her while she was in this state.

"I wanted to try, one last time, to dissuade you from going to Higgins Patch tonight. There could be danger. I know Virginia will follow your lead and do whatever you do."

"Charlotte said you were presumptuous, and she was right. We are barely acquaintances and yet you claim to know us well enough to predict what we will do in a given situation. If you knew anything at all, you'd know that Virginia has her own mind."

"Yes, but she looks up to you. You have great sway over both your sisters, as you well know."

"You're wasting your time, sir, and mine." Kate returned to the andiron on the floor.

"You don't trust me." Joshua walked across the room, stopping only when he stood on the drop cloth. "You don't believe I'm going on behalf of your father. Tell me, Miss Kate, why do I feel we are back in my room with the razor case?"

"Have we ever left it?"

"I've tried, but you refuse to let us. We need to put our differences aside or we'll never be able to work together. We need to *trust* one another."

Kate picked up one of the nearby rags and rose to her feet. "That's difficult, sir," she said, wiping suet from her fingers. "Your ability to fabricate lies on a moment's notice is extraordinary. It seems as if you can pluck them from your head as easily as a farmer plucks apples from his orchard."

"I'm a detective. It comes with the territory. And Allan Pinkerton himself will tell you that lying and deception are necessary in our trade. He believes the end always justifies the means if the goal is to secure law and order. But if you're referring to the comment about my wages, I was only trying to help. Trying to keep you from having to deceive your sisters any more than necessary."

"I see. And was it true? All that business about this being your first assignment?"

Joshua Adams frowned. "Did you know that by November the fog in London is yellow? And by January it has spread several miles across the nearby countryside? They say it's the coal stoves in the city that cause it. A ghastly place, London. Full of crime. In my work it's difficult not to judge a place by its crime. But I dislike New York even more, though it has some of the best markets in the world. You can buy almost anything there. Even so, that hardly makes up for their infamous Five Points district."

"So you have traveled. Congratulations. But that still doesn't answer my question."

To Kate's horror the detective pulled up his waistcoat and shirt a few inches, exposing a patch of skin just below the ribs on his right side.

"Mr. Adams, *please* this is . . . ." She stopped when she noticed a scar, the length of one of his ivory-handle razors.

"But Cincinnati was the real surprise. I didn't expect trouble there. The crime rate is moderate compared to the other two cities, and I was only sent to pursue a certain John P. McCartney, 'Prince of Counterfeiters', and not a man of violence. But instead of the prince I ended up tangling with a petty thug and his derringer. Did you know that even a small pinefire cartridge can handily destroy a liver, or part of it anyway? Luckily, a skilled surgeon was able to save most of it."

Kate dropped her rag and stepped closer. "That's . . . a large scar." She resisted the urge to touch it, and was embarrassed by her boldness in even thinking of doing such a thing. "I'm . . . sorry for doubting you."

"But I wasn't always a detective." Joshua adjusted his clothes. "I was once a teacher. For a year, anyway. But instead of teaching history, I though I'd like to be part of it. Maybe make some myself. I just wanted you to know that."

"Well, perhaps you'll make history tonight, at our meeting, by uncovering evidence that will clear my father."

"So you *are* going."

"I am."

"Then before you go you should wipe that sooty grease from your forehead." Then he turned and exited the room, leaving Kate feeling foolish but a little pleased, too. Maybe this brash, outspoken detective could be trusted after all.

Charlotte stood staring at the large gray-stone mansion. She couldn't believe her nerve or the fact that she had come here again. Still, she wasn't sure she had the courage to enter. But why this obsession, this need to see the Women's Home? Was it because of her acute disappointment in that slovenly amateur, Joshua Adams? After his confession that this was his first case, she realized all could be lost. How had her entire future happiness come to depend on such a deficient character? How was he to clear Father's name and repair her standing with the Gaylord's? Oh, how could Kate trust such a lout? Kate, who was normally so wise and level headed?

When someone raised the canvas shade on one of the windows, she stepped backward. No, she wouldn't go in. This was foolishness. Still . . . maybe she should . . . just once to see. . . . She had to make up her mind. Time was running out. She had finished her chores earlier than expected, leaving her an hour before she was needed to help prepare dinner, and she had spent half of it walking to the Women's Home just outside Sweet Air.

Yes or no. She ran her damp palms down the skirt of her day dress. *What was she so afraid of?* Inside, there were only women. Poor, sick, indigent women. But that was the point, wasn't it? This was what she feared most, to see what she might become. If she lost Benjamin it could happen. Yes, if conditions were right, she too could become like these women inside: fallen, destitute and unloved, with no means of support. No family, no friends. Hadn't Hester told them about the family just outside Pottsville that had been decimated by illness, leaving behind the youngest daughter, as sole survivor, to fend for herself? Yes, it could happen.

She found herself moving toward the large wooden porch, as if in a dream. She just had to go in. She had to see for herself the kind of women who were inwardly scorned and detested by the likes of Mrs. Gaylord and Hester Roach, while outwardly provided with so-called Christian charity.

When had they started seeing her this way? Charlotte mounted the wide, sturdy steps. Was it when Father had been accused of murder? Or during the trial? Or was it when he stood on that scaffolding with the rope around his neck, a white hood covering his face?

If Mrs. Gaylord and others considered her one of the "fallen" then Charlotte must see what she really looked like in their eyes. She took a deep breath as she walked to the large wooden door in need of painting, then placed a trembling hand on the round brass knob and twisted. When it didn't turn, she realized her perspiring palm had failed to grasp it firmly enough. She ran it down her skirt and tried again. This time the door opened.

It wasn't what she expected. From the entrance she could see into a large parlor, clean and neat though a bit musty smelling and sparsely furnished with few adornments. And sitting around in well-worn chairs were ten women, of various ages, all neatly clothed in modest apparel, quietly reading or knitting or dozing; each one looking quite normal.

When the woman in the chair nearest the entrance saw her, she smiled and began running her hands over her poorly arranged hair as if embarrassed by her appearance. Then suddenly a matron or nurse, Charlotte didn't know which, appeared.

"I'm sorry for the intrusion. I'm . . . sorry," was all Charlotte managed to say before bolting down the stairs, but as she did she glanced one last time at the woman still trying to arrange her hair with her fingers.

Kate was happy to have Joshua Adams by her side as she and Virginia walked along the dirt road that cut through the center of Higgins Patch. She didn't know why she felt so uneasy. There was no cause for concern. She knew many of the people, having come here with Mother numerous times. Though never at night. And that was the point. Things tended to look different at night.

In the fading light she could still make out the poorly constructed houses. Huddled together in tired clusters, they looked like patchworks with their odd pieces of wood fastened over gaps in the wall boards. Even some of the roofs sagged as though weary of bearing up under years of coal dust. How did these people survive the harsh Pennsylvania winters in such lodgings? Why didn't the colliery take better care of their property? All these houses were company owned, for which they collected rent; rent, that many said bordered on robbery.

She tried to ignore the odd smells that floated through windows and swirled overhead, and how they changed as the ethnic nature of the streets changed. But two smells remained constant: the first of coal fires; the other of outhouses—the ones that stretched along the backyards like a string of miniature sheds, many without doors, and each one shared by two families.

"It's not much further," Kate said, directing them deeper into the patch toward the Irish quarter, and one of the poorest, where houses were little more than shanties that sometimes sheltered up to thirty people who slept in shifts. But the Germans, Welsh, and Italians had their sections, too. So did the mine bosses and supervisor who lived in the best houses. In reality, the entire patch was divided by both class and culture.

They were heading for Mary O'Brien's house, a fact that Joshua Adams had only shared while on the way here. It still peeved Kate that he had kept the meeting place a secret as if he were afraid she'd go without him. As they veered off the main road and onto a small rutted path, she tried vanquishing her suspicions. She wanted to trust him, to give him the benefit of the doubt, but it was hard.

"Over there," Kate said, pointing to a shack with small windows that appeared like sad eyes on each side of a poorly-hung rough-hewn door.

"I didn't expect it to look . . . like *this*," Virginia whispered. "So . . . *sinister*."

"It's just the darkness playing tricks." Kate mounted the rickety boards that served as a front step. She tried looking more confident than she felt in hopes of comforting Virginia who seldom came to the patch, and never once to the O'Brien's.

Before she could knock, the door partially opened and there stood Mary O'Brien. "Well, it be herself now," Mary said with a thick brogue and a surprised expression on her face. She ran her hands over her tightly bound hair, then down her soiled dress. "Oh, mercy me!" she cried when she looked over Kate's shoulder and spotted Virginia standing beside Joshua Adams. "'Tis another one!" She rubbed her hands together. "I had no idea you'd both be comin' with him or I would have made some tea cakes for the visit."

"Be at ease, Mary." Kate took the woman's hand and squeezed it in friendship. "The fault is ours. Forgive my rudeness in not letting you know. And don't trouble yourself. All we've come for is information."

That seemed to placate Mary, for she smiled and opened the door wider. "Well then, come in. You are welcome."

The three filed into one room that served as both kitchen and sleeping quarters for the adults. And though Kate had never been up-stairs, she knew that overhead was a small attic where all the children slept. The downstairs, itself, was cluttered and dimly lit. Aside from the coal stove, there were assorted cooking utensils, food barrels of varying sizes, a table, two wooden benches, and a collection of rolled bedding.

"Please sit," Mary said, taking the only oil lamp in the room and placing it in the center of the table. "And I could manage some tea, if it pleases you."

Kate nodded. "That would be lovely."

Once the stove was stoked and the kettle positioned, Mary went to where a few crude shelves had been braced and nailed to the wall. Reaching to the top, she pulled down what looked like a bundle of rags. Then bringing it to the table, she carefully unfolded the cloth, exposing four lovely china cups and saucers, all delicately painted with pink and red and yellow dahlias.

"Part of me dowry," she said beaming. "Carried 'em all the way from Donegal, I did." As she placed each cup and saucer in front of her guests, a sudden rustling noise made her turn.

A little boy had scrambled down the attic ladder, and even in the dim light Kate recognized him as the one whose fingers she had bandaged at the Mattson Colliery. He stood in bare feet and shabby nightshirt, grinning and holding up his hands. Kate supposed it was to show her that his fingers had healed, but in the poor light it was impossible to see if they actually had.

"And just what do you think you're doin', Sean Muldoon?" Mary moved toward the boy. "You should be in bed now! That breaker whistle will be blowin' before you know it."

To Kate's surprise, the little boy swore under his breath; then barely dodging the back of Mary's hand, retreated up the ladder.

"That's right! You best be gettin' up there now before I wash your mouth out with soap! And don't think I won't neither!"

When he disappeared, Mary sighed and began fussing with her cups. "'Tis Catherine Muldoon's boy, God rest her soul. I make him wash and say his prayers every night, and even try to teach him his 'please' and 'thank-yous' but 'tis a losing battle with him at the breaker now. All that them breaker boys learn is how to cuss and smoke and chew tobacco. Catherine is surely turnin' over in her grave, but I'm doin' my best with a house full of my own brood and the extra men I've taken in for the room and board money."

Kate nodded. "It's a good thing you are doing." She had not known Catherine Muldoon or her family but she had heard how the woman died in childbirth, along with the baby, and left five young children behind. And since it was impossible for a widowed mine worker to care for his children alone, it was common practice in most patches for other families to take them in.

As Kate sat with her back to the wall feeling the wind blow through the bare, poorly fitting boards, her heart ached. She and her family had so much, even in their reduced circumstances. Why couldn't she be grateful to God? Why couldn't she be satisfied with her life as it was? *Like Mary O'Brien. Like . . . Mother.*

When the tea had steeped and Mary filled the cups, including the fourth cup that sat in the empty place by Virginia, Joshua Adams cleared his throat. "Thank you, Mrs. O'Brien, not only for the tea but for carrying the notes back and forth between your husband and me. I am most eager to hear what he has to say." Joshua looked around. "But he doesn't appear to be here. Will he be home soon?"

"Not likely. He's at the pub drinkin' his tonic of whiskey and beer. It's for the lungs, don't you know. He's losin' his wind. Claims he's got the miners' asthma. I kept tellin' him no, then the other day he coughed up blood, and that was that. No use sayin' any more about it. But 'tis not him you need to be talkin' to. He knows nothin' that would interest you. It is himself you need to be askin.'" Mary pointed to a corner cluttered with barrels.

It took a moment to see him, the man who had been in the shadows all this time. He seemed to blend into the dark like a vapor. Then he moved. He was a large man, with broad shoulders and strong, sinewy arms well suited for wielding a pick or drill or shovel. Even his overalls and heavy boots were the garb of a laborer. He moved slowly, and Kate wondered if it wasn't so he could size them all up. When he reached the sphere of lamp light, Kate saw that he was a plain man with blunt features, dark brooding eyes, and thick unruly, black hair that made him look wild.

He stood by the table, studying each of them in turn, then finally took the empty seat beside Virginia. "I'd not be speakin' to you at all if my sister had not talked me into it." His voice was deep, his brogue even thicker than Mary's. "She said I owed it to your mum, a woman well known here in these parts for her Christian charity. And since you're stirrin' things up now, my sister thinks your mum needs to hear what I know, though I'm not at all sure what good it will do. And I doubt it will bring her any peace."

By the thickness of his brogue, that it had not time to soften, Kate guessed he had only been in this country a year or two. To be sure, he was an "Irish speaker" like his sister, and spoke Gaelic. And he was from Donegal. Kate knew that many Irish in Higgins Patch came from County Donegal, that part of Northern Ireland that was rural, poor and Catholic. And though Kate was Irish herself, she was not only third generation American, but her Irish roots were from the soil further south, in Protestant County Dublin. And the two couldn't be further apart.

Dublin was heavily influenced by the English, having once been the seat of British rule in Ireland, while Donegal was mired in Gaelic culture and superstition. People claimed it was County Donegal that many of the Molly Maguires had called home, but Kate never believed it. Until now.

"I appreciate your willingness to see us," Kate said, suddenly wanting this meeting to be over. "And thank you for your kind words concerning my mother."

"Shall we get on with it?" Joshua Adams pushed aside his tea and leaned over the table.

"Can we not know your name first, sir?" Virginia said, one eyebrow arched and looking so fetching Kate cringed from worrying that this dark stranger would think so too. Virginia had removed her hooded black cloak and it now lay folded on the bench beside her. Out of a desire to not embarrass their hostess with a show of finery, Virginia's dress, like Kate's, was void of the normal frills associated with feminine fashion. Even so, she looked lovely.

"Your name, sir?" Virginia repeated.

"It's Patrick. Patrick O'Brien," the man said, still looking as disagreeable as a snake while he studied Virginia. "And I'll not be rushin' now, Mr. Adams." He turned to glare at the Pinkerton. "Do you not learn manners where you come from? Here, in this house, we allow our guests to finish their tea before talkin' business."

"I thought I was being mannerly, Mr. O'Brien. My only intention was to conclude this matter as quickly as possible and leave you to your rest. I assumed you'd want the balance of the evening to yourself."

"I would, indeed. But it will be the devil to pay if my sister thought I insulted you by hurryin' your visit. She places great store in Mrs. Farrell's friendship, and would not be pleased if my treatment of you was less than proper." He glanced at his sister, and for the first time the darkness left his face as he smiled.

Joshua Adams picked up his cup and drained it. "Excellent tea, Mrs. O'Brien." Then he returned the cup to its saucer. "Your gracious hospitality is most appreciated."

"Ah, there now." Patrick O'Brien planted his large hands on the table. "Let us talk about more serious matters. But first I would see the money you promised. My sister didn't want me takin' it, but I'm not ashamed to say we could use it. A day's wage is still a day's wage."

Kate pulled a handful of coins from her cloak pocket, and making sure all ninety-six cents was there, put it on the table in front of him. To her surprise he didn't even look at it.

"Shortly before Mr. Blakely's death, two men came askin' if I wanted to earn some money." Patrick looked directly at Joshua Adams. "When I inquired just how would this money be made, they said they had need of a man my size, a man who could scare some sense into the likes of Mr. Blakely. 'Convince him,' they says to me 'to sell to the railroad and make it look like the work of the Mollies.'"

"Why would these men come to you? Why would anyone think you'd be interested in that kind of job?" Joshua said, making Kate want to give him a discreet kick under the table, but she restrained herself.

"Is that your way of askin' if I'm one of 'em? One of the Molly Maguires?" Patrick's face darkened as he leaned his elbows on the table. "And if I was now, would I be tellin' the likes of you?"

"Patrick, be civil," admonished Mary O'Brien as she left her place by the stove and stood near her brother.

"I know what the newspapers say. How they call the Mollies 'wild Irish' and 'illiterate brutes' who drink too much and use their fists instead of their brains to settle matters. But what they don't say is how the English and Welsh always get the best jobs while the Irish are passed over and forced into doin' the work of butties or laborers, fillin' sometimes as many as six to seven coal cars a day and gettin' only one-third the wages. And though we're willin' to work full coal that's hardly good enough for the new masters. Now that the railroad has taken over the Mattson they want us to do more work for less pay. Imagine anyone tellin' them swells in their fancy suits that they should haul more coal and be paid less for the privilege. But they can do as they please, can't they now? Haven't they got their railroad police crackin' the heads of anyone they think is makin' trouble for them at their collieries? And that's not all. Them newspapers don't tell you how the collieries force workers to buy everything from their company store, do they? A store where they charge three times what a thing is worth. The 'pluck-me' store, everyone calls it."

"Patrick O'Brien, enough of that talk, now!" His sister placed her hand firmly on his shoulder.

"You see what I have to put up with? A razor tongue she has." Patrick gave his sister's hand a pat. "I was only tryin' to tell Mr. Adams, here, that the Mollies are just men like himself, hopin' to make a better life. Is it wrong for a man to want a better life? For him and his family? To want to be paid fair wages? To work in a safe environment? And not havin' to purchase his goods at the company store for fear of losin' his job? And if this good life can't be had for the workin' and strivin', and if a man finds himself facin' injustice at every turn, with no one to help or even listen to his grievances, then I ask you now, doesn't that man have the right to use his fists if need be? What difference the means? 'Tis the *end* that matters."

"Oh saints preserve us! You're wearin' these good folks out!" His sister nudged him with her elbow. "Get to the part they've been waitin' to hear."

"Yes . . . you want to know about those two men. Well, didn't I show 'em my knuckles. And the toe of my boot, too. And what I told 'em was that I'd have nothin' to do with any business that meant harmin' old Mr. Blakely. He was a fair man. His colliery one of the best. Didn't he keep a Widow's Row for those who lost their husbands in the mine? And never forced 'em to take in so many boarders they had to sleep in shifts, neither. And I never did hear any talk of him orderin' the coal cars to be topped off. Not like the Mattson Colliery who makes it a practice of framin' their cars with extra boards so they can hold four tons each but only pay the miners for three. I bet you didn't know that now, did you?

"Mr. Blakely looked out for his workers, too. Never skimped on laggings or shorin' timber. You could trust his roofs not to come down on a man and bury him alive. Same thing when it came to 'robbin' the pillars'. If it looked like there'd be trouble, he'd send men in to shore the roof, or he'd leave part of the pillar standin'."

He paused, and as Kate watched him take the delicate painted cup in his large, rough hand and gulp the strong inexpensive Indian tea, she remembered the stories her mother had told her about the dangerous practice of "robbing pillars" where solid pillars of coal, which were left to hold up the roof while the rest of the coal was extracted from a chamber, were finally removed, causing the roof to cave. Two of Mother's relatives had died while robbing pillars.

Patrick put down his cup. "Just know I respected Mr. Blakely and would never be part of doin' him harm. There's not a man in Schuylkill County who wouldn't have been proud to work for that man if ever there was an openin' in his colliery, and that's a fact."

"So these men wanted you to scare Mr. Blakely into selling, and you refused? Did they ever tell you who they were working for? Who hired them?" Joshua Adams asked.

"Yes."

"Who?" returned both Kate and Joshua at the same time.

Patrick O'Brien reached over and slowly gathered the coins lying on the table, then slipped them into the pocket of his overalls. "They said Jim Farrell sent 'em."

"That's a lie!" Kate said, springing to her feet. "How dare you defame my father's name like that!"

Patrick's face clouded, but instead of the expected scowl, there was compassion in his eyes. "It may be a lie but 'tis not my lie. 'Tis what the two men told me, and that's the honest truth."

Joshua Adams tugged on Kate's arm forcing her to sit down.

"Why didn't this come out in the trial?" Kate said, feeling utterly miserable.

"You think any here in the patch would willingly involve themselves in matters concernin' the likes of Franklin B. Gowen? Everyone knew Mr. Farrell was in his employ. And it was clear they were goin' to hang him anyways. My sister said all things considered, 'twas no need of bringin' any more hurt to Mrs. Farrell. A wife can't be held responsible for everything her husband did."

For a long time all that could be heard was the sound of wind whistling between the boards.

"It seems to me we need to look at this logically," Virginia said, finally breaking the silence. "Either Father sent them . . . ."

"Virginia!"

"or someone else did. The question we should ask is 'who had the most to gain?' Some would say Father. There was, after all, a goodly commission involved but . . . ."

"Virginia, this is hardly the place . . . ."

"Kate, we must look at this objectively. You want the truth? Then let's search for it. With open eyes. If we do that then we must say, yes, Father had something to gain, but he wasn't the only one. Franklin B. Gowen had an even bigger stake. Everyone knows he's looking to own all the mines in the county. And everyone agrees that the Blakely Colliery would be a great prize. But how would blaming the Mollies for any mischief serve Father? One could say it would divert attention from him and onto others. But it would help Mr. Gowen even more, for in order for him to realize his grand scheme of controlling the mines he must destroy the WBA, and he must destroy the Molly Maguires; the two things that stand in his way."

"Miss Virginia, I hardly think Mr. Gowen wants to destroy the Workingmen's Benevolent Association or any other group seeking justice and working within the confines of the law." Joshua rose from the bench looking agitated. "But we can explore these theories at a later date. I think we've taken up enough of Mr. O'Brien's time."

Kate added her agreement with a curt nod. But when she rose she was startled by the expression on Patrick O'Brien's face as he watched Virginia unfolded her cloak and drape it over her shoulders. The hardness had dissolved and was replaced by one of surprise—as though discovering something unexpected—and also by what Kate could only describe as, awe. His lips formed a slow, broad smile; his eyes glistened as if looking at a holy thing; as if he were watching an . . . *angel*. And it took all of Kate's willpower to keep from snatching Virginia right then and there, and dragging her from the house.

⌣

"What do you mean by behaving so flirtatiously?" Kate said, her question exploding like a keg of blasting powder in Virginia's face. All the way home from the O'Brien's Kate had been fuming. Had been biting her tongue. Had not said a word fearing to make a scene in the patch or in front of Joshua Adams. And when they got home Kate had said nothing even while dragging her sister all the way upstairs and into her room. But as soon as the door was closed, the words spewed from her mouth.

"'Can we not know your name first, sir?'" Kate mimicked her sister's earlier words, fluttering her eyelashes in an exaggerated manner and placing her folded hands beneath her chin.

"You look ridiculous."

"Just as ridiculous as you tonight!"

"If you're referring to my effort at politeness when I spoke to Mr. O'Brien . . . ."

"Politeness? Your behavior exceeded the limits of proper conduct and bordered on . . . on . . . ."

"On *truth*? Admit it, Kate, what you're really angry about is that I didn't react the same way you did when Mr. O'Brien told us those two men said Father had hired them. I spoke my mind and you resent it."

Kate sighed as she walked to the bed and sat down. She was slowly getting accustomed to her tiny room that had once been the linen closet housing all the family's curtains, bed sheets, quilts, table cloths and such before being converted into a bedroom so her real room could be rented out to boarders. Even now she could detect the smell of camphor that still lingered in the cramped space which, aside from a bed, contained only one small side table holding a Bible and a chipped green oil lamp. Now, the sight of the Bible helped dispel her anger.

"You sounded like you thought Father was guilty." Kate's forehead crinkled. "You . . . never hinted at anything like that before. Do you? Do you think Father killed Mr. Blakely?"

Virginia removed her cloak and sat beside her. "I don't know. I don't want to believe it, but I really don't know."

"I couldn't bear that," Kate said. "I couldn't bear it if I thought Father was guilty."

CHAPTER 4

Kate entered Martin's Dry Goods Store feeling confident that her strategy would work. She clutched her quilt as she glanced around the spacious room full of shelves, wooden barrels, flour and sugar sacks, and a large L-shaped counter. But the store was empty of customers, and even the Roaches were nowhere to be seen. They must be in back unloading stock. She'd just have to wait. Perhaps she'd use the time shopping; see if anything interested her. Now that she didn't have to use her quilt money to pay Joshua, she could buy a few necessities. She spotted a glass and brass oil lamp that would make a fine replacement for that battered one in her bedroom, then decided it was a silly luxury.

Next, she examined the bin of cast iron molds and pots, then the cluster of shelves containing assorted crockery, decanters and writing implements. Seeing nothing of interest, she went to the counter and placed her quilt on its polished wooden top. As she stood waiting, she scanned the wall behind the counter. It contained dozens of long shelves, each holding several bolts of beautiful fabrics. Hester certainly had an eye for cloth. Her collection included bleached muslin, percales, sateen, ginghams, India linen, calicoes, batiste and wools.

But Hester also carried accessories for ladies who preferred "fancy work." The shelf on the end with its embroidery and crochet goods was one of Kate's favorites. She sighed as she scanned the collection of floss and hoops, embroidery patterns, crochet and knitting needles, thread and yarn. These days, with all the work of running a boardinghouse, she had little time for such pleasures. Next, she scanned the glass cases on the counter that contained ribbons, pins, thimbles, snaps and hooks. She could use a packet of snaps. Only yesterday Charlotte complained that two of her dresses were missing theirs. And come to think of it, Kate had a button missing on one of her favorite dresses. Surely she would find a match in one of the many glass jars containing assorted buttons. But not today. She couldn't spare the time.

Her eyes went back to the fabrics. Now where was that beautiful wool she had just seen? Oh, there. It would be perfect for making one of those bolero jackets Virginia loved. Maybe she'd buy a few yards and make one as a Christmas gift. She'd have to buy a paper of needles, too. And some thread. She shifted her feet. But she didn't want to spend all day doing it. She looked around again.

"Hester? Mr. Roach? Any one here?"

A rustling noise came from the stockroom, then the bulbous figure of Martin Roach stepped into the open doorway. "She's not in. You just missed her." As usual, he was impeccably dressed, wearing his customary dark brown frock coat, low cut vest, and lighter-color tubular-shaped trousers. His small bow tie came to little points just below the folded collar of his white shirt. His short brown hair was parted to one side, and oiled to lay flat on his head, making his ears appear, to Kate, as large as endives. But what she found most amusing was the wide mustache resting across his upper lip like a fat, hairy caterpillar.

"Will she return soon?"

"Hard to say. She went on an errand, and no one can lose track of time like that woman."

Kate's heart dropped. So much for her plan. The only reason she had come this late in the afternoon was because Martin was usually at the Tavern by now, downing his first beer of the day, and talking politics. Oh, why did Hester have to leave? She was ever so much easier to deal with than her husband.

"I've come to sell my quilt," Kate said, marshaling her resolve. "Hester has always favored my work." She lifted the quilt carefully over the round-headed nails lining the inner edge of the long wooden counter; nails that served to measure the yard goods. "She has always liked my interesting patterns and small, even stitching."

"Well, she doesn't have the most discerning eye." Martin had maneuvered behind the counter and now stood gathering the quilt in his hands as he examined the seams. "Adequate. It's adequate."

As he ran his hand over the spot where Joshua Adams' muddy boots once stood Kate smiled. Thanks to some good strong soap and white vinegar, no trace of the footprints remained.

Martin looked up, his eyes as emotionless as the buttons in his jars, his lower lip forming a thin rigid line beneath the mustache. His "poker face" she had heard Hester call it. "I'll give you three fifty for it."

"It's worth five."

"Then try getting it from someone else."

As Kate began folding the quilt, Martin chuckled. "You always were headstrong. I once had a horse like you. Stubborn as a board, but I broke him. Yes, sir, I finally got him to see things my way."

"Good day, Mr. Roach." Kate draped the quilt over her arm and was about to leave when he reached across the counter and stopped her.

"Now hold on there. I never said I disliked stubbornness. Turned out that horse was one of my favorites. Well . . . before I broke him, anyway. Yes, sir, I like a little fight, a challenge. So this is what I'm going to do, seeing I'm in a generous mood. I'll give you four dollars, four dollars even."

"Kindly remove your hand," Kate said, squinting at Martin Roach's chubby fingers that were crushing the sleeve of her upper arm. She had always found him disagreeable, even when Father was alive, but lately he had become insufferable, trying to set himself up as unofficial head of Sweet Air and dictate policies no one wanted.

"I won't take four dollars." She pulled against his hand. "But I'm willing to split the difference. Make it four fifty and we have a deal."

Martin Roach released her. "What I find irritating about you, Miss Kate, is that you don't know when you're licked. You still think you have a big important daddy to make you into someone significant. Not like your sister, Miss Charlotte. She knows where she stands. She knows that she needs to keep her hooks into that rich Benjamin Gaylord if she's ever going to be anything now. She understands that he's the only reason she's ever invited to *our* dinner parties. You should have seen her last time she was there. What a timid little mouse! Hanging on young Gaylord's arm like she couldn't take two steps on her own. But she knew her place, I'll give her that. She thanked Mrs. Roach and me most proper and grateful like."

"I'll hear no more about my sister. If you want the quilt, it will cost you four-fifty."

"You're daddy's gone, Missy." He ran his fingers over the back of Kate's bare hand, violating a basic rule that says a gentleman should never touch a lady's skin. He laughed when she pulled away. "You're a little nobody now. But I can change that. If you were to be more sociable, that is. I could open doors for you. Bring you back into polite society."

He unlocked his money box and began counting out the coins. "It always galled me the way your daddy pampered you three girls, like you were princesses or something. Well, you're not a princess anymore, are you?" He placed four dollars and fifty cents in the palm of his hand. "Things have changed. These days, it's my wife and I who entertain the important people. I dare say our guest list rivals yours when your father was alive. You could be part of that again, if you had a mind to." He leaned over the counter, holding out his palm, his eyes daring her to take the money from his hand.

Kate glanced at the coins, then at his disagreeable face. "I've changed my mind, Mr. Roach. I'm not selling my quilt today. I've decided to try to get five dollars for it after all."

Kate was still fuming when she stormed through the front door of her house, nearly knocking the pair of leather fire buckets off their pegs. "If I were a man I'd . . . ."

"I thought I heard your voice. Talking to yourself, Miss Kate?" Joshua Adams grinned as he exited the front parlor, his mop of blond hair tousled as usual. "You look mad as a hornet. What's wrong?"

"Nothing!"

"Well . . . if you say so." Joshua raked his hair. "I've been waiting. I thought you'd be home long before this. Your mother said you just went to the dry goods store to sell your quilt." He looked sheepish. "I'm happy you were able to get the mud . . . ." He stopped when he noticed the quilt dangling from her arm. "You didn't sell it?"

"No!" Kate pushed passed him

"What happened?"

"Nothing!"

Joshua stepped in front of her. "Something happened. You want to tell me about it?"

"No."

Joshua stood his ground for a minute, then shrugged good-naturedly. "All right, then let me tell you my news. Can we go somewhere private?" He glanced at Widow Clayton and Miss Rodgers who were hovering near the front parlor door inspecting a piece of lace.

Kate nodded, then led him down the hallway to the empty back parlor. Once inside, she draped her quilt over the back of an armchair and sat down. She should be in the kitchen helping her mother and sisters get dinner ready. Meal time in a large boardinghouse was always hectic.

"What's your news?" She gestured for him to take the damask-covered chair next to her, and hoped he would be quick.

"I've been checking out your father's notebook." Joshua pulled the book from his rumpled coat. "And what I've discovered is that the listings of the collieries are not random. They are all collieries that have sold out to the railroad, and are, in fact, listed according to the land agent that brokered the deal. But I still don't know why some names are checked and others not. But I'll figure it out soon enough."

He opened the book, and leaning closer to Kate's chair drew her attention to one of the columns. "See? Here and here . . . how they're grouped?" He flipped through several pages. "It took me awhile but I discovered that five different land agents handled these sales for the railroad. I've written the name of each agent above their column as well as the number of collieries they sold."

Kate took the book. "William Carter, nine collieries; Richard Church, fourteen collieries." She turned the page. "Martin Roach, thirty-one collieries." She turned additional pages. "Jim Farrell . . . twelve collieries; Samuel Baxter, *Samuel Baxter?* Two collieries."

"You sounded surprised by that last one. Who's Samuel Baxter?"

"A cooper who owns a small house just outside Sweet Air, with a shack in the back where he makes his barrels. And yes, I was surprised. The others are men of substance, with standing in the community. Which is why the railroad enlisted them. But Samuel Baxter just doesn't fit in with the rest."

"Hmm . . . wonder why his name is underlined?"

Kate shrugged.

"Well, tell me about the others."

"William Carter is a wealthy dairy farmer who owns three different farms in Schuylkill County. Richard Church owns the tavern in Sweet Air, and Martin Roach is owner of the town's dry goods store. And of course, my father."

Joshua tilted his head as if studying her. "I understand he had deep ties to the area. That his father, your grandfather, ran the Little Schuylkill Railroad when it operated between Port Clinton and Mahanoy Junction, and that he operated it for nearly twenty years before your father took his place and before the Philadelphia and Reading purchased it. And your great-grandfather settled in these parts and worked at the anthracite-fired iron furnace owned by John Pott, Pottsville's namesake."

"You've done your homework."

"I'm trying to earn my keep," Joshua said smiling. "But getting back to the notebook, what *I* find strange is the sales figures. Your father, William Carter, and Richard Church brokered about the same number of deals. But then comes Martin Roach, who's way at the top, and Samuel Baxter, who trails at the bottom. You'd think there'd be a more even spread among them."

"Martin Roach is ambitious. I'm not surprised to see his figures exceed the rest. And Samuel Baxter, well, he just doesn't have the influence of the others. Like I said, I'm surprised he was able to broker any sales."

"Hmm . . . warrants further investigation." Joshua slipped the notebook into his pocket. "Now . . . what happened at the dry goods store?"

"Nothing." Kate rested her head against the back of the chair and closed her eyes, trying to catch her breath before entering the mayhem in the kitchen. "I just decided not to sell my quilt."

"Really?"

Kate heard rustling and opened her eyes in time to see Joshua pull his chair closer.

"And just why not?"

"A woman's prerogative," she said with a frown, "and you needn't sit so close, Mr. Adams."

"The move is symbolic, Miss Kate. It's meant to tell you I need to be allowed into your inner circle. Are you ever going to trust me?"

She didn't know why she did it. Perhaps it was the sweet, earnest look on his face, or the resolute way he sat in his chair as if to say he would sit here until he got his answer. Maybe it was just because she was still upset and needed to share it with someone but didn't want it to be her mother or sisters. Whatever the reason, she relayed everything that had happened. It wasn't so much an emotional tirade as it was the repeating of a story, with emphasis on a few words here and there. When she finished she felt a wonderful sense of relief as though the burden of this disagreeable incident had lifted, and could now be forgotten.

"Thank you for listening," she said, rising from her chair. "I don't know why, but telling you has made me feel better." Then she hurried out the room to take up her duties in the kitchen, all the while wondering why he looked so angry.

Pots boiled on the stove, and the smell of baking bread and roasting lamb permeated the kitchen when Kate arrived.

"Finally!" Charlotte said, looking flustered and ready to cry. "How could it take you this long to sell one quilt?"

"I didn't sell it." When Kate saw Charlotte's face drop and her mouth ready to form a string of questions, she quickly added, "But never mind that now, just tell me how I can help."

"I . . . I don't know." Charlotte stood wringing her hands. "Everything is all topsy-turvy. Maybe . . . maybe . . . the table. Should she set the table, Virginia?"

"Yes, set the table, Kate." Virginia stood by one of the long wooden tables breaking up lettuce and dropping the pieces into a deep bowl. "I've already pressed the cloth and it's in the dining room folded across one of the chairs."

"Where's Mother?" Kate said, looking around.

"At Higgins Patch."

"*Now.* So close to dinner?" It wasn't like Mother. She would never leave at this hour unless it was important. "What happened? I heard no breaker whistle."

Virginia dropped another handful of torn lettuce into the bowl, then wiped her fingers on a rag. "She's at Mary O'Brien's. She took them soup and fresh bread and some cheese. She just heard about Mary's husband, Tom, taking ill. He hasn't been to the mine in days. With Tom losing all that pay, Mother figured they could use the food."

"The miner's asthma?"

Virginia looked glum. "The note didn't say, but what else? And there's nothing to be done for that. It always ends in . . . death. What will happen to Mary and her children then? I can't bear the thought of her out in the street with her little ones, and no roof over their heads. How can any woman endure such hardship?"

"What is it? What's wrong? You never cared about the patch before or what happened there. Not even about the people. What has changed?"

Virginia's eyes welled. "You're right, and I'm ashamed. You always said I was a born crusader, only now I believe I've been crusading for the wrong things. I believed getting the vote for women was paramount. And yes, it is important. But . . . now . . . after being there in the patch, and hearing, really hearing about the many abuses, I understand there are far worse things for a woman than being denied a vote. I'm just beginning to realize how difficult it is for women in coal country. I never thought about it before. Not really. But these women are so brave, and they endure so much, and work so hard to keep their families and homes together. But how can any woman survive if her husband dies and leaves her with half a dozen children, and no money, and no house to live in? What is she to do? Must Mary beg in the streets? Where will she sleep? We've all had to give up our rooms, you and Charlotte and I. But we still have a nice clean space to call our own. Oh, Kate! It's not right! It's just not right!"

"I know." Kate put her arms around her sister.

"Oh no . . . oh no! The bread! It's burning!" Charlotte shrieked. "Oh, how are we ever going to get dinner ready without Mother?"

"We're more than capable of doing it," Kate said, grabbing a handful of rags and rescuing the bread. She placed the three loaves, which were browner than usual but not burnt, on one of the long tables. "Now, baste the lamb while I set the table. When you're finished, take the vegetables off the corner bench and wash them. I'll help cut them up."

With that Kate rushed to the dining room and began draping the white linen cloth over the long mahogany table that could easily seat a dozen. Her laced boots moved noiselessly over the green and mauve Wilton carpet as she took pains not to snag the edges of the crumb cloth with her heels. She smiled when she glanced at the green woolen cloth beneath the table. Crumb cloths had gone out of fashion years ago, but boarders could be messy, and Mother was practical.

When the linen was placed, Kate went to the polished mahogany sideboard and pulled out ten sets of sterling silver knives, forks and spoons. The hallmark of a good boardinghouse was that it maintained a dependable routine, one that could be counted on by all.

Here at their house, boarders expected dinner to be served promptly at five. And Kate would see that tonight was no exception. But tomorrow, tomorrow she would sit with Virginia and discuss how they might help the O'Briens.

⌣⌐

Virginia could feel his eyes. They were like a hot wind on her face. Even the simple black dress she wore seemed to flutter beneath his gaze. It had been like this for three days now, though she had done her best to ignore it. She tried keeping her focus on the large black ribbon nailed to the door, and was glad today would be the last time she needed to come. She took comfort in Kate's arm firmly entwined in hers, and Mother's stout body in front like a shield of protection, but from . . . what? Why should his attention unsettle her? If Kate knew, surely she'd laugh. Or would she? Kate could be priggish in her way. She might find Patrick O'Brien's interest, offensive.

They threaded their way through the crowd of mourners, then passed the tall hulking figure of Patrick O'Brien. He spoke in low tones to the other miners but his eyes were fixed on her. Mother was the first to the door, and already knocking. Within seconds it was opened by a distraught Mary O'Brien, all clad in black.

Virginia followed her mother and Kate into the house, happy to escape those burning eyes, and found the room full of women. Today, being a Sunday, and the last day of the wake, a larger than usual crowd had gathered. Yesterday, Mary O'Brien had told her how it would be: that many men, who couldn't afford to take time off from the mine, would come today to join the other men in the street while their wives gathered in the house. Already, a wide circle had formed around the crude wooden box that lay across two chairs. Several women were weeping—friends and not the customary paid funeral

criers often seen at an Irish wake. Mary had told her she couldn't afford such luxury.

And there would be no funeral because Mary had told her she
couldn't afford that, either. But with the help of the "fund" Mary saw
to it that her Tom had his wake, where people could come for three
days and eat bread buttered with roasted chicken fat and drink cheap
Indian tea; where they could come and see Tom in the open pine box
lined with canvas and packed with ice. See his hair combed back, his
face scrubbed, though still tattooed by coal dust; see his hands lying
by his sides, and the coal stained fingers that had worked the Mattson
Colliery for nearly ten years.

They could see him in his best clothes, too: a short Albert jacket,
a waistcoat and trousers all of the same black inexpensive material.
And across his chest they could see the black rosary he prayed every
Sunday during Mass.

Virginia, along with her mother and Kate, walked toward the
casket to see it all for themselves one last time. Mother told them they
didn't need to come since they had been here twice before. But only
Charlotte stayed home; Charlotte who had come the first day and was
so irritable and fussy throughout it all that both Virginia and Kate
were happy she never returned.

When some of the mourners saw the trio approach, they parted to
make room. Mother spent a few quiet moments in front of the casket,
then disappeared.

As Virginia continued looking down at Tom O'Brien she wondered what Kate was thinking. Was she thinking about Father?
Virginia was. Her eyes welled as she thought of his funeral. At least
he had a decent burial. But how would she feel if he hadn't? What if
instead of a proper burial, he were taken, like Tom would be later today, and loaded on a wagon, then driven to the nearest medical school
to be used in their anatomy classes? Oh, she just couldn't imagine

such a thing! Virginia had learned that widows who couldn't afford the burial fee would donate the body of their loved ones to a medical school, allowing it to be handled and viewed by strangers. But since time began, hadn't necessity forced one to bear the unbearable? And like other widows before her, Virginia knew that somehow Mary would bear it, too.

Virginia suddenly felt the need to get away. She'd burst into tears if she didn't. It was as if she was feeling the pain of Father's death all over again. And it made her heart ache that much more for Mary O'Brien. Without a word, Virginia left Kate standing at the coffin, then maneuvered through the crowd, heading for the widow.

"You seem to be bearing up well," she said, giving Mary a hug and still feeling close to tears. "You are in my constant prayers. I pray God makes a way for you and your family, and supplies your every need."

"'Tis a good prayer, Miss Virginia. One I believe God has already answered, for only yesterday afternoon didn't I get a telegram from Pittsburg. I have people there, don't you know. They haven't much, but they do have a roof over their heads, and all with steady jobs at the steel mill. And they say there's plenty of work to be had for the likes of me. Seems Pittsburg is in want of domestics and willin' to hire the Irish. Well, haven't I been cleanin' my house for years? Hard work never frightened me. And I'm strong." She held out her calloused hands. "I can still use a scrub brush with the best of 'em."

Other women were coming up now, hoping to talk to Mary. One spoke to her in Gaelic, and before long the entire conversation was in a language Virginia didn't understand. She left the group thinking she'd join her mother. Over the tops of heads and between milling bodies, she spotted her near the stove helping a handful of women prepare more tea for the guests. Maybe Kate, then. But when she saw her sister all the way in the corner by the barrels, and surrounded by mourners, she couldn't bear the thought of having to wade through the sea of bodies that separated them.

That's when the back door looked inviting. She knew the air would be unpleasant because of the outhouses, but it seemed preferable to this crowded, stifling room full of tears and sad conversation. And it was certainly preferable to the street in front of the house where all the men had gathered.

Virginia worked her way to the door, then opened it and stepped out onto a wide dirt path that flanked the backs of nearly two dozen shacks. Across the way was another dirt path running along the backs of two dozen other shacks. And in the weed-filled patch between the two, was a string of outhouses. Virginia saw a handful of children chasing some chickens, making them flap and squawk and raise dust. A cow, tied to a post by one of the shacks, mooed softly, while two pigs routed nearby in the dirt.

Virginia brushed the dust off a good-sized flat rock that seemed to mark the entrance to Mary O'Brien's little herb garden, and sat down. She wished she and Kate had been able to do something for the O'Briens. But there hadn't been time. Two days after Mother received the note from Mary, Tom O'Brien died. Mother said it was his heart. She said she had seen it before with other miners whose asthma was far advanced. Their hearts just gave out. And Mother had told her that Tom had worked the mines for thirty years. Ten here, the other twenty in Wales and England. And he had started when he was no bigger than Sean Muldoon.

If only there was something she and Kate could still do. But without money? It seemed as if nothing got done without money. Still . . . maybe she and Kate and Mother could plead with the Mattson Colliery to set up a Widow's Row. Or maybe . . . .

"'Tis a lovely sight you make, sittin' here with the wind in your hair," a man's deep voice said.

Virginia looked up, startled, then frightened when she saw the hulking figure of Patrick O'Brien standing over her.

"I come to use the facilities," he said, pointing to the nearest outhouse with a grin, "but I see now a far better reason for bein' here."

Before Virginia could rise, Patrick O'Brien sat down beside her. The rock wasn't nearly big enough for the two and they were forced to sit so close not even a blade of grass could pass between them. It wouldn't do. She had to leave. But how? She was in such an awkward position that the only way to get up was to use the strong shoulders of Patrick O'Brien to push against. And she wasn't about to do that.

"'Tis a grand thing you and your family did in comin' here these past three days. It's meant a lot to Mary."

Virginia's heart raced. It felt strange, improper even, to be sitting so close to a man. "Will you be moving to Pittsburg, too?" She hadn't wanted to start a conversation but feared silence would be even more uncomfortable.

"No, I'll be stayin'. They are Mary's people, not mine. Though she says I'd be welcome enough."

"Mary's people? I thought she was your sister . . . O'Brien . . . of course, she's your sister-*in-law*. And Tom is your brother. I never stopped to consider . . . I didn't think that much about it."

"'Tis plain you gave us no thought at all."

Virginia looked away. "I'm sorry about your brother. But I'm sure you're worried about Mary now, and the little ones. It's so hard for those left behind. It . . . seems wrong that the Mattson Colliery doesn't have a Widow's Row. Perhaps if my sister and mother and I went and spoke to the superintendent; perhaps if we laid out the economic sense of keeping widows here so their children can continue working at the breaker, and so these same widows can provide room and board for the many single, able-bodied miners that need a place

to stay, well . . . maybe then they'd see the wisdom of it and surely
. . . ." She stopped when she felt his hand cover hers.

"You have the heart of a woman and the mind of a man. You're
a wonder, Jenny." His wild black hair fell across his forehead, his lips
smiling, his dark brooding eyes searching hers.

Virginia couldn't say why she didn't pull her hand away. Maybe it
was for fear of falling backward off the rock. Or maybe it was because
his presence was so powerful, so overwhelming she dared not move.
"Mr. O'Brien, you're a bold, fresh man with the manners of a goat.
Do you think it proper to call me by name? Do you think I'm one of
your pub women? Besides, the name is *Virginia*!"

He laughed a deep throaty laugh, then put his face so near hers
they almost touched. "Pub woman? And what might that be? Nothing
good, I'm thinkin'. Oh, you're no pub woman, for sure. You're no
kind of woman I've ever known, and that's a fact. But you are Jenny
to me. *My* Jenny as sure as there's a sky overhead, and as sure as the
breaker will be crankin out coal dust tomorrow. I don't mind tellin'
you that from the moment I laid eyes on you, I was smitten. And
when you first opened your mouth I knew there'd never be another
woman for me."

Virginia pushed backward to free her hand, and as she feared, she
fell right into the herb garden. "Mr. O'Brien! You . . . ."

"Oh, not *Mr. O'Brien*. I won't have it." The large burly man rose,
then took her arm and in one easy motion pulled her to her feet.
"Between us it must be Patrick."

Virginia's cheeks burned. "You are taking liberties, sir, when all I
wanted was to be kind and show you and your family Christian charity and . . . ."

"I'm a brute to be sure." Patrick led her gently by the arm out of
the herb patch and onto the dirt path. "I'm a man used to speakin' his
mind. And not used to polite company, neither. And that's a fact. And

I'll surely never be good enough for the likes of you, but I meant no disrespect. Even so, I'll not call you anything but Jenny." He smiled and let go of her arm. "Tell me your heart, lass. Tell me what it 'tis you want to do for Mary." He directed her away from the outhouses, to a nearby path lined with stones.

Virginia found herself following this strange man, as if pulled along by an invisible cord, though she no longer felt afraid. "Well, I've always wanted to start a newspaper, a paper that championed women's rights, especially the right to vote. But now . . . I believe I'd rather write about coal country. And the issues facing women here."

She walked alongside him, feeling strangely excited and alive. "I'd like to write about the lack of housing for widows, the poor schools, the company store. How sometimes husbands drink away their pay, leaving the family with nothing. And why. And the people here . . . they are so brave and strong and hard working. Oh, there are so many things I could write about!" Her hands swept over the patch. "This place is full of tales needing to be told. And someday I will. Only now, I don't have the money to start a paper."

"And tell me why you'd be needin' to start a newspaper? When there are enough already? 'Tis simpler to just write for one, I'd be thinkin'. Though I doubt it will help Mary none. But maybe others, down the road." Patrick's brogue was as strong as the arm that touched hers as they walked.

"But who would hire a woman?"

"My friend at the *Anthracite Monitor*. He'd be glad for a chance to publish a good solid piece from someone of your class."

"The *union* paper? Virginia eyed him. "Do you have ties to the WBA?"

"Not a one, other than friendship."

Virginia shook her head. "I doubt your friend would want something from me. The name of Farrell doesn't mean anything now. Not after . . . Father's hanging."

"Ah, now there's where you're wrong, lass. 'Tis a well respected name still. And there's many who doubt that your father was guilty at all."

Virginia stopped and in spite of herself smiled into Patrick's earnest face. "You mean that? You're not just saying it? About not everyone thinking Father was guilty?"

"I never say anything I don't mean, Jenny. You best be knowin' that about me."

"Well then, how do I contact this friend of yours?"

"You don't."

Virginia folded her arms across her chest. "Then tell me how in the world I'm supposed to give him my article!"

"I see you have a bit of a temper. I've got one meself. I suppose we'll be buttin' heads like a pair of ibex before long."

Virginia laughed. "I'm sorry. What I mean is how do I get my work to him?"

"It's that simple, Jenny. You'll be givin' it to me. And if I like it and think it's worth the publishin' then I'll be passin' it along to my friend. At my say-so he'll put it in his paper, sure enough."

"You . . . read?" Virginia said, as they resumed walking.

"And write. My friend at the *Monitor* taught me years ago when we were in the old country. We're still friends, even now. And sometimes he'll bring me one of his papers hopin' I'll see the light and join the WBA." He pulled her to a stop, his large hands cupping her upper arms. "I know you thought me illiterate, and I'll not be holdin' that against you. I'm a rough man, to be sure. But a man can be many things, Jenny, and each of them warrin' against the other." He let go of her. "Bring me somethin' and if I like it I'll be passin' it along."

"You'd do that? You'd help me, a woman, write for a paper?"

"If coal country can be changed by your pen, and the pen of others like you, then I'm not so much of a fool as to want to be stoppin' it." He smiled and offered her his arm, and as Virginia took it, she noticed they had walked a good distance. "But it will cost," he added, "for there's somethin' I'll be wantin' from you."

"Oh?" Virginia said as they turned and headed back to the house. "And what is that?" she asked, not at all certain she wanted to know the answer.

"You must swallow your pride, that pride which is as flamin' as that red hair of yours, and call me Patrick. And don't go lookin' at me sideways, neither. 'Tis only a name. I'm not askin' for a kiss or to hold your hand. 'Tis no indecent thing I'm wantin', Jenny."

For a long time Virginia didn't say a word. And the silence wasn't the unpleasant thing she had imagined. It was, in fact, rather comfortable. But his request troubled her. He was a sly one, this hulking enigma of a man, for he knew full well this wasn't about a name. What he was really asking was this: was she willing to consider him an equal?

Finally, when she sighted his house, Virginia leaned closer, so that no one would hear. "You'll have my article at week's end, Patrick."

CHAPTER 5

Virginia sat at the small desk in the upstairs library trying to finish her article for the *Monitor*. She yawned as she dipped her pen into a circular blown-glass inkwell. She was tired. She had been dressed and writing for hours, but still wasn't finished.

She breathed deeply, hoping to draw inspiration from the room with its large wooden bookcases that reached the ceiling and filled entire walls. The "treasure chest" she called it. And great pains had been taken to protect this treasure. Green pleated-silk covered the glazed doors of each bookcase, protecting the leather bound volumes from dust and sun.

She was grateful Kate had been able to talk Mother out of converting the library into a bedchamber for boarders. Trust Kate to come up with a solution, though it had cost Virginia her bedroom. For in order to save the "treasure chest", Kate had to convince Mother to turn their upstairs sitting room into a bedroom that both Virginia and Charlotte shared, thus freeing up their own rooms for renters. But how could she complain? The converted sitting room was still roomier than Kate's linen closet, even with two people sharing it.

Absently, she picked at the soft shalloon cloth protecting the desktop from nibs and ink, then adjusted the lighting of the tall-chimney oil lamp. She thought of Father, and how he had bought her this lamp, with its milk-glass base, to use while "writing." It was one of his many attempts to reconcile himself to a forward thinking daughter he never understood. What would he think, now, of her writing for a union paper? She doubted he'd be pleased, though perhaps a small part of him would be proud, too. She sighed and glanced at the tall mahogany clock that told her time was slipping away. With a flurry of her pen, she completed the last paragraph.

Would Patrick like it? She had tried framing a convincing argument for including a Widow's Row in all collieries. For the past week, every free moment had been spent gathering information. What she found was both expected and surprising. She already knew that anxiety ran higher among women living in patches without a Widow's Row. But what she hadn't expected was the fatalism that permeated every patch. Miners lived in constant fear of weak rock support, the presence of explosive fire damp, carbon monoxide, flooding, and the ever present threat of a mining mishap that could leave them dead, or disabled and incapable of ever working again.

She learned, that over time, this boulder of anxiety ground down to acceptance. Death was likely, and the miners powerless to prevent it. It was this preoccupation with death that accounted for some of the heavy drinking. Miners, believing it could be just around the corner, often looked for distractions. Others succumbed to superstition. Their work, after all, took them deep into the bowels of the earth— Satan's territory. Often these miners wouldn't move or start a new job on Friday; always ate in the same place; discouraged the presence of women at the mines, and so forth. And though Virginia didn't believe in such superstitions, all her research, even of those seemingly foolish things, seemed to knit her heart to coal country and to the people who lived and worked and died here.

Quickly, she reread her work, then made corrections, added new lines, deleted others. When she was satisfied, she copied it onto a fresh sheet of paper, folded it, then secured it with red sealing wax stamped with her father's signet ring. It was all in keeping with how she had told Patrick to expect her correspondences.

She wondered again if Patrick would like her article, then laughed at her boldness in calling him by his first name. Neither Mother nor Kate nor Charlotte would approve. But already it seemed so natural, so comfortable. At least in her mind. She never thought of him as Mr. O'Brien anymore. But speaking his name, actually saying it aloud, that still stuck in her throat.

She tucked the folded paper inside her small cloth purse. If Patrick didn't like the article, he'd certainly tell her. One thing she had already learned about him, he had no trouble speaking his mind.

She ran her hands over her hair as she glanced at the clock. She wanted to get to Main Street and back before anyone missed her. She'd have to hurry. Already the sun, streaming through the window, was warming the faded damask-covered cushions of the window seat. She extinguished the lamp, then flew down the stairs, grateful that the carpet, held in place by silver-plated stair rods, muffled her noise. Already the house was waking. Boarders could be heard milling about in their rooms. And from the large, back-hall window on the first floor, Virginia saw Colonel Smyth heading for their tidy little outhouse that sported both elaborate wood trim and a cupola.

The clanking of pots in the kitchen told Virginia her mother was already busy preparing breakfast. There would be no time to waste. Without making a sound, Virginia darted through the door and out into a glorious morning.

A warm, pleasant breeze fluttered the tendrils of her hair as well as the dogwoods that seemed, to Virginia, to wag like bushy tails among the thick crop of white and yellow pines. She hurried along the narrow path leading to Main Street. Through the trees, she spotted a few merchants unlocking their doors while others were busy pulling merchandise onto the wooden plank sidewalk. But for the most part, the sidewalk and street were empty. It made it easier to spot the little boy who stood on the corner.

Virginia scurried past the large hardware store, the coppersmith, the tavern, the milliner's shop, apothecary and book shop, the clothing store, Martin's Dry Goods, then stopped in front of Antonio Carbonetti's new grocery. She felt guilty that seeing it still gave her perverse pleasure since it was the cause of that disagreeable Martin Roach having to eat humble pie after he tried, but failed, to stop the Carbonettis from opening their shop.

She smiled down at the little boy who stood near its door. He appeared only a few years older than Sean Muldoon, and wore clean but worn overalls, scuffed boots, and a little cloth cap. He held his right arm close to his body as though trying to conceal the fact that there was only a one-inch stump where his hand should be.

"Are you Michael O'Malley?"

The boy grinned and nodded. "You Miss Virginia?"

"The very same." She opened her purse, pulled out the folded paper and three pennies, then placed them all in his open left hand.

Patrick had told her about Michael, about his accident at the breaker and how after he lost his hand he was discharged by the breaker boss. Patrick also spoke proudly of how Michael continued working by picking coal from the dangerous culm bank whenever the company police weren't around, then sold the burlap bags of coal for ten cents each—though Virginia wondered why Patrick didn't consider this stealing. But now that the Mattson Colliery had buried the culm bank beneath mounds of dirt due to the recent fire, Michael had lost that livelihood as well.

So the boy came to Sweet Air every morning, the community considered affluent by miners, in order to do odd jobs. Merchants gave him pennies to run errands or sweep and wash the walk in front of their establishments. And on slow days, Michael collected dog excrement or "pure" as the tanner in the next town called it, the one who purchased it from Michael for his leather processing.

It was Michael O'Malley who would carry the articles and notes between Patrick and Virginia. It sounded simple. Patrick had made it sound simple. But sooner or later people would find out. And then what? Would she be prepared for the consequences?

Kate hated flies. They were especially bad this year, and seemed to be everywhere. She was glad they were finally going to deal with the pests. She and Mother had already taken all the cheap, yellow cambric from the trunk in the garret and brought them down, placing a pile in every room. And all morning Kate had worked to finish the best parlor: securing all the windows with gauze blinds, then covering the large gilded mirror and paintings with cambric. She had also hung strips of sticky spiral flypaper in corners; then for good measure tacked red-berry asparagus clippings over the door.

Ridding a house of flies was a big undertaking. Everyone was needed. Even now, Charlotte was working in the dining room and Virginia in the back parlor. Before nightfall, the entire downstairs, including the three downstairs bedrooms, would be done.

That still left upstairs. And since Kate still had an hour before she was needed in the kitchen, there was time enough for one more room, provided she worked quickly. For days, Clarence Thumbolt, the retired railroad man, had been complaining how the flies were pouring into his room like a Biblical plague. Mother was there now remedying the situation. So Kate decided Jasper Wright's room should be next since he had shown a prickly nature whenever inconvenienced by even petty matters like his bread not sufficiently toasted or his linens improperly ironed.

But when Kate reached the top of the stairs and glanced into the partially opened door of Joshua Adams' room and saw it empty, she changed her mind. Time to test her resolve. No temptation would induce her to violate his privacy this time.

She entered and saw that his bed was made and everything neatly arrayed with the exception of the razor case lying open on his desk. Ignoring it, she went straight to the task of securing the gauze blind over the window.

"I'm glad you're here, Miss Kate."

She turned toward the familiar voice and smiled. "Mr. Adams, you'll be pleased to know that tonight you'll have a fly-proof room."

"I need to talk to you," he said, stepping into the room and closing the door behind him.

She would have protested if it were not for the worried look on his face. "What is wrong, sir? You look distressed."

"Remember I told you Mr. Pinkerton had an inside man? The one sent to infiltrate the Molly Maguires?"

"Yes."

"Well, he has successfully penetrated the AOH."

Kate frowned. "The Ancient Order of Hibernians? I thought it was a respectable organization." Hadn't Mother told her it was an Irish Catholic fraternity that helped its dues-paying members with favors, advice, and sometimes money? It even had a benign motto, 'friendship, unity, and true Christian charity.' And didn't Mother tell her that Mary O'Brien's husband and some of his friends belonged to it?

"Yes, it's respectable." Joshua tossed his large farmer's hat onto the polished mahogany desktop. "At least in other locals where it's just similar to Protestant societies like the Knights of Pythias. But here, in Schuylkill County, the AOH appears tied to the Molly Maguires. It seems that most of the bodymasters, the so-called leaders of these chapters, are men from Donegal. And even the Catholic clergy in Schuylkill have condemned many of their activities.

"But the good news is that the AOH has accepted our man. He's one of them now. He's taken their secret oath; learned their passwords and handshakes. They trust him. And because they do, he's been able to learn much."

"Anything relevant to Father's case?" Kate laid the wad of netting on the bed, then joined him by the desk.

"No. But our man is slowly compiling a list of those who might be involved with the Mollies. And . . . it seems your friend, Patrick O'Brien, is one of them. I thought I should warn you. I know how friendly your mother has been with the O'Briens. But now that Mrs. O'Brien has moved to Pittsburg, she should distance herself from Patrick. It would be best. If our agent is able to build a case against him, it may not go well with his associates. Questions will be asked."

"You're *not* suggesting that Mother will be linked to the Mollies?"

"No, only . . . well, with your father's trial still so fresh, I thought you'd want to avoid any notoriety." He touched her sleeve. "Truthfully, I was thinking mostly of you. I didn't want you to experience any-more embarrassment or . . . pain." He removed his hand and let it drift to the dusty hat on his desk. "But there's another point. Our agent thinks Patrick O'Brien might be dangerous. He may be linked with some violence in the past. You and your family need to under-stand that."

"I see. Of course I'll let them know," Kate said, leading him to the door. "And thank you for telling me."

Joshua raked his mop of hair. "Someday I'd like you to see me as I really am, properly dressed and groomed." He looked at her a bit too intently and stood a bit too close. His hand went to the knob, and before she could say a word, he opened the door and there was Mother coming from Mr. Thumbolt's room. She paused, lowered her eyes, then quickly descended the stairs. But the expression on her face told Kate she was clearly scandalized.

Goodness. How was she going to explain this?

⸻

Kate wished her black-laced boots didn't make such a loud tapping noise as she walked across the large terra-cotta tiles of the kitchen floor, a floor covered in rag carpet only in winter. Even the cheerful walls, freshly painted with yellow ocher wash, failed to elevate her mood.

Normally she loved being here. It was the only room she really enjoyed, now, other than their back parlor. She loved its spaciousness, and the fact that it ran across the entire left side of the house instead of the back, which was more customary. But this position afforded them a wonderful panorama of the hills and woods without the clutter of an outhouse or clothesline. It also gave them a good view of their prized tulip garden—the envy of Sweet Air, and which was, even now, ablaze with color.

Ignoring the wafting orders of herbs and drying meats hanging among the pots overhead, Kate went to the corner where Mother often spent time checking the barrels of buckwheat meal, flour, corn meal, and salt. No sign of her. But near the wall filled with shelves of crockery was the cloth-lined plate-rack. Kate noticed it already held dishes ready to be rolled in front of the hearth for warming before dinner. Mother's handiwork to be sure. She was here somewhere.

Kate rounded the corner and there she was, her plump body wrapped in a white apron, plucking a chicken. Kate's stomach churned, though she didn't understand why. Mother was reasonable. She would understand, once Kate explained things. Even so, Kate's courage waned with every step as she passed the large double sink, the ovens and stoves, then crossed to the opposite wall where two sizable work tables were nestled beneath a large window. Kate came along side her mother and picked up a potato from the nearby pile. Then she peeled potatoes while her mother plucked chickens and all without either of them saying a word.

By the time Mother plucked her fifth chicken, Kate had worked up her courage and finally shared Joshua's information about Patrick O'Brien. She watched her mother salt and wash the chickens. Watched her tuck them into two large roasting pans. *Why didn't she say something?* When her mother opened a small cask of raisins and stuffed them, along with several sprigs of rosemary, into the chicken-cavities, and all without a word, Kate blurted, "I've explained all this so you would understand why Mr. Adams and I were behind closed doors."

"I'm sorry to hear Patrick O'Brien is under suspicion." Her mother wiped her hands on her apron and turned to Kate. "He's an intense man but that doesn't mean he's dangerous or has done anything wrong. Your information will not change my attitude toward him, nor my involvement at the patch."

"No . . . I . . . didn't think so."

"But it's not Patrick O'Brien I'm concerned about. Don't you know I never doubted your conduct? You don't need an open door to behave like a lady. But it's the others, those living with us. You know most of our boarders have little to occupy their time, so they fill it with gossip. Sweet Air is a small town, Kate. Something seen and misunderstood by a boarder could easily turn into a scandal. Surely you understand that. Scripture cautions us to flee even the *appearance* of evil." Her mother folded Kate in her arms and kissed her cheek. "A woman's reputation is a fragile thing. She must protect it."

Kate rested her head on her mother's shoulder. Oh, how she wanted to weep like a child and tell her mother everything, the way she used to when things went wrong or were too hard. She wanted to tell her why Joshua Adams was really here, and about the rent money she had been collecting from him, and how she had violated his privacy, and even how she *shouldn't* be behind closed doors with him because of the strange way he made her feel. Confessing to Mother always seemed to make things better. And perhaps she would have if her sisters had not suddenly burst into the kitchen and shattered the moment.

When there was a knock on her door, Kate knew who it was. Earlier, she had asked Virginia to come to her room before retiring. She wanted to tell her about Patrick O'Brien, and this out of Charlotte's hearing. There was no need to burden Charlotte with Joshua's news. Charlotte never went to the patch so there was little likelihood of her ever seeing the man. And what good would it do to have Charlotte fretting over Mother's continued patronage of Patrick O'Brien and how it might affect her standing with the Gaylords, should they find out?

But Virginia was another matter. She had changed—running to Higgins Patch and the nearby collieries every minute. And for reasons she wouldn't divulge. And Kate had not forgotten how that awful Patrick O'Brien had looked at Virginia when they had visited the patch with Joshua Adams. And afterward, too. She had seen how he stared at Virginia in a most brazen manner during Tom O'Brien's wake. And even how the two had walked the path together.

Another tap, and Kate opened the door.

"You wanted to see me?" Virginia said, in her customary forthright manner. Her beautiful long hair, cascading over her shoulders and shimmering like fire in the dim lamp light, looked freshly brushed.

Kate directed Virginia to the bed, where they both sat down. Then she quickly relayed Joshua's information. "I've already told

Mother. But I failed to dissuade her. I fear she'll continue helping out at the patch without making the slightest effort to avoid this man, even though I stressed how dangerous he might be. Perhaps if you were to voice your concern, maybe that would do it. Will you try?"

Virginia rose, her face nearly as red as her hair. "I will not. Why should we take the word of this . . . amateurish Pinkerton? And how did he come by his information? A rumor, an unkind remark, dropped at the Sweet Air Tavern?"

"No . . . not the tavern. I'm sure his information is credible."

"Why? Because you like him? Because bringing him here was *your* idea. Because you . . . . But never mind. Just know I won't try to dissuade Mother."

Kate was all astonishment. Though Charlotte was the purported beauty of the family, Kate had always considered Virginia even prettier with her flaming red hair, her dimpled cheek, her flawless skin, and dancing green eyes. And though Kate knew people teased Virginia about how all redheads had a temper, the truth was, Virginia rarely showed any, and only when she cared deeply about something. So why was she acting this way now? It didn't make sense. "Virginia, I . . . don't know what to say. You're behaving so strangely. Why is this such a hard thing?"

"Because . . . I have made his acquaintance, and I believe I know Patrick O'Brien well enough to say I have nothing to fear, therefore no reason to stop seeing him."

"*Stop seeing him*? Oh, Virginia, whatever do you mean?"

"If you must know I'm planning to write articles for a friend of his at the *Anthracite Monitor*. In fact, I've already written one."

"The *Anthracite Monitor*? What about?"

"The need for more Widow's Rows."

"So that's what you've been up to this past week; running out to all the collieries."

"Yes, and if Patrick likes it, he'll . . . ."

"*Patrick*? You say his name as if you were more than acquaintances. Is this what it's come to? You running wild all over the countryside and keeping secrets and . . . ."

"I'm not the only one keeping secrets. What about *your* secret?"

"What secret?"

"The one between you and Joshua Adams. Just how is it that he has been here nearly a month and you're still able to pay him? With what? You haven't even sold your quilt. And don't tell me it's because he's only charging half price. Our money should have run out long ago."

"Well . . . I . . . that is . . . ."

"Don't bother explaining. You see, that's the difference between us. Whatever the reason he's still here, I know it's all right, and I know it because I *trust* you. Why can't you trust me, too?"

"Maybe I know things you don't; things I'm not at liberty to share. But believe me, Virginia, I do trust you. I just can't say the same for Patrick O'Brien. He might be dangerous. You could get hurt. Your reputation could become sullied." She folded her hands on her lap. "'A woman's reputation is a fragile thing. She must protect it,'" she said, quoting Mother and feeling like a hypocrite. "I love you, Virginia, and wish to spare you grief. And of course we must consider Father's investigation."

"Ah . . . Father's investigation. Now it comes out." Virginia took the few steps to the door. "I'm sorry we don't see things the same way, Kate, but I'll not do as you ask, and that's final." She opened the door, then turned. "You know . . . I loved Father too. And things can't always be your way." With that, she left.

Virginia hurried along the narrow, dusty path, clutching her good moiré skirt, trying to keep the hem from getting soiled. She moved so quickly she barely missed twisting her ankle in one of the ruts. *Slow down, slow down, he'll still be there.* She tried ignoring the heat. It was unusually hot for this time of year, and the absence of a breeze made it uncomfortable.

She wondered what Patrick wanted. His note arrived this morning, just before church, carried by little Michael O'Malley who had waited in front of her house while she penned a reply agreeing to this meeting.

"Must see you," was all his note said. Michael had to fill in the rest, relaying details of the time and place they were to meet. Thankfully, the house was in an uproar with everyone trying, at once, to ready themselves for morning service. Virginia knew it was only this confusion that prevented the appearance of a little one-handed boy, clad in overalls, and carrying a crumpled piece of brown paper, from being noticed.

It had been difficult for Virginia to sit through the service and pastor's sermon on "the importance of maintaining a clear conscience before God." It had been difficult for her to help Mother and Kate and Charlotte prepare lunch for their boarders, then wait patiently while everyone ate like snails. And it had been difficult to hear the clock strike two and still be in the kitchen washing dishes, when that was the very hour she was to be at the old Catholic Church near Higgins Patch.

Finally, at quarter after, when every dish was dried and put away, she took off her apron and declared she was "going for a stroll." A nice, long Sunday stroll. And everyone believed her. Everyone except Kate, judging by the look on her face.

Must see you. That sounded urgent. Virginia quickened her pace. What could it mean? Maybe it wasn't urgent at all. Maybe she was reading too much into it. Maybe he just didn't like her article. She found herself growing angry. That was hardly a reason to summon her like this. They had agreed that her articles, and any correspondences pertaining to them, would be couriered by Michael O'Malley.

Perspiration dotted Virginia's forehead. She should slow down. If it was important enough to send her this note, he would wait. But oh what a sight she must be! Surely by now the heat had spoiled the lovely curls she had taken such pains to create. She had pulled back her hair—to accentuate her high cheekbones and the delicate curve of her chin, though she'd be hard pressed to admit it—then fashioned long curls that cascaded down her back. She fingered her hair. Everything still seemed to be in place.

Her clothes had been carefully chosen, too: a tan bolero jacket that hugged her slim waist and was partially open to reveal a white blouse and green silk tie. Her long brown skirt was sleekly tailored and swept backward, and boasted a modest bustle. And a straw hat, ornamented only by a thin white ribbon, completed the picture, a picture meant to convey to Patrick that she was no flighty female to be taken lightly.

But all her fussing seemed silly now. Thankfully, the path was nearly deserted. The Masses were over, and most of the parishioners were home, eating. At least few would see her heading toward the patch, though the ones that passed gave her odd looks.

Finally, between the thicket of dogwoods and mountain laurels, she saw the church just outside Higgins Patch. The building, itself, was an old brick structure with three arches leading to a narrow portico. Little stain-glass windows dotted the periphery and gave colorful illustrations of the life of Jesus; a useful reminder, Virginia thought, to those heavily burdened, that there was Someone who wanted to carry their load. A red and white brick cupola topped it all off and housed the large bronze bell that announced deaths and Sunday Masses.

There was no one in sight except for the tall, imposing man who stood among the old headstones of the little adjoining cemetery. His hair was combed back but not oiled, and his face was clean-shaven. And instead of overalls, he wore dark trousers and a jacket. He held a cluster of wild honeysuckles, and Virginia wondered if he was visiting a grave. He saw her too, but stood in place, waiting.

The little wrought-iron gate creaked as she opened it and stepped inside, then carefully maneuvered the weed-encrusted tombstones. "Is everything all right?" she said, when she reached him.

"You're late, Jenny." He shoved the handful of drooping vines in her face. "But 'twas worth the wait. 'Tis a fine sight you make."

Virginia looked at the flowers, then realizing they were for her, frowned and took them. "What has happened? What's wrong?"

"There's nothing wrong, lass."

"It's my article, then. You didn't like it."

"Oh, it was a grand piece. I've sent it off to my friend and he thinks so too. He'll be publishin' it in his paper next week. And he says to send him others, as long as they are as good."

"Then why have you sent for me? I don't understand. I thought something terrible had happened and . . . ."

She suddenly felt Patrick's large hands on her shoulders pulling her closer. "I was achin' for the sight of you, Jenny, and just had to see you. And oh, how lovely you look, too. And I'd like to be thinkin' it was on account of me that you fixed yourself up so. 'Tis the image of your face that I've been takin' into the mine with me. The tunnels don't look nearly so dark now."

Virginia pushed against his chest, trying to distance herself, but his hold was too strong. "Please don't talk that way. I won't stay another minute if you do."

Patrick's dark eyes smiled into hers as he let her go. "'Tis no use. It can't be helped. I'll be sayin' what's on my heart. And you can listen or no."

"Patrick, you mustn't send for me like this. We must confine our correspondences to letters or notes carried by Michael O'Malley, as we agreed. People will talk and . . . ."

"Ah, 'tis that awful pride of yours that's speakin'. Do you not like me, Jenny? Even a wee bit?"

"Yes, of course I like you but don't you see . . . ."

"See what? That you and me are so much alike we are as one breath? That I know your heart and mind better than you do? And that I'm the very man for you. Will you not give me a chance?"

"What you ask is impossible. Impossible! And we're not alike. Not at all. We're from different worlds, we're . . . well . . . it's impossible!"

"Impossible is it? Do you want to know what's impossible, Jenny? What's impossible is a man going into the bowels of the earth, and diggin' and scrapin' out a livin' with his hands, then walkin' out alive. Every day a man goes into a mine could be his last. Every day is *precious*. And I'll not be wastin' any part of it. I love you, lass, and you'll not be changin' it, say what you will."

"I . . . I won't be coming again. Either we correspond by mail or not at all." She headed toward the gate.

"I suppose it will have to do, for now at least," he said, coming up beside her and taking her arm. "But might I walk you home? Part way at least?"

Virginia shook her head. "We'll say good-bye here."

He looked at her so intensely that for a second Virginia feared he was going to kiss her. "Ah, how cruel you are, lass," he finally said. "Not even willin' to give a few crumbs to a starvin' man."

"God speed." She turned to leave.

"One more thing, Jenny," he said, stopping her. "I've been lookin' for those two men I told you and your sister about, the two who said it was your father who wanted to hire me for a bit of mischief. And when I find 'em I'll be havin' a nice long talk with the pair. Who knows what I'll be shakin' out of 'em?"

"You . . . won't do anything rash, will you? You won't make trouble for yourself by assaulting them?" She thought of the accusations Kate had leveled against him. They would be watching him now. "And these men . . . they could be dangerous, you know."

A big grin split across Patrick's face. "Ah, Jenny, I fear your heart has betrayed you. 'Tis plain you care about me for otherwise you wouldn't fret so."

"You're a ridiculous man!" The muscles of her face tensed with anger as she opened the wrought-iron gate and stepped onto the path, all the while tightly clutching the flowers in her hand.

Charlotte was as nervous as a cat. Any minute, Benjamin Gaylord would come walking through that door. She glanced around the back parlor for the hundredth time, seeing if everything was in place. Her sisters had helped tidy up, and even helped organize the tea table beside her. It was covered with a lovely embroidered cloth, and arrayed with two delicate gold-rimmed English tea cups, a plate of buttered bread which Kate had helped her make, a nosegay of four purple pansies in a crystal bud vase, and Mother's best teapot hidden beneath a handsome quilted bonnet.

Charlotte had been planning this since yesterday, after Benjamin stopped to present his calling card and ask that he be allowed to visit Charlotte promptly at four the following afternoon during tea. And oh, how it made Charlotte fly into a tizzy! What was she to wear? And should her buttered bread be left flat, or rolled as Mrs. Gaylord was prone to do?

She finally settled on rolled bread and her prettiest tea gown; a ruffled green dress with long puffed sleeves and tight bodice of expensive polished cotton. Around her high collar was the string of pearls Benjamin had given her, and around her wrist, a simple gold bracelet; both in keeping with the time of day and the custom dictating that glittering gems only be worn for more significant occasions.

But her hair had caused her no end of grief until Kate came to the rescue and helped create the elaborate braiding Charlotte desired; skillfully securing them in attractive loops across the back of her head.

All this had taken hours, and Charlotte marveled at Kate's patience, for it was time spent away from doing the many chores required to properly maintain their large house, a house that once boasted a staff of five servants. Charlotte hoped, by all her effort, to give Benjamin something pleasant to remember when he was surrounded by this year's bevy of London debutants. And it seemed worth it, for even Virginia, who preferred casual living and plain fashion, complimented her by saying that she and her tea table had never looked lovelier.

Now, Charlotte sat in one of the damask-covered chairs, smoothing the ruffles of her skirt and thinking how kind Benjamin was to make time for a visit. Tomorrow, he and his mother would leave for New York, and from there board an ocean liner to England. Surely, he still had much to do in preparation. And she had been careful to point that out to her sisters, who agreed it was most congenial of him to think of socializing today. She was certain this visit was meant to allay her fears; to tell her all was well with them in spite of his mother's protestations; that he still loved her and wanted her to be waiting for him when he returned.

Her heart jumped when she heard his familiar voice offering all manner of polite salutations and warm felicitations to her mother who ushered him into the parlor.

Charlotte rose, allowed Benjamin to salute her with a shallow bow, then resumed her seat. He placed his black silk top hat on the empty rocker before taking the damask-covered chair beside her. Before Charlotte could remove the bonnet from the teapot, her mother disappeared, leaving the parlor door slightly ajar.

"Your visit is timely." Charlotte poured tea into the cup containing a slice of lemon, which Benjamin favored. "I was planning to send a note wishing you God-speed on your journey. Now I can wish it in person. How excited you must be! The Derby is sure to be thrilling. I understand that even now Parliament is preparing to adjourn in anticipation of this year's racing season." She was glad she had overheard Colonel Smyth mention this.

Benjamin took the cup from Charlotte's extended hand but said nothing, making her wonder why he was so quiet when normally he was a fountain of polite conversation. She offered him the plate of bread, and was disappointed when he refused. "I made these especially for you."

He placed his cup, untouched, on a nearby table, then began drumming the arm of his chair. "If you must know, I am far too upset to partake. It is best I come right out and tell you that this is not a pleasant social call. I'm here to discuss the rumors circulating around town."

"*What* rumors?"

"I am too much of a gentleman to repeat them. But I shall skirt the edges and leave it to you to fill in the rest." He straightened in his chair. "For one thing, I've heard about the disgraceful way your sister, Kate, has been conducting herself with your cousin, Joshua Adams.

I've been told that undeniable improprieties have occurred of such a delicate nature I dare not repeat them, but you can well imagine.

"And as for this cousin of yours, in addition to his ungentlemanly comportment toward Miss Kate, other aspects of his behavior must be called into question. What does he mean by running all over town? Stirring things up? Prodding and poking into matters best forgotten? How are we ever to get past the disgrace of your father's hanging if these unseemly relatives of yours continue to bring it up?"

"I . . . I think we . . . I think our family has every right to try and clear its name. And as for Kate, she is the picture of feminine virtue. I resent your implication and . . . ."

"But that's not the half of it. Your mother is not without stain. Always traipsing off to the mines or Higgins Patch, and associating with *riffraff*. Has she forgotten she is still a woman of some stature?"

"I will not hear another word against my mother! She is . . . ."

"And imagine my shock when I heard that you, too, actually visited that dirty pesthole. What reason could you possibly have for doing such a thing?"

"I attended a wake. He was a friend of . . . ."

"But worst of all is your sister, Virginia! When I heard she was writing for the *Anthracite Monitor* I refused to believe it. Then her article came out. An article that criticizes the Mattson Colliery, the colliery recently acquired by the railroad. The very railroad from which *I* derive my employment! In addition, I am told your sister has taken up with one of the miners, a rough, coarse man, I understand. How is such a thing to be tolerated? You know my family enjoys great standing in the community."

He was sitting on the edge of his chair now, and Charlotte found herself half expecting him to fall off.

"You know how hard I've worked. First at my studies; trying to finish strong at Harvard, then for the past two years at the railroad."

His hand pulled on his beard. "Don't you understand that the very eyes of Franklin B. Gowen are on me! And he has great plans, Charlotte, and I am to be part of them. My family has plans, too. I'm expected to follow in my father's footsteps. To be a captain of industry. And my father left large footprints, to be sure. Footprints that can only be filled with an understanding wife by my side. A wife worthy of the honor. How then am I to countenance all this behavior?"

Benjamin rose and began shifting his weight from one polished black boot to the other. "In truth, my mother believes you and your family have breached all bounds of proper behavior, and she has even suggested I consider a more suitable wife."

Charlotte's cup and saucer rattled in her trembling hand as she placed them on the table. "Then sir, I suggest when you are in England you search out a possible bride from among the many debutants you shall encounter!"

Benjamin appeared taken back. "I . . . I'm not going to England, much to my mother's strenuous objection. I have told her I must stay and guide you through this rash and foolish time before it's too late. Thus far I've been able to convince her that this is all a product of you and your family's great loss, and that a proper Christian attitude would be one of forgiveness and a willingness to steer you and yours away from these unfortunate indiscretions and back onto a more proper path."

Charlotte rose, gripping the arms of her chair. "Since I and my family are so repugnant to you, I see no reason to continue our relationship. I release you from your pledge. You are free, Mr. Gaylord, to find the suitable wife both you and your mother so crave."

The color drained from Benjamin's face. "My only thought was to avert a possible disaster for both of us. I assure you, it was never my intention to break our engagement."

"Then I shall break it, sir. I pray you and your mother have a pleasant voyage. Good day."

Benjamin picked up his hat. "As I said, I shall not be going to England. My one hope is that you will come to your senses and consider my position. When you do, perhaps we can work things out."

Long after Benjamin Gaylord left, Charlotte remained in the parlor, weeping inconsolably, and nothing her sisters or mother said could comfort her.

⁓

Kate's head felt so heavy she could barely move it. And why was it so difficult to see? Yes . . . that was the problem. The dense fog. And was that a prison yard? Everything looked gray. Was it raining? No. Only a shower of pebbles being scattered about the yard by the crowd of people—important people, by the look of them. Why had they come? Her heart pounded when she saw the gallows. Oh . . . yes . . . it was today. She heard other voices, hundreds of them outside the prison walls, voices of those not important enough to be allowed to attend the hanging but who would be allowed entrance after the execution, when the gates were opened to the public. Even so, she could see some enterprising onlookers in nearby treetops, those who had come early enough to get a place on one of the limbs.

The mist was so heavy now it almost felt wet. Surely it was raining. Through it, she managed to see others filing into the yard. Who are . . . ? Oh, the jurors. She knew their faces: every line, every contour, every blemish. Hadn't she watched them all throughout the trial? Searching for signs of how it was going?

Her eyes returned to the gallows. There it was in front, where everyone could see, tall and solid; a single rope dangling from the center of the crossbeam. On the scaffolding floor laid a white hood and two sets of steel manacles. And what was that on the ground just below? A coffin? Had the undertaker already come to measure the prisoner? Yes . . . he must have . . . and now the coffin sat open and empty, waiting . . . waiting.

Suddenly, there was a stir as heads turned and bodies rose up on toes to see. Kate tried to push up too, but couldn't. Who was coming? She had to wait until the little procession reached the gallows. And there he was, wearing a black waistcoat and dark gray trousers beneath a black velvet-collar frock coat. His collared shirt was so white it looked almost blinding in the mid-morning sun. And his shoes . . . how polished! How they glinted in the sun as he walked! Oh, what a fine figure of a man! Tall, strong, dignified. But how could he look so calm? Didn't he know what was about to happen? Didn't he *understand*? In his hand was a small, black Bible. Oh . . . and there was her pastor walking alongside him, whispering. Words of comfort? Perhaps that explained it. Oh Lord, thank you for pastors! But she didn't like the look of the two men leading the procession: the stately prison warden appeared far too pleased with himself, and the beefy middle-aged sheriff staggered when he walked. Surely he wasn't drunk?

When the prisoner reached the steps, he hesitated, but only for a second. Then he began his climb. How many steps were there? She couldn't count. But it seemed to take the prisoner forever to climb them. When he gained the platform, a large man, who now held the steel manacles, took the Bible, handed it to the pastor who had finally arrived at the top, then began shackling the prisoner. Oh, how rough he was. No, don't . . . . You needn't be so forceful! He won't run away. He'd never run away.

Now his hands and feet were fettered. Oh, what a sight! She couldn't bear to see anymore. *Close your eyes, just close your eyes*. No use. There was the hangman, clear as day, taking the noose and tightening it around the prisoner's neck. Next came the white hood. Take it off! Let me see his face, his kind, dear face one more time! Just one more time.

She heard the pastor praying, then he moved away. All was quiet now. She could hear the wind sighing through the trees. Oh, it had to be raining. She could feel it on her face, her clothes. She held her breath. Then came the terrible thud of the trap-door dropping and the sight of the body twisting and shaking, the legs drawn up, then swinging forward, until finally a shudder and then . . . nothing but stillness.

"Father!" Kate shot up in bed, perspiration soaking her nightgown, tears drenching her face. She had not had this dream for some time. Why now? Was it because she had been stirring things up? Making everyone relive this past heartbreak? Bringing it to the forefront of everyone's mind, including hers? Why hadn't she listened to Mother? Why couldn't she just leave it alone?

She covered her face with her hands. "Oh Lord, what am I doing? To myself? My family?" She thought of how Charlotte had wept after breaking her engagement. And Virginia, how she was running wild, aligning herself with danger, and pitting herself against the powerful railroad. And Mother, broken hearted and praying for them all. *Oh what had she done?* She was destroying her family. How could she have been so selfish? Mother was right. Why did she think she could bring about justice on her own?

"Oh, Lord, forgive me. Please restore me and my family . . . our lives, our peace. Turn me back to You. Help me walk in Your ways."

CHAPTER 6

Charlotte knew she had been rash. Throwing her future away like that. Releasing Benjamin from his promise of marriage. She blotted her eyes with her fingers. *Oh why did she do it?* Maybe it wasn't too late. Maybe she could still make it right. She rose from her bed where she had been languishing since finishing her chores, and rubbed her forehead. *But how?* How could she possibly correct her folly? She walked to one of the small tables and picked up Benjamin's card, the one he presented to Mother the day before coming to tea. As she felt the expensive heavy paper, the raised lettering of the monogram, the answer came.

She hurried across the hall to the library, a room she rarely used. It intimidated her. She was sure Father and Virginia, and even Kate, had read most of the volumes housed in the tall mahogany bookcases, while she had barely read a dozen.

The green Windsor chair felt stiff to her back as she pulled out several sheets of paper, dipped her quill into the inkwell and began her letter. *Dear Benjamin . . . .* What was she to say? Forgive me? Take me back? It was all a mistake? I was hasty?

She pursed her lips. No . . . it wouldn't do. Groveling and fawning was not the way to win Benjamin's affection. She crumpled the paper and threw it into the nearby leather receptacle. Besides, what was she to ask forgiveness for? For being a Farrell? For having a father who was hanged for murder? For having a tender hearted mother who loved and blessed the people in the nearby patches? For having a clever sister who was unconventional and wanted to enter the male dominated world of newspapers? For having her eldest sister try everything she knew in order to clear the family name? How could Charlotte ask forgiveness for any of these? Yet, they all conspired to ruin her, to ruin the life she had envisioned for herself.

If only there was a way she could end this nightmare. If only she could remember something Father had told her. Something that would prove important to the case. Something that would bring it to a satisfying conclusion. Then maybe she could forget. Then maybe the town could forget. Then maybe Benjamin could forget. And things would return to the way they were. She rubbed her forehead trying to block out the sound of the nearby clock ticking away the time. It was useless. There was nothing more to remember. She had given Joshua Adams all her information, all her recollections, and though he had carefully recorded them in his notebook there was not one that seemed to impress him as being important.

She stared down at the blank sheets of paper spread across the desk. If only they had found that note Mr. Blakely sent Father. It would prove Father had not lied. And perhaps he'd still be alive, and she'd still be engaged to Benjamin. Oh, she was so tired of crying herself to sleep! If only . . . . She picked up the quill. What would the note have said? She suddenly found herself writing.

Dear Mr. Farrell:
I have an urgent matter to discuss with you. Kindly meet me at my colliery tonight after the breaker whistle sounds.
                              Sincerely,
                              Roger Blakely

She put down the pen. The note was simple enough; probably much like the one Mr. Blakely wrote Father. Could such a simple note really have made a difference? She stared at the paper. How easy it would be to pretend she found it stuck behind one of the desk drawers. What would people say then? "It seems your father wasn't a liar after all." And maybe if they realized that, they would also realize he wasn't a murderer, either. It wouldn't bring him back but maybe it would bring back their reputation, their standing in the community. But of course this was just silly conjecture. All anyone had to do was compare her handwriting to Mr. Blakely's to know it was a forgery. She was about to throw it away when she heard Virginia's voice.

"I didn't expect to find you here. I came to finish my . . . writing, but I'll come back later." She smiling over Charlotte's shoulder as if pleased to see her employed in this manner. "What are you doing?"

Charlotte crumpled her page and tried tossing it into the waste receptacle but it landed on the floor by Virginia's feet, instead. "Give it back!" she snapped, when Virginia picked it up. "It's . . . private . . . just something silly to pass the time."

Virginia frowned. "What's this? What does it mean?"

"Honestly, Virginia, why must you always be so full of questions? Can't I have any privacy? Or time to myself to pursue . . . to write a letter or two?"

"A letter or two? It looks like you were forging Mr. Blakely's note to Father."

Charlotte grabbed the paper from Virginia's hand. "I never intended to use it or show it to anyone, truly, Virginia. I was just sitting here thinking what if . . . and then I found myself writing it." She ripped the paper and watched the torn pieces flutter, like moths, over the polished desktop. "Oh, Virginia. I'm so miserable! Why did this have to happen to Father? And why must we go on paying and paying for it? Everyone hates us. To them, we are all 'fallen' women. What's to become of us? Are we to pay the rest of our lives?"

"I don't know," Virginia said softly, bending over and kissing Charlotte's forehead. "I really don't know."

Don't stare, Kate told herself as she wiped down the horsehair clothesline. But she had never seen Charlotte so glum. And it was all her fault. As she secured the ends of the line around two wooden posts, she determined to put the matter to rest. She would stop the investigation. It was the only way. Maybe then Charlotte and Benjamin Gaylord could resolve their differences. Maybe then joy would be restored to their home.

Out of the corner of her eye, she watched Charlotte place the basket of wet linens on the ground. Her face was pale; her eyes puffy and red. And her lovely blond hair, normally so neatly arranged in curls, was simply pulled back and netted at the nape of her neck. And all morning, as they stirred dozens of linens in boiling water with their clothes sticks, Charlotte didn't utter a word in spite of the fact that Kate tried to entice her with comments on fashion and parlor games; topics which had always delighted Charlotte in the past.

"Help me with this sheet," Kate said, pulling it from the heaping basket that represented hours of work. The weather was hotter now. That meant bedding had to be washed twice a week rather than once. "I'm almost looking forward to winter!"

Her sister gave no response as she stretched her end of the sheet over the line.

They hung three sheets in silence before Kate's patience waned. "You must stop this moping! Honestly, Charlotte, he's not worth it."

"That's just what I'd expect you to say. You never did like Benjamin. Though he's truly wonderful, really."

"How wonderful can he be? If he really loved you, he wouldn't care what others thought, not even his mother. He would defend you, and not worry so much about his reputation."

Charlotte began to cry.

"I'm sorry." Kate flung the end of her sheet over the line and turned to her sister. "I don't want to add to your sorrow, but you must face facts. Don't you think his coming here and lecturing you was arrogant? Surely it proves he cares more for his reputation than he does for you or your feelings."

Charlotte blotted her eyes with her fingertips. "Can't the same be said of you? Aren't you bent on clearing Father's name to save *your* reputation no matter who it hurts? Truly, Kate, it pains me to say it, but I see no difference between the two of you in that regard."

Kate had already faced this truth the night she woke up drenched from her dream. Even so, Charlotte's words felt like the snapping of a tree branch across her face. "Oh, my darling." She took Charlotte's hand, feeling very much like crying herself. "You're right of course, and what can I say except that I'm sorry? My bullying of you and Virginia has made a complete mess of things. Please, *please* forgive me. I don't know how else to make it right except by telling Mr. Adams he must suspend his investigation at once. Let us get back to picking up the tattered threads of our lives."

"Do you mean it? Oh, Kate, I think it would be best, truly it would, for all of us."

Kate nodded as she watched the rumpled figure of Joshua Adams head down the path toward Main Street. "I do mean it, Charlotte, and I'll prove it." Gathering her skirt in her hand she hurried after the Pinkerton. "Mr. Adams. Mr. Adams!"

At the sound of his name, the detective stopped and turned. When he saw her, he began retracing his steps.

"I'm sorry to detain you from any business you might have in town," Kate said, trying to catch her breath, "but it's important you stop the investigation at once." When he looked puzzled, she added, "I mean my father's investigation. Naturally, you may remain here as long as it takes you to conclude your investigation for the railroad."

"What brought this on? Why do you want me to desist?"

"For my family's sake." She was determined to abandon all pretenses. Honesty was the only course now. "It's ripping them apart." She gestured with her chin to where Charlotte stood hanging a pillow case. "She's been so glum, so miserable since breaking her engagement with Mr. Gaylord. And Virginia . . . I fear for her. I fear she is courting danger. I cannot search for truth at the expense of those I love."

"Perhaps not finding it would be worse."

"What do you mean?"

"Kate, it seems that you and your sisters are learning things about yourselves that you need to learn. This entire investigation is perhaps the very process God is using to reveal what's in your hearts, perhaps forcing you to see things you might not otherwise see. And suppressing the truth would not be wise."

Kate frowned. It was the first time he had spoken to her in such a familiar manner. And though inwardly it pleased her, it would hardly do. She had no intention of developing a relationship with a man who would soon be traipsing off to who-knows-where in search of danger. "I've . . . never heard you mention God before. I didn't know you were religious."

"There are many things you don't know about me. But never mind that now. Getting back to your father; I've uncovered some important information. I think it would be foolish to stop the investigation. May I speak to Miss Charlotte? Not only about my findings, but about something more personal, as well? And if I can ease her mind about the investigation, will you continue it?"

"I . . . well . . . there's Virginia to think of, too. She . . . didn't believe me about Patrick O'Brien, though I told her everything you told me, without mentioning your source, of course. She's writing for the *Monitor* now, and I fear she's becoming even more involved with that man."

"Perhaps nothing I say will alter Miss Virginia's course. But in the end, the truth will be just as important to her as it is to the rest of you. The question is, do you have the courage to see it through?"

Kate bristled. "Courage? Who was it that sent for you in the first place?"

"I'm not talking about vengeance, Kate, or about wanting to restore your family honor. I'm talking about truth. Do you want to find it?"

"Well . . . of course . . . naturally."

Joshua leaned closer. "Because your motives are important to me now. It matters what's in your heart. For how can you love anyone while you're seeking revenge? And I'd . . . I'd like for you to consider me a suitor. But even if you never see me that way, for your own sake you should continue the investigation. If you stop now, I think you'll regret it the rest of your life."

Kate's heart jumped. "I hardly know how to answer that, Mr. Adams, but . . . ."

"Joshua. Please call me Joshua."

"but you are presumptuous as usual."

"Then you don't want me to speak to your sister?"

"That's not what I was referring to. And . . . yes, if you think it will do any good . . . then by all means talk to her."

"And if I make her comfortable about my investigation, will you allow me to proceed?"

Kate nodded as she headed for the clothesline, shaken by Joshua declaring himself a suitor. And just what was this personal matter he spoke of? And why did he want to share it with *Charlotte*? Maybe she shouldn't have agreed. Maybe she should have heard it first, to see if it was fitting. She felt a prick in her heart. No, it wasn't jealousy. It couldn't be. If Joshua Adams wanted to tell Charlotte something personal, who was she to object? But for some reason she did.

"Mr. Adams has something to say to us, Charlotte." Kate dodged the sheets flapping in the breeze, and headed toward a large spreading maple and the wooden bench beneath it. Without a word, Charlotte followed. Kate was the first to sit, then Charlotte beside her. Joshua was already settled on a tree stump a few feet away.

"I've tracked down all the previous owners of the collieries that sold out to the railroad through your father's initiative." He directed his attention only to Charlotte. "And not one of them claimed they were coerced. In fact, they all said your father went to great lengths to innumerate both the benefits of keeping their collieries and the benefits of selling them. So we can consider, as false, any accusations that your father hired thugs to intimidate Roger Blakely."

In spite of herself, Kate heaved a sigh of relief while Charlotte remained as emotionless as a Grecian urn.

"I don't know about the other land agents for I've not had time to investigate their sales, but regarding Samuel Baxter, my inquiry has revealed him to be reprehensible. Both colliery owners said they were threatened, and told they would see no end of mayhem if they didn't sell. They said the thugs claimed to be Mollies. But that hardly makes sense since the Mollies oppose the purchase of any more collieries by the railroad; fearing conditions will worsen under their ownership.

"My next step is to visit Samuel Baxter, but I won't proceed unless you, Miss Charlotte, feel comfortable with me doing so. And I have, in fact, assured your sister, Kate, that I will drop the case at your say-so. However, before you give your answer I'd like to share something with you. Something personal that you might find interesting. May I?"

Kate held her breath as Joshua stopped and waited for Charlotte to respond. Charlotte seemed to think about it a lot longer than she normally seemed to think about anything, making Kate realized, once again, how difficult all this had been for her.

Finally, Charlotte folded her hands that were red and chapped from the morning's laundry, and glanced at Kate. "Does he mean it? Will he really stop the investigation if I wish it?"

Kate nodded.

"And *you* will agree?"

"I give you my word. And there will be nothing more said about the matter or any hard feelings on my part, I promise you that."

Charlotte tilted her chin upward. "Then I agree. Please share what's on your mind, Mr. Adams."

Joshua leaned over and rested his arms on his thighs. "My father was a preacher. A zealous man of God. Many would say too zealous. But I understood him. Like the woman with the alabaster jar, one who is saved out of great sin and is forgiven much, loves much.

"I suppose that's why I chose my profession, too. Knowing my grandfather's past, I wanted to fight evil, to write a history I could be proud of. Because, you see, my grandfather was a second son. The family estate was a large one in England, where his father, my great-grandfather, was a wealthy landowner. But because of the law of primogeniture, where the entire estate goes to the first son, my grandfather found himself with a taste for rich living but no means of supporting it. That's when he came to America, to pursue opportunity and riches. And he found them both in the slave trade."

Charlotte's eyebrows knotted. "Pardon me, Mr. Adams, but I don't understand the purpose of this, or how it could possibly connect to my circumstances."

Joshua smiled but there was sadness in his eyes. "My grandfather told us stories about his life as a slaver. He had expected my father to follow in his footsteps, and even made him serve on the slave ships. Through his stories I became acquainted with many of the prominent slavers of his day as well as those in times past. I heard names like Winthrop, Waldo, Fanueil, and . . . Gaylord. And other names too, of prominent families who were among the chief slavers and made their money not through respectable means but through selling rum and human cargo."

"The *Gaylords*?" Charlotte gasped as though his words had just penetrated. "You can't mean Benjamin's family."

"The very ones. In fact, Benjamin's grandfather, Richard Gaylord, was one of the most notorious slavers of all. Oh, many of these families are now in respectable businesses to be sure, and far removed from slaver days, but their hands are not clean. Their inheritance is tainted by blood and human suffering. Not like your family, Miss Charlotte, which, I might add, I investigated thoroughly. Do you know what the name 'Farrell' means?"

Charlotte just looked at him as though still too astonished to speak.

"It's Gaelic, and means courageous, a man of valor, and by extension, a man of honor. Always remember that, Miss Charlotte. You have ancestors to be proud of; ancestors who have lived up to their name."

Charlotte sat gazing at her lap as though trying to take it all in. Kate, on the other hand, stared boldly at Joshua, her heart swelling with gratitude. Oh how they needed this! They were all sinners in the sight of God; not one good. No not one. Not the Winthrops or Waldos or Gaylords, nor any of the prominent families who ruled the world. Not even the Farrells. All were splattered with shame. How was it that she had forgotten this? As her gaze continued to rest on the handsome detective, she hoped her eyes conveyed what was in her heart as she mouthed the words, "thank you." Something had happened. Something wonderful. God had used Joshua—his words, his story—like the balm of Gilead, to set Kate free; to utterly erase the shame of her father's hanging, and bring healing to her heart.

"Please forgive this unseemly display," Charlotte finally said, looking up, her face tear-streaked. "I now understand how foolishly I've behaved in being so enamored with the Gaylords, in worrying about offending them, and in my concern about their thoughts on every matter. It has exposed my deep pride, and I'm thoroughly ashamed. Mr. Adams, you must continue your investigation. And thank you for your candor."

Joshua rose. "Then I shall waste no time in seeing Mr. Baxter."

Kate rose too, feeling strangely lighthearted. "And I'll accompany you. I would very much like to hear what he has to say."

For a moment it looked as if Joshua was going to argue, but then he smiled as he tugged on the edge of his rumbled vest. "I think I've come to know you Farrells well enough to understand when arguing is futile. I must go now and attend to other business. But first thing in the morning I will pay him a visit, and you may come, Kate, provided you let me do the talking."

Kate returned his smile. "It shall be as you say, Joshua."

"'Pride goeth before destruction, and a haughty spirit before a fall,'" Charlotte muttered under her breath. Wasn't that what Proverbs 16:18 said? And oh how prideful she had been! She was on her knees now, digging through the small trunk where she kept her childhood treasures. When she found her old wooden hand mirror and comb—the ones Father had given her when she was five—she pulled them out and rose to her feet. She couldn't stop thinking of Joshua's words. Like darts, they had pierced her heart, made her see her great deficiencies and how she had become so like Mrs. Gaylord and Hester Roach, the two women she feared most, but least admired.

This in turn made her think about that woman she had seen at the Home. Even now she recalled that sad, sweet smile. And the shame, too, that covered her face as she tried fixing her hair. Had she been fastidious once? Taken pride in her appearance? That is, before life had stripped her of everything, even the most basic necessities such as a comb and looking glass?

But it seemed the woman still had some pride left, even in her dire circumstances. It showed what a hard thing pride was to overcome. What would it take for Charlotte to overcome hers? Would she have to lose everything, too? For some reason the thought of losing all didn't seem as frightening as it once did.

Charlotte turned the mirror over in her hand. The large flat wood made a good surface for a painting. But what should she paint? Flowers? Butterflies? Birds? She closed her eyes and pictured the woman again. What would *she* like? Had she loved sitting in her garden, like Charlotte did? Had she owned a cat that delighted her when it curled up on her lap? Or was it music that had thrilled her heart? Charlotte thought a minute. Yes, a butterfly . . . perhaps in a bed of tulips. That should make her happy.

She thought of Father and wondered if he'd mind her giving away his gift? Then remembering his generous nature, concluded he'd be rather pleased by her gesture. And it would please Charlotte, too. For some reason, one she didn't quite understand, she wanted this woman to have something nice. Something to delight her and remind her that she was still valued; that she still mattered.

Was that pride, too? Wanting to matter? And be valued? She didn't think so. At least not the same kind of pride she had felt around

Mrs. Gaylord and Hester Roach. The kind of pride that made her think she was superior. Made her want to look down on everyone else. Made her afraid that others were looking down at her, too. The kind of pride she now saw as ugly.

She tucked the mirror and comb under her arm. It had been ages since she had painted anything. She quickly gathered her box of paints, then dashed out the bedroom door, feeling more excitement than she had in a very long time.

Kate hadn't expected this. The small house that was once as rundown as the shacks in Higgins Patch now looked bright and perky with a new shingled roof, a fresh coat of white paint, and new green shutters. It was obvious that here is where Samuel Baxter had spent some of his new found money.

She had always considered Baxter an enigma. Coopers normally made a good living since they were skilled and important to a community; after all, barrels were always in demand. But Samuel Baxter had a reputation for shoddy workmanship, and this kept him from being prosperous. It was well known he was only given jobs calling for "slack cooperage," barrels that were used for non-liquids such as grains, and didn't require tight fitting staves. Because of this, the Baxters were always in want. But all that appeared to have changed.

Kate followed Joshua past the side of the house, then down a dirt footpath leading to the back. Even the path seemed freshly cleaned, and was lined with stones. The surrounding yard had also been cleared of dead brush and debris, and now chickens and pigs could be clearly seen roaming about.

She and Joshua made their way to the workshop which was part enclosed shack and part lean-to, and where a stocky, broad-shouldered man stood pounding staves into an iron hoop. It seemed business had picked up. Kate noticed that various size barrels lined one wall and a pile of saplings, for additional staves, filled a nearby corner. And his collection of tools had increased, too. Last time she was here he only had a handful. Now the long wooden workbench was cluttered with hoop drivers, hammers, a broadax, drawknife, different sized planes and other tools she didn't recognize, while three saws, a compass and two adzes hung on nails in the wall boards. But the biggest surprise was the pile of oak shavings nesting around Samuel Baxter's feet, indicating he was working on a whiskey or wine barrel. Her father had once told her, after ordering a wine barrel from Pottsville for a large holiday party, how oak was the preferred wood for such casks due to its fine grain and ease at which it could be waterproofed. As she approached she wondered who would be foolish enough to hire Mr. Baxter to do a "tight cooperage."

The steady tapping increased as she and Joshua drew closer. Kate was certain Samuel Baxter had seen them coming, but he neither looked up nor acknowledged their presence. Even so, Joshua was not put off, and over the noise of the hammer, told Baxter what he had learned from the colliery owners.

"So, what I need to know," Joshua said, as he finished, "is why you hired two thugs to scare the owners into selling, then had them claim to be Mollies?"

At last, the broad shouldered Baxter stopped his pounding. "You have some nerve coming here and accusing me. Whoever told you I hired men to threaten anyone is a liar."

"I can get sworn statements if I have to," Joshua returned, looking as calm as the duck floating in the nearby pond.

"Go ahead. Get anything you like. It wasn't me that hired them." Baxter's muscular arms glistened with sweat as he smacked the hammer against the palm of one hand, making Kate fear he might use it on Joshua. "Now, get off my property. Both of you. And don't come back!"

"This is not over," Joshua said, returning his glare.

"I haven't heard any complaints from the railroad. If they're content with the way everything was handled what's it to you how that business got done? Just who do you think you are, going around accusing people?" He raised his hammer and this time Kate was sure he planned to use it. But when he moved around the partially formed barrel, he dropped his hand, and Kate wondered if it wasn't because he saw that Joshua had him by a foot or more.

"This is all your doing, Missy." Baxter turned to Kate. "Calling in your no-account kin to bother respectable folks. Well, just send him back to his cow pasture or there's going to be plenty of trouble."

"It would go easier on you if you cooperated," Kate answered, no longer feeling the need to defend herself. Justice was the only thing she wanted now. "Because sooner or later we will get to the bottom of this, and sooner or later your involvement will be exposed."

When she turned to leave, Joshua took her arm and smiled. "Couldn't have said it better myself."

Virginia was glad that the cemetery was less weedy today. Someone had put a sickle to the taller growth but left the cuttings on the ground where they remained like matted straw. Still, it made navigating the tombstones easier. She worked her way toward Patrick O'Brien who stood tall and straight in his black suit, holding another clump of wilting honeysuckles, and *smiling*.

This time she knew the meeting was not about her articles. Two more had been sent to Patrick through Michael O'Malley, and both had already been published in the *Monitor*. But once again, his note had caused her untold anxiety, for it simply said he had information about her father. But *what* information? All morning she had wondered about it. Had Patrick found the two thugs? If so, what had he learned? Did they continue to insist that Father had hired them? These questions had eaten her like a cankerworm, making her unable to touch a morsel of her Sunday lunch, though Sunday lunches were always special at their boardinghouse.

But why should she worry? Kate had told her about Joshua's findings. There was no reason to believe Father had had anything to do with the bullying of Roger Blakely. But Virginia always needed double proof before she let a matter drop. Kate said it was the newspaper woman in her while Virginia wondered if it was simply a lack of faith.

"'Tis a lovely sight you are," Patrick said, still sporting his grin.

Virginia ignored the compliment, though she had taken pains to look her best. "Please, give me your news quickly. I don't think I can stand another minute of not knowing what you've learned."

Patrick handed her the flowers. "No, Jenny. You won't be rushin' me. For as soon as I tell you, you'll be leavin' quick as the wind. And I'm in sore need of your company. I've been longin' to see you these past many weeks, but I honored your wishes and didn't send for you, though it took all me willpower, I can tell you."

Virginia accepted the honeysuckles and brought them to her nose. The fragrance was as sweet as the feelings she had at seeing him again. She could hardly admit it to herself, but she had missed him, too.

"Will you walk with me, then?" Patrick took her arm even before she could respond and led her out of the church cemetery. Then his large, rough hand guided her to a path she had never walked before but one she knew led to a deserted saw mill nestled deep in the woods.

"Why bother asking if you're not going to wait for an answer?" she said, suddenly noticing the nasty-looking cut over his right eye.

"Well, truth is I wasn't willin' to have you say 'no'. People from Donegal tend to be superstitious. We believe in fairies and curses and holy wells, don't you know, though the Church frowns on it. Some priests have even threatened our people with excommunication." His large muscular frame bent closer to her. "I guess I didn't wait for an answer for fear of jinxin' things."

"Then am I to assume I'm walking with a pagan?"

"Oh, no, Jenny. I have the fear of God in me, to be sure. You need not worry on that account. But though I'm a prayin' man and partake of the sacraments, I'm a wretched example of Jesus, for sure. The blood of Donegal is in me and besides bein' superstitious, we can be a contentious lot.

"But enough of that talk, now. I need to be tellin' you how much I liked your articles, especially the one about the outhouses being too close to the wells. 'Twas a good one, and maybe answers the question of why so many of our wee ones get the flux durin' the rainy season. You did a grand job on it. Maybe it will stir up the new owners into doin' somethin', though I won't be holdin' me breath."

"Patrick, you are such a contradiction. A man who reads and writes and picks flowers for a woman, but prefers to use his fists is a man I cannot hope to understand."

"And who'd be sayin' I use me fists?"

"Your right eye."

"He pulled her to a stop. "Ah, Jenny, you are a delight. And I might as well tell you all about it, for there's no holdin' back now. You see, it was like this. Me and Powderkeg Kelly . . . ."

"Powderkeg Kelly? *Who is that?*"

"Ah darlin', he's a man down on his luck, don't you know. Sometimes I give him a few coins to do an odd job for me here and there, though I know he'll just be spendin' it on the drink. He used to be fire boss at the Mattson Colliery. Before the workday began he'd inspect the breasts and crosscuts and gangways for gas and other hazards. But his whiskey drinkin' made him sloppy, and that made him dangerous to himself and others. He was finally let go. But he's right handy with blastin' powder, too, so for awhile he was still able to earn a livin' by goin' from colliery to colliery takin' on the most dangerous blastin' jobs that others didn't want. But even that he lost by showin' up drunk one too many times. Some say it was Powderkeg who blew up Mattson's culm bank and timber mound out of pure revenge for bein' fired. It's possible, for to be sure the man can be spiteful, and I still resent that the blame fell on the Mollies when they had no part in it at all."

"Then why would you go anywhere with such a man?"

"Because, darlin', when you set out to break heads, you need someone who's not afraid of doin' it. And Powderkeg's such a man. Some say he's crazy, and maybe he is but . . . ."

"Oh, Patrick, what did you *do*?"

Patrick slipped a strong muscular arm around her waist and pulled her closer. "I see your concern, lass. And I appreciate it." His face was intense, his eyes so full of love that Virginia stood unable to move as he quickly shared how he and Powderkeg found the men who had tried to hire him, and how after several minutes of persuasion, when more than a nose was broken, the men gave up that name.

"*Martin Roach*?" Virginia repeated in disbelief. "And not Samuel Baxter?"

"No, 'twas the name Martin Roach that we shook out of 'em, and no mistakin' the matter."

Virginia frowned. How could that be when both Kate and Joshua Adams suspected Samuel Baxter and told her how belligerent he had been at his cooperage? Could Patrick be wrong? One look at his injured eye told her no. Who would lie to such a man and face the threat of Patrick returning to extract punishment? She would just have to let detective Adams sort it all out. And as she stood looking at Patrick, at his earnest face, at the large gash over his eye that was still red and swollen, she couldn't stop herself from touching his wound with her fingertips.

"So, you got this for me."

"Jenny, don't you know that I'd get a hundred such wounds for you, if I had to?"

She felt the warmth of his arm around her as he drew her even closer, felt the steady movement of his chest, saw the searing look in his eyes, and knew that if he tried now, right this moment, to kiss her, she'd let him. But he just ran his large thumb down her cheek, his eyes telling her that he knew it, too.

"Best we be gettin' back, now," he said with a sigh as he let his arm drop from her waist." And the moment passed.

Kate was stunned by Virginia's news. Could Martin Roach really be behind all their troubles? She just had to find out. But when she went to Joshua and told him, and insisted they revisit Samuel Baxter, he convinced her they should wait a few days until he could gather more information.

Now, as her feet kicked up dust from the path, she felt like a fool for waiting. Three days had passed and Joshua had come up with absolutely nothing. That was three days wasted, and she wasn't about to waste a minute more.

"Kate, will you listen to reason? This is rash," Joshua said, trailing behind her.

"Let me finish investigating Martin Roach and collect some evidence."

Without answering, she continued toward the cooperage.

"It's never wise to reveal what you know, or *think* you know, too early. If your sister's information is credible, we could tip our hand prematurely and end up warning Mr. Roach before we're ready."

Kate quickened her pace.

"Will you at least slow down! I'm eating your dust back here!"

Kate stopped and turned to squint at the detective as he traversed the few yards separating them. "Joshua, I respect you and your abilities as a Pinkerton," she said when he finally reached her. "But since we don't know how reliable Virginia's source is, we must use other means to verify it. Human nature always betrays itself. If we confront him, we will learn the truth by his reaction. My instincts tell me that no matter what, Samuel Baxter knows more than he's telling."

Joshua fingered the brim of his dusty farmer's hat. "Did you really mean it? About respecting me and my abilities?"

"Of course." Kate smiled, glad that the hat hid his eyes, those eyes she found so unsettling. "But sometimes, Joshua, you're too cautious. I see no value in waiting to question Mr. Baxter. And I'm determined to go with or without you."

"I can see that." Joshua tilted his hat backward and when he did, she saw that his blue eyes shimmered with pleasure. "But the way Samuel Baxter wields a hammer you just might want to rethink the matter."

"Then be my bodyguard. I'll even let you do all the talking." Kate offered him her arm. "Peace?"

"Peace," he said, laughing.

It was full sun by the time they reached the cooperage where Samuel Baxter was busy cupping the inside of a stave with a shaving tool. This time he made no pretense of not seeing them. He dropped his work, and picking up the broadax from his bench, held it in a threatening manner. "I thought I told you to stay off my property!"

"I came to apologize," Joshua said. "Seems I was out of line when I accused you of hiring those two ruffians to bully the colliery owners. We now know it wasn't you at all, but Martin Roach."

"You . . . don't know what you're saying. And Mr. Roach won't appreciate talk like that." He brushed his dirty fingers across his lower lip and glared at Kate. "He's a powerful man in this town now, and you, Miss Farrell, don't have an important daddy to protect you anymore."

"I have the truth, sir, and need no protection. But I do have one question. When you found out that Mr. Roach was using threats and intimidation to broker his colliery sales, is that when you confronted him and demanded a bribe? And is that how he paid you for your silence? By listing his last two sales as yours?"

Samuel Baxter's face dropped. "Your presumption is staggering, Miss Farrell. And you have more nerve than any woman I know. But can you prove any of this?"

"All in time, sir. For when Mr. Roach hears of this he'll not be happy. As you said, he's powerful, and the powerful always find someone else to blame. I'm sure he won't have to look any further than right here for his scapegoat."

"No one's going to make any kind of goat out of me!" Samuel Baxter growled, pointing a nubby finger at her, a finger that looked surprisingly like the butt of a cigar. "You be careful, Missy, or you're gonna find yourself in a heap of trouble! Mr. Roach knows how to protect his friends."

"And just what makes you think you're Mr. Roach's friend?" Kate saw a look of panic sweep over Baxter's face. And as she and Joshua turned and walked away, Kate could still feel the cooper's eyes on her.

They went a good distance before Joshua, who had remained silent all this time, pulled Kate to a stop. "I thought you were going to let me do all the talking."

"I was. But then the words just popped out. He made me so angry when . . . ."

"You were rash back there, Kate. Sometimes you let your feelings get the best of you. I know it's because you are a woman with a passionate nature, one who feels deeply. Maybe that's one of the reasons I have become so . . . fond of you. But passion in itself is not a virtue unless it's coupled with self-control."

As they walked the rest of the way home in silence, Kate replayed Joshua's words in her mind. He was right. Her emotions needed to be tempered by self-control. That's why she was determined not to lose her heart to someone who would be here today and gone tomorrow. Someone who lived in the cross-hairs of danger. But as they continued walking, she knew it was already too late.

⁓

Kate sat in the back parlor listening to Joshua lay out what he claimed was a promising beginning toward proving her father's innocence. She was glad that in addition to her sisters, Mother was present, too. It was the first time Mother had taken an interest in any of Joshua's findings.

They all sat quietly while Joshua stood by the hearth, now covered with the hand painted screen Charlotte had decorated in delicate yellow, blue and magenta flowers, and which would remain in place throughout the warm weather.

"What we know for certain, Mrs. Farrell," Joshua said, focusing on the elder Farrell, "is that your husband did not hire anyone to frighten Roger Blakely into selling,"

"I could have told you that." Mother sat in the old rocker, knitting a new winter blanket for one of the many bedrooms.

Though her voice was sweet and not a bit condescending, Joshua appeared embarrassed. "Yes, well, I think we can also add this additional fact to our case—it was Martin Roach who did the hiring.

Further investigation is necessary, but I wouldn't be surprised to find that most, if not all, of his colliery sales were coerced. And if this proves true, then based on Samuel Baxter's reaction today, it's possible he found out and began blackmailing Roach, which would explain how Samuel Baxter shows two collieries to his credit when, according to the railroad, he was never officially enlisted as one of their agents. Even so, the railroad wasn't bothered by his involvement, being more than happy to add those collieries to their string."

Kate watched Joshua smile with obvious pleasure at being able to give them such good news. She then glanced at the others. They didn't seem excited at all. Mother was the most disappointing, for she hardly looked up from her knitting, and when she did, her face was so blank it was as if Joshua had just read the coal tonnage figures for Schuylkill County.

Charlotte, too, showed little emotion. She just sat in one of the damask-covered chairs with her hands folded, looking a bit confused. Kate sighed. She shouldn't be disappointed. Charlotte's disposition had markedly improved since Joshua's revelation about Benjamin's grandfather. Her grooming, too. It was as fastidious as it had always been. Even now, she sat with her pretty ruffled dress spread about her just so, and with every blond curl neatly arrayed. But one thing hadn't changed, she still refused to wear the pearls she was once so proud of.

Virginia was another matter. She appeared deep in thought, her brow knotted. Finally she spoke. "I have two questions. The first is: if, as you say, all this coercion took place, why didn't the railroad know about it? Were contracts not signed? Opportunities for the truth to come out? How could Martin Roach perpetrate such a travesty, if indeed he did so? And the second question is one I don't believe anyone has ever asked, even at the trial, and has only now occurred to me as well. What was the information Mr. Blakely wanted to give Father?

According to Father, Mr. Blakely's note indicated he had something important to discuss."

Everyone looked at Mother. And for the first time, she stopped knitting. "Yes, that's correct. Your father and Mr. Blakely, together, had been looking into a matter for some time. But I can't say what, since he seldom involved me in his business. However, on that night he did tell me he was going to meet Mr. Blakely about something important, and when I asked him if it concerned the selling of the colliery, he said, 'no,' and as you remember, that is what he maintained throughout the trial."

Virginia sat on the edge of her chair. "Then we must ask, was this information important enough for someone to kill him in order to keep it a secret?"

Kate pressed her hands together. "Virginia, you're amazing! Absolutely amazing! I'm shocked no one has thought to ask this before." She turned to Joshua. "Do you think it's possible that Father and Mr. Blakely also found out what Martin Roach was doing, and were trying to gather evidence?"

Joshua shrugged. "According to the transcript of the trial, your father claimed he never learned what Mr. Blakely wanted to tell him since he was already dead when he arrived. Besides that, he never indicated they were investigating Mr. Roach. If your father had possessed any proof that could clear his name, surely he would have used it during the trial. And his notebook is inconclusive, though one could argue, by the way he listed the collieries, that he had been checking into them. But it's hardly credible evidence, nothing that would hold up in court."

But Kate wasn't convinced. She knew Virginia had a sense about these things; that Virginia could smell a story where others couldn't. Even before all her articles in the *Monitor*, which Kate had been secretly reading, Virginia had a nose for news and a way of piecing things together. Once Virginia had even helped uncover the corruption of a former sheriff by observing how he dealt with the Irish Sheet Iron Gang and the Welsh Modocs—rival gangs that often clashed on weekends in Mahanoy City and the Shenandoah area. She had noted that only members of the Sheet Iron Gang were ever arrested, and when she pointed that out and someone finally got around to investigating, it turned out that the Modocs paid the sheriff a monthly sum to protect their members.

Kate settled back in her chair. Yes she had always been proud of Virginia's fine mind and deductive powers—the very qualities Kate hoped would ultimately save Virginia from her reckless relationship with Patrick O'Brien. For surely Virginia's good sense would prevail in the end.

"Well," Joshua said, walking up to Kate's chair and smiling at her in a way that belied he realized there were still others in the room, "I think we're getting close to solving this case."

"I hear speculation, nothing more. Where is your *proof*?" Mother said, resuming her knitting.

Two days later, Jasper Wright, who seemed to extract more than teeth in his dental office, and who knew what was going on in Sweet Air well before most others, told Kate that the cooper, Samuel Baxter, had suddenly up and moved without a word to anyone, and wasn't that strange after fixing up his house like that? But Kate didn't think it strange. In spite of Mother's misgivings, it told her they were closer than ever to clearing Father's name.

CHAPTER 7

Virginia held her breath as she hurried to the front door. Widow Clayton had just told her a young boy was waiting outside, a boy with only *one* hand.

"Hello, Michael." Virginia smiled down at the ragged child and tried to appear calm as she wondered what had brought him here.

"Miss Virginia, there's been a mishap at the mine."

"It's not *Patrick*, is it?"

"No ma'am. He's as fit as ever."

She heaved a sigh of relief then frowned. "I heard no breaker whistle."

"No ma'am. Superintendent Foley wouldn't let no one sound it." Perspiration-soaked ringlets hugged his forehead like soggy wool as he clutched his cloth cap and squinted at her through the blinding sun.

"Well come in and tell me about it," Virginia said, wanting to give the boy some relief from the heat.

"Oh, no Miss Virginia! I'm not fit for a respectable parlor. My clothes . . . ." He swept his cap across his tattered overalls and scuffed, dusty boots.

"Then come into the kitchen. I'll pour you a lemonade while you tell me what happened." Virginia pulled him into the house.

The house was nearly empty. Mother, Kate, and Charlotte had gone to the large furniture store in Pottsville to purchase a small tufted chair and footstool to replace the hard Windsor chair in Widow

Clayton's room; the chair Widow Clayton insisted was giving her lumbago. And of the boarders, only Widow Clayton was in the parlor, quietly engrossed in needlework.

Would she have invited Michael in if the house had been full? She thought of Patrick's accusations concerning her pride and knew they were true. But little Michael O'Malley seemed pleased enough by her invitation, for he accompanied her without a word, his eyes growing larger when he saw the beautiful front parlor then the huge, well-stocked kitchen.

She pulled a chair up to one of the long wooden tables and gestured for him to sit. And as he settled in, she retrieved the pitcher of lemonade from the large oak icebox that Mother claimed was lined with zinc and insulated with cork, then poured him a tall glass. From a cloth-covered platter, she took two sizable oatmeal cookies, put them on a small plate and placed it, and the glass, in front of him.

"Miss Virginia, is this all for *me?*"

"It is, and before you go, I'll wrap two more cookies in paper for you to take."

Michael began stuffing the cookies into his mouth, first one then the other, as if he had never tasted anything so good or perhaps fearing she'd change her mind and take them back.

Virginia waited for him to finish; able to do so only because she already knew his information didn't concern Patrick O'Brien. Still, she felt uneasy. No mine mishap was good news.

He drained his glass, then wiped the crumbs from his chin with dirty fingers. "It was a bad mornin' at the Mattson. Patrick, he don't know I'm here. I came because I thought you should know that two of his friends died today. 'Troublemakers' the mine boss called 'em, just because they was complainin' about how the railroad wanted everyone to do more work for less pay."

Michael ran his tongue over his lips as though still tasting the lemonade, then frowned. "And you know what they do with trouble-makers—assign 'em to monkey holes where the coal seams can be so narrow a man has to crawl on his hands and knees. Or they send 'em to work in knee-deep water, or where the roof is unstable, which is where they sent them two. And that's what did it. The roof collapsed right on top of 'em. They never had a chance."

"Oh, Michael, how terrible! I'm so sorry. Naturally I'll be at the wake. Tell Patrick that. When is it?"

"Won't be no wake. They were single and left no kin, and no money neither. And the keg fund is empty on account of it goin' to Mrs. O'Brien so she could give her Tom a nice send off, and for travelin' money to Pittsburg for her and her brood."

Virginia knew about the keg fund, a fund miners contributed to monthly to help widows pay funeral expenses and, if possible, a month or two of rent. "Then . . . what will happen to these men?" Though she knew the answer she was praying she was wrong.

"Oh, they've already been loaded on a wagon and are on their way to one of them medical schools. Though from what I hear there's nothing of use left except maybe a few organs and a limb or . . . ."

"Thank you, Michael." Virginia couldn't bear to hear any more, and marveled at the boy's calm demeanor. She looked at him, his feet dangling, unable to touch the floor, but oh how old he seemed, more like a little man than a boy. Hardship had aged him, robbed him of his childhood. "I'd like to send a note to Patrick. Will you wait?"

When he nodded, Virginia wrapped up two more cookies and handed them to him before going upstairs to the library where she wrote Patrick a hasty note telling him how sorry she was about his friends, and that if he wanted, she'd be willing to meet him at the church, Sunday. After taking a few pennies from her purse, she returned to the kitchen in time to see Michael shove his last cookie into his mouth. She tried not to smile as she wrapped up a few more before sending him on his way.

But as she watched him disappear down the path, sadness overwhelmed her. Two men had died today without the world taking any notice. It was as if they had never existed.

But she was wrong. Someone had noticed, for the next day she heard how Superintendent Foley received a note with a drawing of a coffin and crude lettering telling him to "leev town or die." And the only thought that came to Virginia's mind was: *Did Patrick O'Brien send it?*

A storm was brewing. Virginia could feel it. Her articles and research had connected her with Higgins Patch and those who lived there. In heart and mind, she was one of them now. That's why the fomenting tempest troubled her so. But what could be done? The Philadelphia and Reading Railroad now owned more than eighty thousand acres of coal country and ninety-eight collieries, and they were well on their way to defeating many of the independent holdouts with their price fixing and restricting the amount of coal they would haul regardless of how much an independent colliery mined, making it impossible for the independents to compete with what had become a huge corporation. And though no one liked it, this brewing storm was kept at bay by the heavy hand of the Coal and Iron Police, and everybody knew it was only a matter of time before something gave way.

So Virginia was not surprised when, that morning, she and the boarders learned how Superintendent Foley, who had failed to heed the coffin notice, was beaten and left for dead on one of the dirt footpaths leading to the Mattson Colliery.

What would Father think? Would he regret his role? After all, as a land agent for the railroad he was not blameless for the current problems. Would he try to dissuade Franklin B. Gowen from gobbling up the remaining lower anthracite region? Would he speak out against the railroad's harsh, unfair tactics, and its abuse of the miners? She thought so. Father had been a fair-minded man who believed in justice.

But Patrick O'Brien also believed in justice, though it had little resemblance to Father's. Had Patrick been part of the attack on Superintendent Foley? Her heart fell. Patrick was rash. He would want to avenge his friends. And he was powerful; powerful enough to kill someone with his fists. She had to dissuade him from further folly; to stop him before someone did die. If she told Patrick about the new article she was working on—a scathing piece concerning the railroad, and backed by data from the respected Pennsylvania Bureau of Industrial Statistics—perhaps it would convince him there were better ways of winning an issue other than violence. The Bureau's recent "Report on Labor" extolled the WBA for their peaceful work in trying to better labor relations while warning of the danger posed by the unbridled acquisition of collieries by the Reading Railroad.

Surely Patrick would see the need for patience, and allow public opinion to have a chance to turn back the storm. Even the Reading Railroad wasn't impervious to scorn and outrage. The course of many events had been changed by both. This was the way to go. Violence only begat more violence. But he was working in the mine now. If she wanted to see him tonight she'd have to send a note. She thought of Michael O'Malley. He'd be able to find Patrick after work and give him her message to meet at the church. And Superintendent Foley? What if he died? What would happen then?

Oh, God, keep Patrick from further folly. And please don't let Superintendent Foley die.

Virginia hurried to the library and scribbled a note, then rushed down the stairs, passed the front parlor where several of the boarders were still discussing the morning's news. And before anyone could see her, she darted out the door heading for Main Street and Michael O'Malley.

⌒

Though the wind was warm, Virginia clutched her hooded cloak as she tried to avoid the dips and holes in the narrow footpath. The hovering shadows and red sky told her little daylight remained. She quickened her pace. She wanted to reach the church before dark, and before the rain came. Even now she could smell it in the air. Any minute the heavens were sure to open.

But this was madness, heading for Higgins Patch at this hour! She had tried to leave earlier. But dinner and dishes had taken longer than usual. And when finally done, she had donned her brown broadcloth cloak, then darted out the kitchen door mumbling something about taking a walk.

What was she going to tell her mother and sisters when she returned? How was she to explain where she had been, and why? Oh, she couldn't think of that now. Best to think about how to dissuade Patrick from doing more harm. But would he even be there? He never replied to her note. Perhaps there just hadn't been time. Still . . . what if . . . .

Thunder rumbled in the distance as an owl screeched in one of the nearby trees. The wind had picked up, and now whipped her cloak, flapping it like wings. And when she reached the church, she felt a sense of dread as she peered through the dim light and saw that the grounds were deserted.

Should she wait? Maybe . . . yes, certainly . . . but only for a minute or two. As she gathered her cloak around her, she heard a familiar voice and saw a man step from the shadows of the arched portico.

"Jenny? Is that you, lass?"

Though it had started to rain, Virginia removed her hood as the figure approached. "Patrick, I'm so glad you're here."

"What has happened to make you come like this?" His voice was laden with concern as he led her to the shelter of the portico. He smelled of sweat and coal dust, and his dirty black overalls and heavy black boots made him nearly invisible in the ever growing darkness. "Why have you come, lass?" he repeated.

"Superintendent Foley. Oh, Patrick, if he dies they'll hunt you down like a dog."

"And why would anyone be doin' that?" He leaned closer as if to better see her in the fading light. "Ah . . . so that's it. Well, put your mind at ease. It wasn't us that done it. We had no hand in the Foley beatin'."

"We? So . . . it's true. You *are* one of them . . . a Molly."

"Be certain you want to know a thing before you ask, Jenny, for I've already told you I'll hold nothin' back from you. I'll speak plainly, and I'll speak true."

Virginia's insides quivered as she leaned against one of the arches. "Are you . . . part of the Molly Maguires, Patrick?"

"If you're thinkin' there's some sort of organized group by that name, you'd be wrong. But if you're askin' if I'm one of many men who want to improve conditions in the mines, if I believe in retributive justice, and that more wealth should be redistributed so working men can live like human beings, and if you're askin' if I'm willin to use force to accomplish it all, then yes, I'm a Molly."

Virginia's breath caught. "Have you ever . . . ?"

"Killed anyone?" Patrick put his arm around Virginia's waist and drew her closer. "No, my sweet lass. I've derailed a coal car or two in my time. Even wrote a few coffin notices for them that couldn't write. But I've never taken a life."

"If you want to change things why not work through the WBA? Like your friend at the *Monitor*?"

Patrick released her and began pacing. "Open your eyes, Jenny! Look at what the railroad is doin' to coal country. It's clear they mean to own everything before they're done. Don't you see the writin' on the wall? Gowen is already goin' after the WBA. And that's not me talkin', neither, that's from my friend at the *Monitor*, who like you, always thought he could win by peaceable means. But now even he believes that sooner or later, Gowen, with the full power of the railroad behind him, will try to crush the union."

"No matter what you say, you can't justify violence, Patrick. You must work within the confines of the law."

"The law?" The rain was falling harder now and pounded the roof of the portico. "You mean the Coal and Iron Police? The ones that crack a boy's knuckles for tryin' to earn a livin' by collectin' a few bags of coal from the culm pile? Or throw a man and his family out of their home for accusin' the company store of cheatin' 'em by not deductin' all they had paid on their bill? *That* law?"

"Oh, Patrick, I don't want to argue. I just want you to be careful. You must not try to avenge your friends." She quickly told him about the article she was writing. "Wait it out. Give my pen, and the pen of others, a chance to change things."

Patrick stopped pacing and stood staring through the archway into the night. "You have a good heart, and you mean well, and what you're doin' might help some, I'm not sayin' it won't, but you've never been hungry, Jenny, or cold, or desperate. You've never seen your wee ones with rat bites on their arms or die from the stinkin' squalor they're forced to live in. But I've seen plenty of it. And my people have seen plenty of it. Just how long must *they* wait?"

Virginia stood beside him, listening to the water cascade off the roof and feeling its spray as it covered the open arch like a veil. "You overwhelm me, Patrick. And frighten me, too. You love with such intensity, but you hate with as much intensity, too. You're like a wild man, capable of anything."

He turned and drew her so close Virginia felt the air from his nostrils brush her cheeks. "All I know is I love you, lass. And the kindness and concern you show me gives me hope that someday . . . you'll be strong enough to admit that you love me, too. It's what I live for. And I'll not be doin' anythin' to spoil it. You have me word on that. Me and the other Mollies will not be makin' trouble. I'll see to it. And I'll see to it that the one who did this will not be doin' any more damage."

"You know who did it? Who nearly beat Superintendent Foley to death?"

"I might."

"Then you must report him to the authorities. You must tell what you know."

"What manner of man would turn on his own? I'll not be doin' that, for sure, Jenny, and I'll not hear another word on the matter. We, in Higgins Patch, handle our own affairs."

The rain had slowed, though it still made a soft pitter-patter noise on the roof. It was useless to push the matter further and Virginia needed to get home. Patrick had already given her his word that he had no hand in injuring Superintendent Foley. He had also promised there would be no further trouble. And she knew she could count on his word. If he really knew who assaulted Superintendent Foley, perhaps in time he'd be willing to bring him to justice. It was something she'd pray for, but now she was content he had no hand in the Foley matter. And that was no small thing.

"Thank you, Patrick," she whispered.

Only a sliver of moonlight penetrated the archway, but it was enough to see the fire in Patrick's eyes as he leaned closer and cupped her face in his large coal-stained hands. Without a word he tilted her chin upward, then kissed her. Virginia felt his love and passion flow through her, felt her heart stir, and just as she was about to put her arms around him, he dropped his hands, then gently drew the brown hood over her head.

"I'll be walkin' you home now, and no use arguin'. And when I see that you're safe, I'll leave, though to be sure it will grieve me to part from you."

And so they stepped out into the dark, damp night.

Virginia didn't realized how long it had taken to get from the church to her house until she saw that all the windows were dark except for those in the front parlor. Just how many hours had she been with Patrick, anyway? It's true, they had walked like snails, as though neither wanted to reach their destination. And it's true they had stopped numerous times along the way and just stood on the dirt path, she listening, he talking—telling stories about the old country: what it was like growing up in a family of ten in County Donegal, its limestone cliffs, the smell of the bogs, the rocky soil that wasn't much good for farming but fine for raising sheep.

He spoke of how his father, and his brother, Tom, who was only five at the time, left Donegal eight years before Patrick was even born, to work in the mines of Wales and England, and how they sent money home every month, but only managed to come themselves once a year. He talked about the poverty, how most nights he and his mother, his brothers and sisters, had only potato mush to eat, and how he would hunt red deer or rabbits to help feed them; how when he was twelve, he finally joined his father and brother in England and worked as a butty, carrying tools and equipment for the miners, and helped shovel several tons of coal into railcars each day. He described how his brother, Tom, met Mary, and after a few years wanted to take his young family and Patrick to America where there was more opportunity, and ended up settling in Schuylkill County; and how it was another seven years before Patrick could join him because their father had come down with miner's asthma and Patrick didn't want to leave him, so worked by his side then tended him while he was dying.

But there was a noticeable hardness in Patrick's voice when he spoke of how he had not wasted those years in England, but had learned to be a top notch miner, skilled in setting props, and drilling and blasting coal, and how when he came here his skills didn't mean anything because all those jobs were given to the Welsh and English, and the only work he could get was the same work he did as a butty when he was twelve years old. His stories had made her both laugh and cry.

Now, as she climbed the steps to her house, while Patrick remained on the path below, she realized they must have been talking for a very long time. She braced herself for what lay ahead, then opened the front door and tiptoed inside. She wondered who was in the parlor, and found herself hoping it was anyone but Kate. By the time she took off her damp cloak and hung it on the corner rack, the parlor door opened and there was Kate, fully dressed, standing with her hands on her hips.

"*Where have you been?* We've been worried sick! Only this past hour was I able to persuade Mother to drink some hot milk and go to bed, though I had to promise I'd wait up, and if you weren't home by midnight, I'd wake both her and Charlotte, and then we'd all go looking for you. I've rarely seen her so upset."

"What time is it?"

"After eleven!"

Virginia shook her head. "No, it can't be. Not that late, surely." She followed Kate into the large front parlor, surprised to see the overhead crystal chandelier lit. Its light, bouncing off the two giant pier-mirrors between the windows, made it painfully clear that Virginia's muddy boots were leaving a trail of dirt across Mother's prize English loom carpet. But she dared not stop for Kate was too angry. So she tried walking on tiptoes as she maneuvered her way around half a dozen chairs, two marble-top tables and their piano from Paris. Her breath caught when the small clock on the thick marble mantel sounded eleven-thirty. She realized, for the first time, the heartache she had caused her family.

"Oh, Virginia," Kate said, taking her sister's hand when they settled on the moss-green sofa by the fireplace. "What is going on with you? You are normally so sensible."

"I had to see Patrick O'Brien. To find out if he had any hand in the Foley matter."

"And did he?"

"No, and I believe him, Kate." Virginia looked at her sister, wanting desperately for her to say she believed him, too.

But Kate just sighed. "I suppose that was Patrick I saw from the window."

"It was. He wouldn't hear of me walking home alone in the dark."

"Yes . . . that was thoughtful, but did it have to take so long?"

"I know. Time . . . well, it just got away from us. He started talking, and oh, my, how that man can talk! He told me about Donegal and his childhood, and . . .well here it is eleven-thirty. I'm so sorry, truly. I never meant to worry anyone."

"You'll have to face Mother in the morning."

"I know."

"But she's always liked the O'Briens, so I doubt she'll say much, though you gave her an awful fright."

"But you don't, do you? Like Patrick, I mean."

"Does it matter?" Kate frowned. "You don't care for this man, do you? I mean *really* care for him? You haven't gone and lost your heart now, have you?"

"No . . . no . . . of course not. But he's a decent person, Kate, though a complicated one. And this I must tell you so you understand that I'm not hiding anything or covering for him . . . you were right. He is a Molly. He told me so himself. Still, believe me when I say I have nothing to fear. I ask you to trust me in this." Virginia leaned her head against her sister's shoulder, suddenly feeling very tired. "But he sees things so differently than we do. He believes violence is justified in the face of injustice."

"Isn't that a contradiction in terms?"

"Yes . . . but we haven't lived his life or walked in his shoes. Is it right to judge him? I fear having to scrape and scratch for everything has made Patrick bitter. But perhaps we would be, too, if our lives were as hard as his."

"That's a poor excuse. Many people face hardship and don't turn to violence. We must be a nation of laws or crumble into chaos. Might can never make right, nor fists rule the day. I've been reading your articles, Virginia, and I . . . ."

"*You have?*"

"Well, what I'm trying to say is that your articles have pricked my heart. They have brought home what we've known all along, that life in coal country is hard. It's a fine thing you're doing, Virginia. We all need our hearts pricked from time to time. But if Patrick wants to change things, let him do it peacefully. It's time to break the cycle of violence. Time for both sides, labor and management, to settle their differences, to make peace and forgive the sins of the past."

Virginia removed her head from her sister's shoulder. "You can say that with a straight face?"

"What do you mean?"

"Have you forgiven? Have you forgiven the sins of the past? Forgiven the people of this town for what they did to Father?" And by the look on Kate's face, Virginia knew the answer was "no."

⌒

Kate was stunned when the invitation arrived; delivered to their door by a footman. Written on small, expensive linen notepaper and stamped with Benjamin Gaylord's monogram, it requested the pleasure of Mrs. James Farrell, Miss Kate Farrell, Miss Virginia Farrell, Miss Charlotte Farrell and Mr. Joshua Adams' company at a formal dinner party a week from Saturday. And as soon as it was read the tears and squabbling began, with Kate finding herself in the middle. At times like this she hated being the eldest.

"Just tell me again why you don't want to go, Virginia," Charlotte said, clutching the mantel of their back parlor fireplace with one hand while holding a handkerchief, dampened with tears, in the other. "Don't you see that by inviting all of us, even our *cousin*, Benjamin means to make amends? That he is extending an olive branch and saying he wishes to put aside our differences? If you don't go, it will be a slap in his face; a clear rejection of his kind overture."

"I really don't think I'd be very welcome. My new article for the *Monitor* is coming out tomorrow, and is sure to vex your Mr. Gaylord and many of his guests. It's best for all concerned that I don't attend. I think only of you, Charlotte."

Charlotte twisted the handkerchief in her hands. "Kate, tell her it's not true. Benjamin has swallowed his pride in extending this invitation. He well knows Virginia's involvement with the *Monitor* and that their sentiments differ greatly. *Please* tell her that to refuse would be a gross insult."

"Well . . . ."

"Oh, I know you think I'm foolish for still wanting Benjamin after all he's said, and even after what Mr. Adams told us about the Gaylords. But I still love him, Kate, though I'm not as impressed with his family as I once was. Nor will they be able to influence me to the extent they once did. But that doesn't negate Benjamin's fine qualities. In the end, I suppose we can't always help who we love." Charlotte left the fireplace and settle in a nearby chair. "Can't you both see how important this is to me?"

Kate sighed. How was she to resolve this? Like Virginia, she, too, would prefer not to go, but for different reasons. She had no desire to socialize with the likes of Martin Roach or any of the other prominent citizens sure to be there. Still . . . her heart went out to Charlotte.

"I do know how important this is to you, Charlotte. But you must understand Virginia's position. Her new article will anger those associated with the railroad." Virginia had let Kate read her last article before sending it off with Michael O'Malley. "It will put her and many of Benjamin's guests in an uncomfortable, perhaps even contentious, position. And I must confess, I'm not eager to be in the company of some who will be guests that night. But I understand your dilemma, too, Charlotte. You hope to win back the man you love, a man who has humbled himself with this gesture. So, for your sake, dear, I shall go." She turned to Virginia. "And I hope you will, too."

As Virginia rested her elbows on the arm of the chair and tented her fingers, Kate could see the struggle going on within her. "You're right, Charlotte, we cannot always help who we fall in love with. And I don't want to do anything to spoil your opportunity to mend things with your Mr. Gaylord. So, yes, I'll go, too."

When Kate entered the back parlor she was startled to see Joshua sitting in one of the damask-covered chairs. She couldn't say why she was surprised, after all this was where they had agreed to meet as soon as they had finished dressing. Maybe it was the way he looked, so . . . .

"You are *stunning*," Joshua said in a hushed tone. He rose to his feet as she walked to the center of the room, his eyes following her every move.

"It has taken Charlotte the better part of the week to get all our gowns ready for Mr. Gaylord's party. You can't imagine what a dither she's been in, heading operations like a general, and removing and replacing bows and sashes and the like so we would be fashionable enough to suit her. I managed to bear up well enough, but we all had to beg Virginia's indulgence since she was tired of the whole affair by the second day."

Joshua's eyes sparkled with pleasure. "It was worth the effort."

Kate fluffed the many layers of lace decorating her outer skirt. "I would have preferred a simpler dress, but Charlotte insisted that since there are so few balls and operas in the area it has become the custom of some women to wear more elaborate gowns to an elegant dinner party, which, Charlotte assured us, Mr. Gaylord's always qualifies, and therefore she wouldn't hear of us wearing a cotton dress of subdued color sporting nothing but a bit of lace around the cuffs and neck."

Joshua's grin widened, making Kate suddenly self-conscious of her plunging neckline and short, off-the-shoulder sleeves. Her bustle and silk underskirt rustled as she walked to the fireplace. "Please sit, sir. There's no need for you to remain standing."

"I prefer it," he said, walking over to her.

"I . . . see you have purchased a new suit."

"Well, I did promise Charlotte when she first told me about the invitation. And luckily the gent's-ready-to-wear store had something only requiring a modest amount of alterations."

Kate knew she was staring but she just couldn't take her eyes off him. She had never seen him look so handsome. His black coat, that had extended narrow lapels faced with silk, was short in front, with long tails in back, and was neatly pressed. Its low cut design revealed a good portion of his starched white shirt and elegant black waistcoat. A crisp white bowtie sat perched beneath his cleaned-shaven chin. Creaseless black trousers hit his highly polished black boots at just the proper height. And his sandy hair was neatly combed, parted on one side, and held in place with only a modest amount of oil.

When Kate continued to stare, Joshua shifted his feet. "I . . . hope you approve. I've wanted you to see me like this for some time."

"Oh . . . you look . . . quite fine, actually. And yes, I approve, very much."

"Then you'll not be embarrassed to take my arm at the Gaylord's when we are summoned to dinner?"

Kate fingered one of her pearl teardrop earrings and smiled. "I shall be honored to take your arm, sir."

He leaned closer, nearly touching her bare shoulder. "You look so beautiful, Kate, that when you first entered the room, you made my heart stop. Literally stop. It will be difficult to see any other woman tonight, but you."

Before Kate could say a word, Mother, Virginia, and Charlotte entered, their silks and satins rustling like dry leaves, their lace fluttering around them like butterflies. But they all looked beautiful: Mother with her elegant rose-colored silk dress and a rose-colored velvet ribbon around her neck; Virginia with her less ornate green gown that shimmered like an emerald in the lamp light; and Charlotte, who wore the most lace and ribbons of all but looked perfect in them. And everyone's hair was elaborately set with braids and curls and pearl-studded hair pins.

"Oh, I'm so nervous." Charlotte wrung her gloved hands. "Though I can't imagine why. This is sure to be a wonderful evening. So gay with good conversation and sumptuous food. And afterward, well, afterward there will be parlor games enough to make everyone laugh and feel cheerful." Her face flushed as she directed her comments to no one in particular. "We are all sure to have a most happy time."

Mother just nodded, while Virginia sighed and looked pained. Then one of the boarders yelled from the hall, "The carriage is here!"

Kate tried to ignore Charlotte's incessant babbling as the large enclosed Brougham coach bumped and jiggled along the dirt road heading for the outskirts of Pottsville. It was difficult to see through the dark overcast night with only the coach's front lanterns to illuminate the road, but judging from the time spent traveling, Kate guessed they were nearly there. And it wouldn't be too soon. With so much lace and satin and silk filling the interior, the carriage was stuffy. Even the little air coming through the coach window gave no relief. And Charlotte was adding to the overall discomfort.

Though Kate was unable, in the dark interior, to see the expression on anyone's face, she was certain that others were also growing weary of her sister's effusive manner in extolling the goodness of Mr. Gaylord for sending his carriage, and for the tactful way he avoided acknowledging that the Farrells no longer owned a carriage or even a barouche, having sold both, along with all their horses, soon after the hanging.

"I've always said Benjamin was thoughtful, haven't I? And this illustrates the point," Charlotte continued. "And one can't take these kindnesses for granted."

But just as Kate was about to implore Charlotte to be silent, Mother's soft voice broke in. "Yes, Charlotte, we quite understand about Benjamin's kindness, as you have made it amply clear . . . numerous times."

And that put an end to the matter, and just in time, too, for the coach rattled past the two giant marble lions marking the entrance of a lengthy driveway, a driveway that curved in front of the sprawling Gaylord mansion.

Kate quickly forgot her discomfort in the profusion of light that greeted them. The entire length of the driveway was lined with lanterns hanging on ornate black wrought-iron poles, and every window of the house brimmed with illumination.

"Oh, dear, we must be late." Charlotte gestured toward the many carriages filling the crushed-stone driveway as their coach pulled to a stop behind the last in the caravan.

Within seconds, the coachman opened the door, then helped everyone disembark, beginning with Mother.

Kate and Joshua were the last to exit, and while Charlotte continued fussing about the lateness of the hour, Kate stood gazing at the three-story brick mansion nestled among large sprawling maples. Nearly half a year had passed since her last visit; the evening the Gaylords entertained Franklin B. Gowen and numerous railroad executives and their families. Like most Gaylord parties, it had left Kate feeling uncomfortable and irritated. She was exceedingly grateful that Joshua was here to help her through this one.

She took his arm and allowed him to aid her in maneuvering the paved walkway with her trailing gown. Then up three broad steps which ran the length of the covered porch, past the huge white columns, until they stood before an ornate mahogany and stained-glass door where a doorman greeted them.

Kate didn't recognize the doorman, and wondered if the rumors of Mrs. Gaylord firing her help for the slightest infraction were true. The doorman ushered everyone into a spacious entranceway boasting a Bavarian crystal chandelier that looked, to Kate, as large as her dining room table; then into a parlor that could swallow three of her own front parlors with ease.

It was difficult not to be impressed, even for Kate who was usually unimpressed by such things, and even after having seen it several times, as well as being instructed by the matronly Mrs. Gaylord on the origin and value of nearly all the furnishings. Long flowing red velvet drapes adorned the floor-to-ceiling windows. Lush couches, chairs and side tables filled the center of the room; a piano and sideboard hugged one wall, a massive gilded pier mirror with lamp sconces covered a good portion of another, while an enormous fireplace, with a large scrolled pink-marble mantel from Italy, dominated the fourth. The walls themselves were adorned with massive paintings of various members of the Gaylord family along with numerous country scenes. There was so much to see, and so much finery, not only in furniture but in statues and urns and the like, that it was easy to overlook the exquisite rug on the floor, until Kate happened to glance down. She smiled as she wondered what Mrs. Gaylord would think if she knew the entire Farrell clan was here trampling her prized Brussels carpet.

And then she saw Benjamin Gaylord, elegantly dressed, right in the center of the room, a room which now held more than twenty people. To one side, she noticed Martin Roach and his wife, Hester, conversing with a tall unpleasant looking man; someone she had never met. She wondered who he might be, but before she could ask, Benjamin Gaylord appeared, smiling, then extended his greetings to each of them.

"I'm so gratified you were able to come," he said after protocol had been satisfied. His eyes were fixed on Charlotte. "Was the coach satisfactory?"

Charlotte's blond curls bobbed as she nodded her head. "Yes, quite."

"I was most anxious over your comfort."

"It was kind of you to send your conveyance but there was no need for you to be anxious." Charlotte's gloved hand flitted in the air like a dove.

Kate was sure this bland discourse would have gone on forever if that tall, gangly man she had seen with the Roaches hadn't stepped into their circle and begged an introduction. Upon closer observation he appeared, to Kate, even more unpleasant, with tight thin lips, a long nose, and the dark beady eyes of a raven; a stingy-looking man by all accounts.

At first Benjamin appeared disturbed by the intrusion, then, after some hesitation, introduced each of them in turn. When he ended with, "And this is Mr. Walter Hill, the new Superintendent of the Schuylkill Division of the Reading Railroad," an awkward silence fell over them.

Kate studied the intruder through squinting eyes. So, this was Father's replacement. And well pleased about it, too, judging by his smug manner. She had heard of him; a seasoned railroad man but one who had no ties to the lower anthracite region and therefore no loyalty to it. She chided herself for being so harsh, for her un-Christian like attitude, but when he opened his mouth she knew she had not been harsh enough.

"So you're the Farrell everyone's talking about," he said, looking at Virginia. "Well, little lady, you certainly have folks at the railroad in an uproar with those articles of yours. And frankly, I'm surprised you'd write such nonsense, being the daughter of a railroad man yourself. Though I suppose a Judas can be found anywhere." He laughed as though making a joke.

"I understand you hail from New York, sir," Benjamin said, obviously trying to change the subject.

But Mr. Hill would have none of it. "How you could side with those malcontents is hard to fathom, Miss Virginia. Did you know that the Company was forced to take that poor unfortunate Mr. Foley by rail all the way to the upper anthracite region and the nearest hospital, where, I understand, a surgeon removed his spleen or was it a kidney? Maybe it was his liver. Not quite sure. But it proves what I've always said, women don't understand the workings of a man's world and should stay home and tend to their knitting."

Kate slipped her arm around Virginia's waist, "Excuse us, sir, but we need to pay our respects to the other guests." Then she whisked Virginia away.

"I'm glad you got me out of that," Virginia whispered, "before I said something I'd regret. I don't want to spoil Charlotte's evening. I only hope that disagreeable Mr. Hill won't be sitting anywhere near us at dinner. Imagine someone so insufferable taking Father's place!"

But they had hardly distanced themselves from the offending Mr. Hill, when Martin Roach cornered them. Perspiration dotted his portly face and his thick black mustache, which seemed fuller than normal, drooped a bit at the edges. He eyed them both, allowing his gaze to linger on their low necklines before directing his attention to Kate.

"Seems you don't need my help after all. Seems all has been forgiven and you've been accepted back into the fold. Though I must say I'm surprised. But now that you've regained your position in polite society, it shouldn't be necessary to continue your investigation. What do you have to gain? You've already gotten what you wanted. You're accepted again. Why remain at odds with the world and seek to prove something that can't be proven? We can be friends." His hand traveled up Kate's arm, to the edge of her short sleeve. "We *should* be friends."

"Excuse me, ladies," Joshua said, walking up to the group and giving Martin Roach a sharp look. "May I escort you both to the dining room? The announcement has just been made. Dinner is about to be served."

Gratefully, Kate took Joshua's arm. Already Benjamin was leading Mother and Charlotte into the dining room, and so they formed a line behind their host, then entered the well-lit room. A large multi-armed candlestick sat in the center of the table. And around the room were numerous patent lamps on gilded tripods, and these, as well as the large adjustable ceiling lamp, all made the dark stucco walls glow; walls that, the portly Mrs. Gaylord once told Kate, were kept free of paper and fabric to prevent the trapping of food odors.

Kate marveled at the huge mahogany table covered with floor-length linen, gleaming English china, sparkling crystal goblets, and small sterling silver card holders marking the place of each guest.

As soon as everyone was seated, the butler and footmen served the first course, a brothy fish soup. And as they poured the accompanying sauterne into goblets, Kate looked down the long table to where Charlotte sat at Benjamin's right. She was smiling and talking and making everyone around her smile and talk, too. It was then that Kate noticed Charlotte's easy grace and natural gentility, something neither Kate nor Virginia really possessed. Why hadn't Kate seen it before? She had always thought Charlotte shallow. And perhaps she was to some extent, but she was also a woman of the times, who understood her place in a man's world and how to fulfill her role in it. And Charlotte and Benjamin did make a perfect couple; well suited in both temperament and interests. Both perfect hosts, willing to sit at a table for hours entertaining people Kate and Virginia often found trying or uninteresting. And after dinner, Charlotte and Benjamin would return to the parlor and play forfeits or charades, where inevitably one of the men, after imbibing too much wine, would crawl on all fours and grunt like a pig or do something else foolish during his charade. But Charlotte and Benjamin would enjoy it utterly, and be charming throughout, while she and Virginia and even Mother sat grinding their teeth.

Seeing it all now made Kate appreciate Charlotte in ways she never had before. Perhaps she would do well to learn from her younger sister's example, Kate thought as she picked up her spoon. But even before she could dip it into her soup, Mr. Walter Hill, who it pleased God to seat across from Kate, as a test, perhaps, or out of a sense of humor, leaned over.

"Well, little lady," he said, looking at Virginia who sat on the other side of Joshua. "Let's discuss why someone of your breeding would align herself with those ruffians at the Mattson Colliery."

Virginia looked up, sipped her spoonful of soup, then said in a clear, sweet voice, "I think I prefer to discuss how Mr. Gowen manipulated coal prices in our area and brought the local collieries to their knees."

Kate put down her spoon and took a deep breath as her hands retreated to her lap. And when they did, she felt Joshua's hand cover hers. It was a comforting, reassuring touch, and instead of withdrawing, she gave him a grateful squeeze.

It was going to be a long night.

CHAPTER 8

Kate needed to take matters into her own hands. Things had gone too far. Charlotte and Virginia were still not speaking, and it had been days since the Gaylord party and their loud, tearful argument. It had to end, even if it meant forcing the issue. So, instead of scrubbing the large kitchen dresser with fine white sand as Mother had asked, she went to where Virginia was busy removing spots from their pewter. Without a word, she took her sister by the arm and pulled her from the room.

"What are you doing? I have no time for games," Virginia said, dropping her oily flannel rag as she tried extracting herself from Kate's fierce grip.

Without answering, Kate continued dragging Virginia. When they reached the front parlor, there was Charlotte on her knees sprinkling dried tea leaves over the carpet.

"Come!" Kate said, jerking Charlotte to her feet while keeping her other hand firmly clamped on Virginia.

"What . . . what's going on? Where are you taking me?"

Kate ignored the question as she towed the pair to the back parlor, shoved them inside, then closed the door behind her.

"Sit," she ordered, pointing to the two damask-covered chairs.

The pair scowled, but obeyed.

"Now," Kate said, putting her hands on her hips, "don't you think it's time you settled your differences? You can't go on like this forever! You're sisters! And grownups! And living in the same house!"

Charlotte pulled a white lace handkerchief from her apron pocket and dabbed the tears that were forming. Virginia just sat looking down at her folded hands.

"All right, if no one is going to say anything, I will. Charlotte, I know you're upset over what happened at Benjamin's party, but I was in a position to see and hear the whole thing, and it was that awful Mr. Hill's fault. He baited Virginia by deliberately starting a discussion he knew was inflammatory."

"That may be so, but Virginia is intelligent, the smartest of us all. It shouldn't have been difficult to keep Mr. Hill in check, not for a woman of her abilities. The dinner party was Benjamin's way of telling everyone he accepts all of us in spite of everything. Then Virginia had to go and ruin it."

Kate waited for Virginia to respond. When she didn't, Kate nodded. "Charlotte's right on that point. Your ability to foil an argument, or refute one intelligently, far surpasses ours. I suppose you could have exercised more self-control."

"I never meant to spoil your evening." Virginia turned to Charlotte. "I knew how important it was to you, but I warned you. I knew there would be a backlash from my articles; that Benjamin's railroad friends might feel compelled to comment. And you know how difficult it is for me to remain silent in the face of gross stupidity."

"You thought only of yourself." Charlotte's eyes clouded with anger. "You made everyone uncomfortable by arguing with Mr. Hill. And once he began raising his voice, well . . . I've never seen people eat so fast. And then when Mr. Hill started flailing his arms like a . . . ."

Kate bit her lip to keep from laughing at the thought of Mr. Hill's long spider-like arms thrashing about and overturning his wine goblet, soiling the Gaylord's expensive tablecloth in the process.

"Well . . . when he began acting like a madman, no one knew where to put their eyes from embarrassment. And then when the butler came to clean the spillage and accidently overturned the soup onto Mr. Hill's lap, it was spoiled. No one had any appetite after that. They all became dyspeptic and barely touched the rest of their meal."

A thin smile managed to evade Kate's efforts as she remembered how the soup had dripped down Mr. Hill's starched white shirt and onto his trousers. And then when he left to wash, how fish fragments dropped from his clothing and left a trail on the floor. And how throughout it all Virginia had remained calm and ladylike.

"But what upset me most," Charlotte said, blowing her nose, "is how you took the part of those ruffians at the Mattson Colliery. How could you defend them against your own kind? Sometimes Virginia . . . sometimes I don't understand you."

Virginia nodded. "I know, dearest. Sometimes I don't understand myself."

"No one even stayed for the parlor games, and Benjamin had such a wonderful evening planned."

"Yes, and I so wanted to play 'Poor Pussy' and meow like a cat," Virginia said, managing to keep a straight face.

At this, Kate could no longer control herself and burst out laughing at the thought of Virginia crawling on all fours and meowing until she forced someone to take her place by making them either smile or laugh. When Virginia began laughing too, it made Charlotte giggle—a soft ladylike giggle which finally escalated into full throaty laughter. Now the three were on their feet, laughing. And soon they were hugging and kissing and asking forgiveness.

Charlotte walked up the steps of the large wooden porch clutching the wrapped package under her arm. She knocked on the white paint-chipped door, timidly at first, then more forcefully. Finally, a tall, middle-age woman with graying hair opened it.

"Yes? Can I help you?"

"I . . . well . . . that is . . . ."

"*Yes?*"

Charlotte jutted her chin. "I'm Miss Charlotte Farrell, member of the Women's Benevolent Society of Greater Pottsville and I . . . ."

"Oh, yes! One of Mrs. Gaylord's ladies. Come in. Come in." The matron slipped her hand under Charlotte's arm and pulled her through the doorway. "You must thank Mrs. Gaylord for that last batch of blankets she sent over. As ever, we are grateful for her kindness."

Charlotte scanned the parlor and was disappointed that the intended object of her visit was nowhere to be seen. She was about to make a hasty departure when suddenly there she was, entering from another room, and taking a chair in the corner. "I will be happy to convey your gratitude," Charlotte said, without looking at the matron. "I'll also mention the superb manner in which your establishment appears to be run."

"We do our best with the little we have." The matron's face reddened. "I mean . . . well, I didn't mean to imply . . . . Of course the generosity of your Society is without peer and we don't take it lightly." She cleared her throat. "Perhaps you'd like a tour of our facilities? I can't remember the last time a member of the Society came for a visit. I would be happy to show you around."

Charlotte shook her head. "I shall save that for another time. Today, I'd prefer to sit and just visit with some of your guests."

"I . . . suppose . . . that would be . . . fine, yes, as you wish." With that she led Charlotte into the parlor and offered her a chair by the window.

Instead of taking it, Charlotte walked over to the woman with the disheveled hair and took the empty seat beside her. "I will sit here awhile, if you don't mind. And . . . I'll call if I need anything."

The matron hesitated, then walked away. When she was out of sight, Charlotte placed the package on her lap then turned to the woman beside her. Sitting this close made Charlotte see that the woman wasn't as old as she originally thought, and something else, too—that she had been pretty once. Despite the unruly hair, outdated dress, and worn look on her face, Charlotte could see that, yes, this woman had been very very pretty. She fingered the package. "I hope you don't think me forward, but I have brought you a little something, and hope you will accept it."

The woman smiled sweetly. "I remember you from last time. And judging from your fine clothes, you must be one of the Society ladies."

Charlotte frowned. She had worn one of her simplest dresses, wanting to draw as little contrast as possible between her and the ladies here. So she was surprised that this woman thought her finely dressed. "My name is Miss Farrell, Miss Charlotte Farrell."

"And I'm Elizabeth Mills, but my friends call me Betsy."

"I shall not be so presumptuous, but may I call you Elizabeth?"

The woman shook her head. "If you feel friendly enough to bring a gift then you must call me Betsy. It's only fitting."

"Yes, well, then please accept this, Betsy." Charlotte handed her the package. "It's just a small thing, but I hope you like it."

In seconds, Betsy removed the brown paper and held the mirror and comb in her hands. "They're beautiful! It's been awhile since I've had anything this nice." Her eyes brimmed with tears. "Thank you."

"I . . . didn't know how best to decorate it. I wasn't sure if you preferred birds to flowers or . . . ."

"*You* painted this?"

Charlotte nodded.

"I . . . don't know what to say."

"There's no need to say anything." Charlotte rose. "I . . . must go now."

Betsy's eyebrows knotted as she fingered the painted mirror. "Why did you do this? You don't even know me. Why would you be so kind to a stranger?"

"I'm not sure. I . . . I . . . think because every woman needs to feel loved and valued and special. And because I thought if I . . . if I were in your place, I'd like it very much if someone did this for me."

Betsy took Charlotte's hand. "Will you come back? Will you come and visit me again?"

The gesture and request embarrassed Charlotte, but when she saw the longing in the woman's eyes as if remembering better days, she smiled and nodded. "Yes, I'll come again." And then Charlotte was out the door and down the porch stairs feeling as light as that butterfly she had painted on the back of Betsy's mirror.

Kate was busy stripping sheets off beds for the second time this week, all the while dreading the ordeal of the washing and bluing to follow. Charlotte was already boiling water; and since it was a beautiful day, Virginia was in the back yard, rather than in the laundry room off the kitchen, laying out the needed wash tubs, scrub brushes, soap and bleaching agents. At least the fresh air and sunshine would be pleasant.

With one final fluffing of the down pillows, Kate finished Mr. Thumbolt's bed, then proceeded to the hall where a pile of dirty sheets lay in a corner. She added Mr. Thumbolt's to the pile then glanced at Joshua's room. The door was still closed. It had been closed since she first came upstairs. Now, his was the only bed left and there was nothing to do but knock. She picked up the last remaining set of clean sheets from the half-table nearby, then knocked on his door.

"*Yes?*"

"I'm sorry to disturb you," she said as she entered. "But I need to change your bedding. Charlotte and Virginia are waiting . . . ." She stopped when she saw him hunched over the desk. And instead of going to the bed, she walked to where he sat. "What's wrong?"

At once, Joshua placed his arms over the papers scattered across the desktop.

"What's wrong?" Kate repeated.

"I'm busy, Kate. You need to leave me to my work."

"You've found something, haven't you? It's about Father, isn't it?"

He scooped the papers into a pile. "I'm trying to codify my notes. Make sense of them."

Kate walked to the nearby Windsor chair and draped the clean sheets across the back, then returned to stand over his shoulder. "May I see? Perhaps I can help." She bent over trying to read the top page of the stack.

Once more Joshua covered the papers. "Nothing you can do. I need more time, and then we'll talk."

Instead of backing away, Kate reached for the top sheet but Joshua caught her wrist.

"No, Kate. Not yet. Let me sort this out. I'll tell you everything in due time."

"Don't you know that's the worst thing you could have said?" She pulled free. "You know how the mind works, Joshua. How it always conjures up the worst scenarios. I'll torture myself for hours. No, you must tell me for I'll not leave until you do."

"Must you always have your way?" When she didn't answer, he sighed. "All right, I'll tell you. But you have to promise you won't go on a gallop. I know how you are, and I don't want you running wild with this. Will you promise?"

"I dislike making open ended promises. Just tell me and be done with it."

Joshua rose from his chair and stood tugging on his rumpled waistcoat as though deciding what to do. "I've investigated sixteen of Martin Roach's colliery sales and not one was coerced," he finally said.

"*What?* That's . . . impossible . . . *isn't it?*"

"However, two of them voiced their displeasure over the price. They claimed they got far less for their collieries than other owners they know, and were still angry about it. But Gowen's hauling practices had nearly bankrupted them so they had no choice but to sell, even for a sum below what their collieries were worth. After hearing this, I went back to some of those I questioned previously. I've only had time to revisit five, and found the same complaint. And early this morning I went to the railroad office in Pottsville. And after showing the office manager my identification and swearing him to secrecy, I pulled Martin Roach's last two contracts, the ones that have yet to be sent to the Philadelphia headquarters. I was looking them over when you came in."

"What are you searching for?"

"The amounts don't match; the amounts between what the two colliery owners said they received and the amounts specified in their contracts." He turned to the desk and thumped the stack of papers. "These contracts list a higher sale price. Tomorrow, I'll take the train to Philadelphia and look at the rest of Mr. Roach's contracts, compare the sale prices and see if there's a discrepancy in what the other five colliery owners said they were paid. If the numbers don't match, I'll speak with the remaining owners on the list."

Kate frowned. "I don't understand. What does it mean?"

"It could mean a great deal. We're talking vast sums of money here when you consider that the largest of these collieries was purchased for three million dollars! But I can hardly take my suspicions to Mr. Gowen until I have proof."

"But you have a theory, Joshua. What is it you suspect?"

Joshua took her hand. "You can't run with this, Kate. You *must* allow me to investigate thoroughly."

"You think he was swindling the railroad. Don't you?" She pulled away. "But how is that possible? How could he . . . ? Unless . . . he made up separate contracts, one for the owners, the other for the railroad. And what? Pocketed the difference? No . . . that's too fantastic. No sane person would attempt such a thing. It's just not possible."

"It could be. Mind you, I said, *could be*. The contracts appear boilerplate, easy enough to duplicate. It wouldn't be difficult to fill out two copies with different prices, and forge the signature on the bogus one."

"Maybe this was what Father and Mr. Blakely were investigating." Kate thumped the desk. "It makes sense now. Yes, all of it. They must have found out, or at least suspected Mr. Roach's double dealings, as you did, from conversations with ex-owners. Samuel Baxter must have found out, too. But he was easy to handle. He could be bribed. That's obviously why Martin Roach had to come up with two quick colliery sales, sales he gained through intimidation and threats, so he could turn them over to Baxter and let him make the commission as a payoff. But it wasn't so easy with Father and Mr. Blakely. *Oh, is it possible?* Joshua, is it possible that Martin Roach hired the two thugs to make Father appear desperate to have Mr. Blakely sell and willing to use force to do it?"

Kate shook with rage. "He must have killed Mr. Blakely, too, or hired someone to do it. He could have sent Father that note. Then timed the murder just before Father's appointment, implicating him as the killer. In one stroke it would rid him of the threat both Mr. Blakely and Father posed." She balled her hands into fists. "Oh, how could he be so diabolical? How could he kill one man, then send another to the gallows, all for profit, for filthy profit?"

"You don't know that, Kate. Such talk is imprudent."

"But it makes perfect sense. You must think so, too, or you wouldn't be going to Philadelphia. Mr. Gowen might not care how an agent made his sales, but he'd care if that agent swindled the railroad in the process. Martin Roach was desperate to keep his dealings secret, and in your line of work you know that desperate men do desperate things." Kate shook her head. "I always thought Mr. Roach of low character but I never imagined . . . I never imagined . . . it would cost Father his life."

Joshua put his arms around her, and when he drew her close she leaned against his chest and sobbed.

"Promise me you won't do anything foolish while I'm away," he whispered when she stopped crying. Then cupping her chin, he tilted her face upward. "I'll only be gone a day or two at the most." When she didn't answer, he sighed. "Kate, you are so prudent and sensible, and yet . . . at times when you let your heart rule, you can be so . . . foolish."

"I know," she said, bringing her face closer to his, and after the briefest hesitation, kissed him.

Kate hadn't planned it, but here she was, the heels of her black boots rat-tat-tatting along the plank sidewalk; her hair bare of bonnet; her faded work dress flapping in the breeze; her heart pounding like one of Samuel Baxter's hammers. The thought only came to her an hour ago when Joshua left for Pottsville to catch the train to Philadelphia. She had tried talking herself out of it, had told herself Joshua would be furious, call her "reckless," perhaps worse, when more than ever she didn't want him thinking ill of her. But nothing worked. Anger shaped her now; anger bordering on a rage that made her mouth sour.

Martin Roach was responsible for Father's death.

How could she let that go? She hadn't even told her mother and sisters what she planned to do. She didn't want to be dissuaded.

She hurried down the walk, ignoring those who smiled and greeted her. A kind reply would only soften her, and that too was a dissuasion. She ignored the gay chirping of the birds in nearby trees as well as the sun streaming in golden waves across her path. She mustn't consider God's blessings. Considering them would force her to consider God Himself. And she refused to think about Him now. If she did, He would speak to her of love. And it wasn't love she wanted filling her heart.

She burst through the door, then scanned the room. Hester was behind the counter waiting on two women—a widow and her daughter who Kate knew had a small farm on the outskirts of town, and who made fine women's corsets and petticoats for extra money. Only one other person was present, an elderly woman examining a cast-iron skillet. *But where was Martin Roach?*

She stormed up to the counter and glared at Hester who was showing the women a wide strip of fine linen whitework full of embroidered eyelets.

"As you can see it's a superb sample of *broderie anglaise* and would make a lovely decoration on any petticoat. Your ornamented undergarments always fetch a good price so you'll have no trouble recovering the added expense."

Before either woman could answer, Kate leaned over the counter. "Where's your husband?"

"Why . . . in the back."

Without a word Kate headed for the stockroom, ignoring Hester's cries of, "You can't go there! Customers are not allowed! Kate!" and ducked through the open door. It was the first time she had ever been in back and was surprised by its size, by how tall and fully stocked the shelves were. But Martin Roach could afford to keep a large and varied inventory. He no longer had to worry about money, did he? She walked down one of the long rows and found him at the end, pulling bolts of heavy woolen fabrics from a box, obviously supplies for the coming colder weather.

He dropped one of the bolts when he saw her. "Why . . . Miss Kate, what are you doing here? Hester's out front. She'll help you if you require assistance. I'm quite busy, and . . . customers aren't allowed back here."

"It's you I've come to see." Her breathing was heavy, her eyes slits. "Tell me, did you think you'd get away with it?"

"Get away with what? What are you talking about?"

"You hired Samuel Baxter to make tight-cooperage barrels, didn't you? As a further bribe? Weren't the two collieries enough?"

"How dare you come in and question me like this! What business is it of yours, anyway?" Sweat beaded his forehead.

"What were you going to do with them? Sell them to the Company Store? Let the poor unsuspecting miners buy them? After all, what difference would it make? The Company Store would never refund their money even if the barrels were defective."

"Why . . . I had no such thought. I was just trying to help a friend. Drum up business for him, as it were. If the barrels were going to be inferior how is that my fault? Besides, they could still be used for grain and such."

"Yes, but for greatly inflated prices."

"Samuel never finished my order so why are we even discussing this?"

"And wasn't that convenient for you? Him leaving town like that? And you must admit you got off pretty cheap with Mr. Baxter. Two collieries and a few barrels. Not like my father and Mr. Blakely."

Martin Roach pulled a handkerchief from his waistcoat and began dabbing his forehead. "I insist you leave now or I'll remove you by force."

"You knew you couldn't bribe them. And you knew that sooner or later they would get the evidence they needed to prove you were swindling the railroad."

"You don't know what you're talking about! I could have the law on you for such slander!" His hand trembled as he raised a bolt of cloth into the air.

"You plan to kill me, too, like you did Mr. Blakely?"

"*What?*"

"That would be foolish. Right here in your stockroom. You could hardly entrap someone else then, the way you did my father."

Martin threw the blot, hitting Kate's shoulder. "Get out! Get out, you brazen little trollop! I've heard the stories about you and that cousin of yours. Don't think I'm unaware of your character! And I'll ruin you in this town. See if I don't!"

Kate shook her head. "You are the one who will be ruined. Even if I never prove you killed Mr. Blakely, you will be going to jail when the railroad finds out how you've swindled them."

"I never killed anyone. I swear!" Martin said, flailing his arms in the air like a drowning man. "I never killed anyone!"

And even as Kate left the stockroom and flew past the counter and Hester and the three customers who all stared with open mouths, she could still hear Martin Roach screaming, "I never killed anyone!"

Charlotte's white-gloved hand clutched the brass ring of the knocker. Her mouth felt like chalk. It wasn't too late. She could still change her mind. *But that would be cowardly.* She took a deep breath and tapped. When a servant came and opened the ornate mahogany and stain-glass door, Charlotte told him hers was a brief "dinner call". Without a word, he escorted her to the front parlor, and there invited her to take one of the many seats. She chose, instead, to remain standing.

Etiquette had brought her here. Protocol demanded that within a week of attending a dinner party the guest return to the host's house to convey his gratitude and to enumerate the joys of the said evening. And the week was up. There could be no more procrastinating. She needed to stay at least ten minutes but no longer than twenty, and wondered how she was going to manage ten minutes of benign conversation considering there were so few joys about that night to enumerate. And then there was Virginia's latest article, and of course Kate's behavior yesterday when she made a spectacle of herself by accusing Martin Roach of murdering Mr. Blakely. The whole town was talking about both sisters, and the gossip had certainly reached Pottsville by now, and the ears of Benjamin Gaylord.

It had become clear to Charlotte that marriage to Benjamin was impossible. Her family would never please him or his mother. And no matter how much she might wish it, she was never going to change her family. She was weary of having to defend them to Benjamin and of having to defend Benjamin to them. And since she couldn't control the behavior of her sisters, nor the prejudices of the Gaylords, there was little to do but sever her ties with Benjamin once and for all.

She walked to the fireplace and studied the scrolled marble mantel, studied the delicate carved leaves decorating the solid lintel over the hearth; studied the lion heads on each side atop wide elaborately carved posts that ended up as lion's paws at the bottom. It spoke of the ambiance of a privileged and cultured life, a life she had no chance of being part of now. But she would do this last required act, to show a character better than Benjamin undoubtedly ascribed to her. And then she would carry on with her life, a life without the Gaylords.

"Charlotte, how . . . pleasant to see you."

She turned to face Benjamin who remained standing in the doorway like a listing ship. He wiped his open palms down the sides of his trousers, then entered the room. "Please sit." He gestured toward the chair nearest her, then took the one beside hers.

"I've come to thank you for the lovely evening at your house. Naturally, I speak on behalf of my mother and sisters, as well."

"The pleasure was mine," he said stiffly.

"The food was superb, especially the green goose. I don't think I've ever tasted better or one with such delicate flavors. Its almond and date sauce was a triumph."

"Yes, one of cook's specialties."

Charlotte lowered her eyes. "Naturally, the games you had planned would have made a perfect ending to a perfect evening. I only regret that the unfortunate incident with Mr. Hill had to spoil it. And I deeply regret my family's part in it."

"Yes . . . yes . . . . But that's all past now."

"All past," Charlotte repeated as she looked him in the eye, daring him to say the obvious—that more than his party had past.

Benjamin picked at his beard and looked away. "Perhaps you haven't heard, but I've decided to join Mother in England. Though the social season is over, I crave a holiday. I leave for New York the end of next week."

"Your mother will be pleased."

"Yes . . . well . . . I suppose, since there's no more to be done here. But I had . . . hoped . . . ."

"Did you see Virginia's recent article in the *Monitor*? The one about the sink holes in the patches caused by all the tunneling in the mines, and how sometimes an entire house disappears when the ground shifts? I especially liked how she made it symbolic for the way the railroad is swallowing up the lower anthracite region." Charlotte fingered the cream broach at her throat. "Did you have occasion to read it?" she repeated.

Benjamin's face clouded. "I did."

"Kate has been reading all of Virginia's articles to us. I think they are rather clever."

"Yes . . . well, Mr. Gowen didn't think so. He was extremely displeased."

"And I suppose you've heard about Kate's performance yesterday, at Martin's Dry Goods Store?"

Benjamin didn't respond, but the look on his face and how he cleared his throat, told Charlotte he had. She smiled and rose to her feet, hoping the appropriate ten minutes had past. "There's no use in pretending any longer, Benjamin. It simply won't work between us. I'm happy you're going to England. We both need to move on. I'm sure you'll find what you're looking for there."

Benjamin was also on his feet, and when Charlotte turned to leave, he took hold of her arm. "I've always had my mind set on you, Charlotte. From the very first, you were the one I chose. It's not easy for a man like me to alter a decision once made, but in this case I believe I must. I'm a thoughtful, cautious man in search of a thoughtful, cautious wife. I still care for you, Charlotte. You are the wife I would prefer above all others, but the obstacles are too many. I *must* consider my family's reputation and standing. I had hoped we could resolve our differences, but it has become all too clear that this is impossible. The task is too daunting with your family's daily displays of shameless behavior. I hope you can see the necessity of my looking for someone more suitable."

Charlotte's heart pounded as anger rose and filled her mouth with what she had not planned to say, with what she had not wanted to say. "You are very smug in your declaration. Perhaps if you had been less so I would have spared you this, but the truth is, Benjamin, I understand your feelings perfectly for *you* are not suitable enough for me. I don't believe I want the grandson of a slaver for a husband, and have decided to find someone more fitting to be my companion in life."

"*Grandson of a slaver?* Whatever are you talking about? My father was well respected, a captain of industry, internationally known."

"Your father, your father, your father, yes, but what of your *grand-father?* Perhaps you should learn more about your family history."

Benjamin released her. "I never knew my grandfather. And I was told little about him."

The look on his face was so utterly desolate that Charlotte felt compassion. "I wish you no ill will, truly I don't. Let us part in peace and friendship, and go our separate ways. Life will go on for both of us. It just wouldn't be as we imagined, that's all. Good-bye, Benjamin. God speed." With that, she quickly exited the house.

⌐⌐

Charlotte hadn't meant to come, but here she was smoothing down the skirt of her day dress, then adjusting her Lamballe bonnet. She wouldn't have come so finely dressed if this were a planned visit, but after her confrontation with Benjamin Gaylord she was too upset to return home, and somehow ended up here. Now she felt embarrassed as she sat beside the plainly dressed Betsy Mills, though she was pleased to see her hair so well appointed and skillfully arrayed in multiple plaits.

"I hope my visit isn't an inconvenience," Charlotte muttered.

"Oh, no! I'm delighted to see you. And I have so enjoyed your gift."

"Your hair looks lovely. It seems you are quite proficient in replicating the latest fashion."

"Yes . . . I almost forgot how much I used to enjoy such endeavors. Your gift has meant a great deal. And this may sound silly, but it's given me hope . . . hope for a better future. And because of that I'd like to give you a gift, as well."

"That's not necessary. My gesture was not meant to garner anything from you, only to . . . ."

"I quite understand." Betsy placed her rough hand over Charlotte's. "But please allow me this."

"Well . . . all right . . . if it's that important to you."

"Can we take a walk? I believe I'm strong enough, and the fresh air will be welcome."

"I suppose . . . if it's allowed. I mean, will the matron permit it?"

Betsy laughed a light girlish laugh. "Yes, if the request comes from you. She wouldn't dare refuse a Society lady."

"Then I shall speak to her." Charlotte rose to her feet, "But you must promise not to overtax yourself."

As soon as Charlotte obtained the matron's consent, she and Betsy were out standing on the dirt path that ran along the side of the Home. Charlotte slipped her arm through Betsy's after seeing, in the bright sun light, how frail Betsy actually looked. "We will only walk a little way, then return."

Betsy didn't answer. Her eyes were closed, her face tilted toward the sun, her chest moving rhythmically in slow, deep breaths. "I'd almost forgotten how pleasant the outdoors can be. The matron would never have allowed me to come out on my own. That's two gifts you have given me." Betsy opened her eyes. "And now for my gift to you—it is the gift of candor. Your demeanor tells me you are a fearful and burdened woman."

Charlotte frowned. "Is this your gift? To insult me?"

"Hear me out, Charlotte, and be at peace. My intentions are good."

Charlotte felt uneasy. What did she know about this woman, really? She could be anyone—a prostitute, a thief, a liar. But when she saw the earnest look on Betsy's face, Charlotte led her through the garden to a marble bench beneath an arbor of unruly wisteria.

"We'll rest here awhile," she said, helping Betsy onto the bench before sitting beside her.

"I once had a garden as large as this. And a big house, too, with many servants."

"I . . . I never imagined such a thing. What happened? What . . . brought you to . . . this?"

Betsy's face darkened. "My husband was . . . *is* two people. Publically, he is a wealthy and influential Philadelphia banker; a deacon at our church; a pillar of Philadelphia society. He knows the best families, moves in the best circles. Privately he is a cruel and brutal man, prone to excessive drinking. And when he drank, he'd beat me so badly I'd often lose consciousness or pray I would. But he never touched my face. Never my face. So no one would know what he did behind closed doors."

Charlotte's hand trembled as she placed it over Betsy's. She had heard such stories from Elmira Crump and Hester Roach, but they were always about a farmer or common laborer or one of the miners, never about someone of the upper class.

"For years I stood it, because of the children. We have two children. Did I tell you that?" Betsy's eyes misted. "Two wonderful sons, one twelve, the other fourteen. Old enough where they don't need a mother so much. At least that's what I told myself when I decided to run away. I just couldn't take the beatings any longer. They were becoming more frequent, more violent, and I feared for my life. I was convinced it was only a matter of time before my husband ended up killing me. I ran three times. But each time, my husband hired a Pinkerton to track me down and bring me back. The last time, my husband told me if I ran again he'd have me committed.

"To explain my running away, he began telling our friends and associates I was mad; that I had gone insane, making everyone feel sorry for him. 'How tragic to be saddled with a mad wife who needs fetching every few months,' they'd say. Some even suggested he put me away in a home for the incurably insane. So I knew he'd make good his threat because he had already set the stage."

Charlotte withdrew her hand. Lucinda Wells had often talked about the improvements made to places like the Women's Home. How they now separated the mentally ill from those only physically infirm or indigent. She studied Betsy. Was she insane? Had she slipped past the doctors who determined such things?

"I know that you're thinking. You're thinking perhaps this woman is crazy after all. I took a chance telling you my story. But you've been so kind I thought I owed it to you. I was once like you, Charlotte. Timid and frightened. But you can change. You can be strong. Though we live in a man's world we need not be helpless or useless. We have worth. And with the right man, we can be a great asset. With the wrong man . . . well . . . it's better to be alone than be with the wrong man."

Charlotte folded her hands. "I . . . I'm afraid of being alone. And I'm afraid of becoming like . . . ."

"Me?"

"Yes . . . and I'm ashamed. I don't mean to be so shallow. I try to fight it." Charlotte shrugged. "But what will *you* do? Has your husband sent someone after you, do you think? Oh, why did you go and tell everyone your name?"

Betsy laughed. "I didn't. Mills isn't my real name. And yes, I believe my husband did send someone. But unlike the other times, this time I didn't stay in Philadelphia. It took me four months to get here, where my husband doesn't have any contacts or influence. I managed to make a little money along the way by cooking for various taverns or scrubbing floors. But I was afraid to stay in one place too long, so most of the time I kept moving, eating out of garbage pails and sleeping in the rain. By the time I got here I was nearly dead. The doctor said I had an abscess on one of my lungs and wouldn't live beyond a week, but here I am, three months later, and getting stronger every day. I'll give myself just a little more time before moving on."

"Where will you go?"

"Out West. I'll be harder to find there. The land is so large a person can disappear. And I'll walk all the way if I have to. You see, the thing is, Charlotte, I'm not afraid anymore. And that's why I've told you all this. You needn't be afraid, either. We women are resilient and resourceful. Whatever your future is, you will find the strength to meet it."

Charlotte's eyes brimmed with tears. How could this woman, who had lost everything, be so brave? She rose, then helped Betsy up, all the while thinking what a pleasant thing it would have been to be married to Benjamin Gaylord and able to help women like Betsy. "I just wish there was something I could do, but the truth is I have little money."

"Oh, Charlotte, you've helped more than you know. Your mirror and comb, your gift, well . . . it reminded me there are still kind people in the world. And beauty and goodness, too. And when I get stronger, I plan to go out and find more of them all. I have some useful skills. I sew and bake and play three instruments. I'll find honest employment somewhere. But whatever I end up doing, I can do it with kindness and love. And so can you."

Charlotte put her arms around the frail woman. "Thank you," she whispered. "Hearing your story makes me think that maybe . . . maybe I can face my own future with courage, too."

⌒

Virginia dropped one of her mother's good English tea cups when the noise of the breaker whistle came shrieking through the open kitchen window. The broken cup was quickly forgotten as she and her sisters rushed to the front parlor.

"No smoke," Virginia said, reaching the window first. "Must be a cave-in." She tried to sound calm, but her heart pounded in her chest. *Oh, God, don't let it be Patrick!*

Charlotte's shiny blonde curls bounced as she craned her neck to look out the window. "I suppose Mother and Kate will be going, and leave us with the task of getting lunch for the boarders."

Virginia glanced at Kate who stood nearby peering at the unchanged landscape. The sun streaming over the tree tops, the green rolling hills in the distance, the cloudless blue sky all made it seem as though it was just another beautiful late summer day.

"I pray it's no one we know." Kate squeezed Virginia's arm.

Had Kate read her thoughts? Virginia studied her sister and felt her heart fill with love. Kate was so wise and stable and loving, but also at times, so very rash. Yet even now, when Kate was burdened with her own problems, she thought of Virginia. Only the downturn of Kate's brow suggested she was troubled. The lovely chestnut-colored hair piled on her head just so, her beautiful violet eyes shaded beneath long thick lashes, the gentle curve of her full lips, the tilt of her head, all evoked, for Virginia, a feeling of serenity, and this made Virginia marvel all the more, for everyone was still angry with Kate, including Mother, over her rash behavior at the dry goods store.

The town was still buzzing, too, and all manner of accusations concerning Kate's soundness of mind had been leveled, not surprisingly spearheaded by Martin Roach. "Mad woman" he had called her, while others had described how crazed Kate looked when she entered the store. Even Joshua Adams, when he returned from Philadelphia, was furious when he found out, and had called her "reckless." But Kate seemed unrepentant, and continued to insist she had done the right thing. It seemed as if she was prepared to withstand them all. *Oh, she could be so stubborn.* Yet, Virginia couldn't help admiring her grit. Maybe if she had more of Kate's courage she'd be able to tell Patrick how she felt about him, though surely he already knew.

"Quickly, Kate," Mother said, heading for the front door without even trying to glance through the window. "Get the bag and clean rags." Then turning to Virginia and Charlotte, she added, "You two handle lunch."

Charlotte gave Virginia a knowing look as Mother issued instructions for cutting up the cooked chicken; for baking the three loaves of bread that were even now rising on the stovetop; for putting together a garden salad; and finally, for slicing the leftover mutton and heating the gravy.

"You should be able to handle that easily enough," Mother said, stopping at the door.

Both Virginia and Charlotte had followed her. "We'll be fine" Virginia said, glancing at Charlotte, who appeared unsettled and confused—a look she had worn for days, ever since her "dinner call" at the Gaylord's. It distressed Virginia to see her sister this way, especially since she knew her articles had contributed to Charlotte's troubles. But it seemed that all three of them: she, Kate and Charlotte, were on different and often colliding paths, and only God would be able to sort it out. She just prayed He'd do it quickly.

"Don't worry, Mother," Virginia said, taking Charlotte by the arm and heading for the kitchen, all the while wishing that this time she could go to the mine, too. How was she ever going to get through the rest of the morning without knowing if Patrick was all right?

Virginia hadn't touched her lunch. Not one morsel. Her stomach was too agitated. All morning she had walked around with a feeling of dread, wanting desperately to know what was going on at the Mattson, but fearing to know it, too. And no matter how many silent prayers she offered up to God, she couldn't dispel her fear.

Even while she and Charlotte cleared the table, then washed the mound of dishes, she couldn't dispel it. So when the knock on the door came and she found Michael O'Malley standing on their front step staring down at his scruffy black boots as though unwilling to look at her, Virginia knew her fears were not unfounded.

"What is it, Michael?"

"You heard the breaker whistle didn't you, Miss Virginia?"

"Yes, of course."

"Well, I just found out it was soundin' the bad news for Patrick O'Brien and some others."

Virginia resisted the urge to clutch the doorpost. "Is he . . . dead?"

Michael O'Malley looked up, damp ringlets squeezing past the edge of his cap. "Can't say. He and them others was robbin' pillars when the whole roof collapsed. There's a crew tryin' to get to 'em. Been at it for hours. Some say they heard voices behind the rubble so maybe some of the men are still alive, but nobody knows for sure."

Virginia grabbed the boy's arm and yanked him into the house. "You must come with me to the colliery." She pulled off her apron.

"Charlotte. Charlotte!" She flung the apron across one of the front parlor chairs. "*Charlotte!*"

Charlotte came from the kitchen, holding a rag and looking peeved at having been called in this rough manner. But she stopped when she saw the little one-handed boy standing in the foyer. "What's . . . wrong?"

Widow Clayton and Miss Rodgers had also left their comfortable parlor chairs and were standing in the hall staring at Michael.

"I'm going to the colliery," Virginia said, without further explanation.

Charlotte's eyes widened. "You can't, Virginia! What if Mother and Kate don't get home until late? Who's going to fix dinner for everyone? I *can't* do it all myself!"

"I'll be back as soon as possible." One of Virginia's hands was on Michael's shoulder, the other on the handle of the front door.

"But if you're not, what will I do?" Charlotte's lip quivered. "What will I make? How am I to cook for all these people?"

Virginia released the knob and Michael O'Malley. "Listen to me, Charlotte. Someone I care about is trapped in that mine and I don't know if he's dead or alive. Now pull yourself together. You're not a child. You *can* do this."

"I . . . I'll try . . . I'll do my best," she stammered as Widow Clayton took her by the hand.

"Don't worry, dearie, I'll help you."

"And so will I," Miss Rodgers added.

"Go on, now." Widow Clayton waved Virginia away. "I know what it is to have someone you love trapped in a mine. You go ahead, and don't worry about us. I haven't forgotten how to make my famous stew with just a little meat and some potatoes and vegetables. Add a few loaves of fresh bread to sop up the gravy and everyone will think they're feasting like kings."

That's all Virginia needed to hear. Without another word, she grabbed little Michael O'Malley and darted out the door.

⌒

Virginia was grateful for Michael's company. Though she had been to Higgins Patch and the outer fringes of the Mattson Colliery numerous times researching her articles, she hadn't been inside the colliery complex for years. It had seemed exciting then: a hub of activity, where strong, brave men spent their days. It seemed to speak of dignity and independence. Now, it frightened her. It was large, dirty and dangerous, with the tall hulking breaker looking like a monster belching coal dust and sounding, with its grinding and crushing noises, like it was busy gobbling up those inside.

Everything seemed to be covered with black grit, even the women huddled in tight frightened circles watching the head frame and pulley above the opening of the mine shaft and waiting for their rescued men and the rescuers, too, who often sustained their own injuries in the process. She tried to take it all in, but couldn't. It was too enormous; a sprawling complex of coal dust-covered structures. On a distance incline, white smoke curled from the six stacks of the boiler house, and in between, like black growths springing from blackened soil were the powder house, water tanks, wash house, supply house, carpenter and blacksmith shops. Then came the buried culm bank, the newer smaller bank, and a criss-cross of steel tracks dotted by wooden cars, most of which were filled with coal and on their way to the breaker. It overwhelmed her.

"I don't see Mrs. Farrell. Do you know where she is, Michael?"

Michael O'Malley, who almost behaved like a little boy on the way over with his jumping and stomping, and who seemed to enjoy holding her hand until now, wiggled free. "No ma'am, but I need to be gettin' back to Sweet Air. There's money to be made. But after quittin' time, I'll come back and check on things." With that, he darted off, leaving her standing alone amid the gloomy, soot-covered buildings.

Where were Kate and Mother? Surely they would remain near the head frame. She scanned the faces around her. Most of the women appeared shy when they noticed her looking their way. But some nodded in greeting. It embarrassed Virginia, but she had become well known in the patch as more and more miners and their families learned of her articles in the *Monitor*. And because of them she was often treated like a dignitary.

"If you're lookin' for your kin, they're over there," one woman finally said as she pointed to a spot somewhere behind the giant pulley. And when Virginia went in that direction, she found Mother and Kate talking to an elderly woman.

"It didn't take you long to get here," Kate said, walking toward Virginia after noticing her.

"How could you know I was coming? I just found out about Patrick. Michael O'Malley came and . . . ."

"I know. I sent him."

"*You* sent him?"

"When he came to the colliery to see what was happening, I told him I'd give him a few pennies to go and tell you. By then, lunch was over and I knew you'd be able to come without leaving Charlotte in a lurch. But he wouldn't take the money."

"Thank you for that." Virginia threaded her arm through Kate's. "Does that mean you are all right now? With the friendship? Between me and Patrick?"

"Not completely. I still have concerns. I know you care for him more than you let on, and he's not the man I would have chosen for you. But who am I to decide such things? These days I'm barely able

191

to manage my own life, and seem to be making a mess of the lives of those I love. And when it comes to men, to matters of the heart, I'm an utter imbecile."

"You're speaking of Joshua Adams, aren't you? I always knew you were sweet on him. He's a fine man, Kate. And I believe he has liked you from the very first."

"He thinks I'm a fool. He's as much as told me so. But I swear, Virginia, when I thought of Martin Roach and Father . . . well, I was like a bull in front of a red flag."

Virginia brushed her cheek against Kate's shoulder. "He'll get over it. And you *were* foolish, Kate. But oddly enough, I respect what you did. I ponder everything, then ponder it again. I wish I knew my mind like you know yours, and then have the courage of my convictions. Like you do."

"Oh, Virginia, what are you saying? You have such a fine mind. I've always admired that about you. And you have plenty of courage, too. I don't know many women who would go to a strange city and picket like you did with Miss Anthony, or defy convention and a powerful corporation to write for the *Monitor*. But when it comes to men, perhaps both of us could use some guidance. I know I could. I'm so confused, Virginia. I do love Joshua. But I'm not sure I love him enough, and even if I was sure I loved him enough to spend the rest of my life with him, I'm not sure I have what it takes to stand up alongside a man like that. See what a mixed up sister you have?"

"Oh, Kate, I'm just as mixed up because that's exactly how *I* feel about Patrick! I suppose we really are imbeciles." It was a blessing to have a sister like Kate. Someone who understood her. Someone who was honest and real, and not afraid to expose her shortcomings; and yet, strong and courageous, too; someone who could withstand the earthquakes of life. Kate would be a comfort if anything should happen to . . . . Virginia couldn't bring herself to finish the thought, and like the other women, focused her eyes on the nearby head frame and pulley.

"Tell me about the cave-in," she said, finally ready to hear the worst.

"I really don't know much. Only that Patrick was robbing pillars in one of the breasts deep in the mine. They say there's so much debris between the gangway and his chamber that they've stopped trying to remove it and are now hoping to reach him and the others through one of the monkeyheads."

Virginia shuddered. Mother had often talked about the workings of a mine; how it was laid out like an underground city with sometimes as many as ten miles of tunnels winding through it. She had talked about how the miners called the main road or gangway, and even the smaller passageways or monkeyheads, by lovely names such as Apple Orchard or Garden Path. She had even explained how a large mine, like the Mattson, often excavated more than one working face or breast at a time, and how a cave-in could seal off several crews at once. Now, Virginia wished she didn't know so much. Maybe then she wouldn't be visualizing Patrick in some dark, dank chamber miles from the shaft and pulley, sealed off from rescue, or perhaps buried beneath the rubble of a collapsed roof. No light, little air, and in pain. *Was he is pain?* She couldn't bear the thought. *Was he even alive?*

"Oh, Kate, we need to pray."

Virginia didn't know how long she and Kate, and Mother who had joined them, stood huddled together praying, but by the angle of the sun she judged several hours had passed. And just when the backs of Virginia's legs were beginning to tighten, she heard the creaking of the pulley.

No one spoke. The entire area was wrapped in silence as the pulley hoisted the large wooden cage through the long shaft. And when it stopped and the wooden gate of the cage opened and a dozen men stepped out, the silence held. Were these rescuers? Survivors? Or both? They were all so dirty. It was hard to tell. One of the men couldn't walk and was held up by two others who half dragged, half carried him to a group of waiting women, while some outside laborers brought over a plank on which to carry the injured man home.

Virginia scanned the others who had come up in the cage, her eyes frantically studying each face. "Oh, Kate, I don't see him," she whispered as two tired-looking stragglers approached. *Oh, how dirty their faces were!* How could anyone identify them? But the women knew their men, for at once they hugged and kissed them, and cried with joy. Now, only one man remained, hanging back it seemed, and moving awkwardly. *Was he hurt?* When she craned her neck to look, her heart stopped. She knew those broad, bulky shoulders, that tilting head, those lumbering hands. *Why had it taken her so long to recognize him?*

Without a word, she ran toward him. He was covered with grit. Not one inch remained clean, but Virginia didn't care. To her, he was the most beautiful sight in the world. When she reached him, she threw her arms around his neck and kissed him so fervently it made her breathless.

"I thought you were dead," she whispered when she let him go.

His smudged face held both surprise and delight, and he laughed in a soft muffled tone as though it pained him to do so. "Ah, Jenny, look what you've gone and done." His breath threaded the tendrils of her hair like a soft breeze. "Now the whole world knows you love me, lass; kissin' me like that in public, and me a decent God-fearin' man. I suppose the only thing left to be done is marry you. How else is your reputation to be saved?" He pulled her closer, then gave her a lingering kiss that seemed to seal his offer.

"Decent? God-fearing?" she whispered when they finally parted. "You're hardly respectable, sir; more of a rake, I'd say."

"Darlin' don't you know it's the wild ones that make the best husbands? And just so we're clear, I'll be wantin' my bath water hot and ready on the stove, waitin' to be poured into our wash tub every night when I come home to you. And maybe I'll even be comin' from our own doghole. I've been thinkin' about it for awhile now. With your brains we can surely figure out how to lease one, or perhaps buy it outright, though leasing seems more practical to my way of thinkin'."

"You are impertinent," Virginia said, trying to sound shocked, all the while pleased, especially about his desire to strike out on his own and work what independent miners called a 'doghole'—a coal seam too small for other, larger operators to mine. It was a way he, too, could be independent and finally employ his skills as a miner; skills that had taken him years to learn. She could see happiness in that.

"Won't you tell me you love me, lass? Won't you say it just once?"

"Patrick . . . don't . . . ."

"Will you at least consider my proposal? For it was real, don't you know," his arms encircled her again.

"Maybe," she said, hardly able to believe she had promised that much, and suddenly realizing what a spectacle she had made of herself. When she pushed against him to free herself, he moaned. "What is it? Are you hurt?"

"'Tis only my ribs. I think I have broken one or two."

"I'm sure he's broken more than that," said a male voice behind her.

When Virginia turned, she recognized one of the men who had come up in the cage with Patrick. "He saved my life. Pushed me out of the way when the roof started falling, putting himself in harm's way instead of scrambling to safety. I fear he received poor reward for his trouble, for he was nearly buried alive." He gave Patrick's shoulder a pat, then walked off clutching the woman by his side.

"Oh, Patrick . . . I thought you might be hurt by the way you walked, only I was so happy to see you I didn't . . . ." She turned and waved for Mother and Kate to come over. "Patrick's hurt," she said when they reached her. She ignored the frown on her mother's face. It was obvious that Mother wasn't happy by what she had seen.

Kate quickly opened the large leather pouch and pulled out a jar of salve and some rags.

"I'll not have you fussin' over me, now," Patrick said, backing away.

But Mother took hold of his heavy shirt, the kind men wore to withstand the constant forty-eight degree temperature of a mine's interior. "Let me see your chest." Her gentle authority seemed to intimidate the normally intimidating Patrick O'Brien, though he continued to protest.

"You're not thinkin' I'll be undressin' right here in front of everyone now, are you?"

Without a word, Mother unfastened the left button of his heavy overalls, allowed it to flap over to one side, then pulled up his shirt a few inches revealing a badly bruised torso. "I'll bind you. It will help the ribs heal and hopefully keep them from moving and puncturing a lung."

Virginia's breath caught. *Puncturing a lung*? "Oh, Patrick, please let her do it."

So the three stood in a huddle while Patrick unfastened his other button, and held the overalls around his waist with one hand and his rolled up shirt with the other, and allowed Mother, using a long wide strip of clean cloth, to bind his ribcage. He groaned whenever she wound it too tight, but the smile never left his face, nor did his eyes leave Virginia's.

When Mother finished, and Patrick put himself in order, he tipped his cap. "Thank you, ma'am. You're very kind. I believe it feels better already."

"Stop your foolish talk. I know you're in pain," Mother said with a sweet smile. "It will be difficult, since you'll not want to lose the pay, but you shouldn't work for awhile. It's important to keep as still as possible and allow those ribs to heal. You're not out of danger yet, Patrick. I've seen this before. Men going back into the mine too soon after an injury, and it killing them. And I know you've seen it, too."

Patrick replaced his cloth cap. "I'll best be goin' now and gettin' washed up, and maybe even rest a spell. You're right, ma'am, I am a wee bit sore. But I'm much obliged to you all for comin' and for your help." His large hand encircled Virginia's upper arm as he spoke. "Would you mind me speakin' with Jenny for a moment?" And before anyone could answer, he pulled Virginia away to a distant spot.

"Quick, now, Patrick," Virginia said in a low voice as she stood beside him, his hand still clutching her arm. "Just say what you want before you scare Mother and Kate into coming over here."

Patrick drew Virginia closer as though not wanting anyone to hear. "I know who killed Mr. Blakely, but I won't be tellin' you now. I learned this yesterday, and only by chance. I saw somethin' . . . then I knew."

"*What! Who . . .?*"

Patrick gently laid a blackened finger across Virginia's lips. "I said I wasn't tellin'. So don't be askin'. Me and him already had a talk, and I think it only right to give him a chance to turn himself in like a man." He smiled and put his face closer to Virginia's. "I know your mind, lass, regardin' the law and all. But I won't be moved. I'm givin' him his week, like I promised. If he doesn't do right, then I'll call in the police."

Virginia was so stunned all she could do was nod.

"Maybe it's best you don't tell your family, or anyone else for that matter, 'til I can settle this." With that, he scooped Virginia up in his arms, kissed her fully on the mouth, released her, then walked away whistling a tune Virginia had never heard before.

She stood watching him go. *Could it be true? Did Patrick really know who killed Mr. Blakely?* The thought frightened her. Wouldn't this knowledge put him in danger? And would he really be able to force the killer to turn himself in? But as she watched him disappear, a different question crowded out the rest: *Oh, why hadn't she told Patrick she loved him?*

CHAPTER 9

"I still can't believe you accused Martin Roach of murder!"

Kate ignored Joshua's scowl as she took the damask-covered chair beside him, then smoothed the skirt of her green linen day dress. She had taken pains with her appearance; had even dabbed two drops of her precious Parisian perfume behind each ear in hopes of distracting Joshua and blunting his expected rebuke. And while this all seemed to disarm him when he first entered the room, she could tell by his face it had not altered his serious frame of mind.

She had invited him here, to the back parlor, so they could talk. She had to remove the barrier that existed between them, a barrier as hard and cold as Mother's prize ice box. They hadn't spoken since Joshua's return from the Reading headquarters in Philadelphia when he managed to share his findings in a semi-civilized manner despite learning of her indiscretion. And for the past week she had missed his friendliness and the pleasant conversations they once had.

"I know everyone believes I went on a fool's errand, and perhaps they're right but. . . ."

"*Perhaps?* Kate, why do you still refuse to admit your blunder; to admit your utter irresponsible behavior?"

Kate stiffened. She had known his scrutiny would be painful, but she had not expected to feel like that little girl who had, on many occasions, sat in this room, on this very chair, while being scolded by her father for some transgression. But truth had always been her ally, and she wouldn't abandon it now. "The thought of Father dying because of Martin Roach's greed was more than I could bear. And yes, I admit I was rash, but the incident was not without profit. Martin Roach may be a lying swindler, as your findings prove, but I don't think he had anything to do with Rodger Blakely's death."

"I have enough on Mr. Roach, on his manipulation of colliery prices and forged contracts, to put him behind bars for years. But even this wouldn't satisfy you unless you truly believed what you said."

"I do believe it. He was nervous and fearful as one who had something to hide. But he was startled by my accusation of murder; so utterly shocked, in fact, that I'm certain it left him little presence of mind to fake a response. Therefore, I must believe his reaction genuine."

"Well . . . I suppose that's something. But see here, Kate . . . that still doesn't excuse your behavior."

"I know." She reached over and took his hand. "And you are the one who most deserves my apology. My bullying forced you to reveal information you were not ready to reveal. On top of that, you asked me to honor your confidence by not making it public." She bit her lip when she felt the tears welling. A woman's tears most always brought a man to his knees. But she was determined not to resort to them no matter how difficult. A pretty dress and a bit of perfume was one thing, but tears . . . no, she'd bear the full brunt of his well-deserved anger without tears. "You trusted me to keep this confidence, and I violated that trust. For that I ask your forgiveness."

"I've already forgiven you, so, if you think I'm still angry about that, you're wrong. But what bothers me, what is a most serious problem . . . ."

"I love you, Joshua." She could almost hear the pounding of her heart. How she had the courage to say that, then look him in the eye, she didn't know. "I just wanted to tell you before you continued and

I lost my nerve. I know you are a man of logic while I am more . . . emotional. I also know I'm not perfect, but . . . ."

"You're wonderful, Kate." His hand tightened around hers. "And you well know my feelings. I've made no secret of them. But it's not your basic imperfections that worry me, though I see few. What worries me is the unforgiveness in your heart. Sometimes it spills into your eyes, your voice. I know it's because of your father's death. I've seen this with other victims of crime. But what you don't understand is that unforgiveness is just as destructive, just as hurtful, as crime itself. And the one who harbors it, ends by making himself its victim. Until you're able to forgive the people of this town, I fear you'll never be free to truly love anyone."

"You say that after my shameless profession?" Kate felt her cheeks burn.

"I say it because I've seen enough of the world to know love can't coexist with bitterness. In the end, bitterness will choke out the most fervent love, even the kind of love I have for you. You must resolve this, Kate, if we're to have any future together."

Kate pulled her hand away. "Then pray for me, Joshua, for I can't forgive the town's people for executing my father."

Before Joshua could respond, the parlor door flew open and there stood Virginia, as white as one of their bed sheets, clutching a piece of brown paper.

"*A coffin notice.* Mr. Thumbolt found it folded beneath a rock, right on our front step! And I think it's meant for *me.*"

Kate rushed to the door and took the paper from Virginia's trembling hand. Joshua had come too, and stood beside her while she read. "Stop pryin if yu no whats gud for yu." Below that was a crude drawing of a woman hanging at the end of a rope, an open coffin near her feet.

"Who could have sent such a thing?" Virginia said.

"Martin Roach. And I don't believe it was meant for you at all, Virginia, but for me."

The look on Joshua's face was one of utter desperation as he tugged on Kate's arm. "Don't even think about . . . ."

"I won't do anything without telling you first. I give you my word."

⁓

Charlotte couldn't stand it—the whole house being in an uproar, and Mother, Kate and Virginia all walking around with frowns. Even the boarders were out of sorts. And it left Charlotte, who seldom did well in a crisis, unable to keep her mind focused on any one thing for long. *Oh what a hateful note.* What kind of person would leave such a thing on their front step? And, oh, what bedlam it had caused. Two mornings in a row breakfast had been late, and one dinner, too. And on laundry day, the beds in all the downstairs bedchambers had been overlooked and never changed. And it took a full day for anyone to notice the oversight.

Now, thoughts of Kate and Virginia kept swirling around in Charlotte's head. Each of her sisters believed the coffin notice was meant for them. Charlotte didn't know what to believe. She only knew she couldn't bear the thought of anything happening to either of them. And it was plain Mother was worried, too. Mother, who was always so strong and dependable, now seemed as flustered as a school girl. And this unnerved Charlotte all the more. But what could be done? What could any of them do, being mere women? She stopped and thought of Betsy Mills. No, she wouldn't put it that way. Women could be strong, too. But wasn't it the role of a man to protect? And where were they? Colonel Smyth was the best they had, and he was well advanced in years. The other men in their boardinghouse, including Joshua Adams—for all his youth and swagger—didn't inspire Charlotte's confidence one bit.

She sighed and ran her fingers across the velvet curtain, inspecting it for holes. When at last she found one, she draped the curtain over others requiring mending, then returned to the work table she had set up in the back parlor. Mother had instructed her to inspect all the heavy curtains before taking down the lighter drapes. She plucked another velvet panel from the pile and smelled the tobacco that had been sprinkled among the folds to discourage moths. It was still strong after all these months in an attic trunk and she found the smell unpleasant.

"You have a visitor," Kate said, suddenly entering the parlor. "Benjamin Gaylord is here. Shall I let him in or tell him you are indisposed?"

Charlotte dropped the curtain then fingered her hair. "How can I see him now? When I look so dreadful? Oh no, Kate, send him away, *please*."

"You look lovely, as usual. You needn't fear on that account. But if you wish, I'll make your apologies."

"Do . . . I? Do I really look all right? I know I shouldn't be so concerned about my appearance, considering what's going on around here, but please don't laugh at me, Kate. I know I'm a silly creature."

To Charlotte's surprise, Kate walked over and gave her a hug. "I'm not laughing, dearest. And you're not silly at all. You are, in fact, a sweet, gracious woman."

"Oh . . . my . . . well . . . thank you." She couldn't remember the last time Kate had been this complimentary.

"So what would you like me to do?"

"Is it urgent do you think? Does he look upset? It *must* be important or he would never have come. Maybe I should see him. But how can I? Like this? Oh, dear . . . ."

"I've already told him we have begun our fall cleaning." She gestured to her own soiled apron and the rag in her hand. "He won't expect to see you in a ball gown."

Charlotte laughed. "Of course you're right, Kate. Send him in. Let me get it over with, otherwise I'll be thinking about it for the rest of the day."

Without a word, Kate disappeared, and within seconds ushered Benjamin Gaylord into the room, then quietly left.

Charlotte remained standing by the work table, still wearing her apron. She had briefly debated whether or not to remove it, then decided to leave it on. Let him see her at her worst. He already thought poorly of her. Why help him change that opinion? But as soon as she looked at Benjamin's kind face, Charlotte wished she had.

"Please sit," she said, removing the curtains from the damask-covered chair and draping them across the back of the old wooden rocker.

He was finely dressed as usual, with his hair and beard neatly groomed, but his face, his eyes . . . something was different. And instead of taking the empty damask-covered chair, he removed the sewing box from the one next to it, placed it on the small end table, then gestured with his hand, "After you."

So Charlotte took one seat while he took the other.

"I've heard about the note you received, the coffin notice, and I am dreadfully concerned."

"Bad news certainly travels fast! We've barely read the note ourselves and it seems the entire Schuylkill County knows about it. But you need not be fearful on my account. I don't believe it was meant for me at all." She narrowed her eyes like Kate was prone to do and wondered if it would have the same effect.

"But I *am* fearful. I'm afraid for you and your family. That's why I've come. I desire to be of service. If you'll permit me, and not think me too bold, I'd like to hire half a dozen men to guard you and your family. They'll remain outside, of course, surrounding the house, but will accompany you or your mother and sisters wherever you need to go. Will you allow me to do this?" His hand trembled as he fingered his beard. "I shall have no peace unless you do."

"Why would my welfare or that of my family's concern you? Or rob you of a moment's peace? And why aren't you on your way to England? Is this some cruel masquerade, a pretext you've devised so you can come and gloat over the fact that, once again, my family is the talk of the town, and we are embroiled in yet another difficulty?"

"How can I leave now? With this going on? When *you* could be in danger? Oh, Charlotte, believe me I think only of you . . . and your family. Please understand that my errand is not one of censure. And when have you ever known me to be cruel or gloat? Over yours or anyone else's misfortune? Do you think so ill of me?" He looked away. "I . . . that is . . . you have every right to despise me, and I'll not try to change your opinion. Only allow me this one thing. Forgive my speaking so freely, Charlotte, but I know your family can't afford to hire protection, while I am well able to do so. If any harm should befall you, and I've failed to do my best to prevent it, I . . . I wouldn't be able to forgive myself."

Charlotte's heart thumped. *Was it possible? Was it possible that . . . he loved her still?* She balled her damp hands into a fist. No. This wasn't love but rather a matter of satisfaction—the satisfaction of a wealthy man coming to the aid of the poor unfortunate trouble-prone Farrells. Her back stiffened. "You are most gracious, but I hardly think your mother would approve, and she'll certainly resent you being thrust into this situation. It's best you distance yourself from this matter at once."

"My mother knows my feelings. I've laid them out to her in a telegram. Would you like me to tell you what it said?"

"If you wish." Charlotte folded her hands so tightly her nails whitened.

"That is not what I asked. Do *you*, Charlotte, want to know what I said?"

Charlotte studied Benjamin's grim face and knew, by it, the importance of her answer. "Yes," she finally said, "I'd like to know."

Benjamin appeared relieved. "What I told her was that I had recently learned of our family's history, and given these facts I would consider myself fortunate if someone as remarkable as you would ever allow me a second chance. I also told her that if you didn't, I would spend the rest of my days in misery since truly you are the only woman I want to marry."

For a moment, Charlotte couldn't catch her breath. When she was finally able to compose herself, she rose to her feet. "You were always a gentleman, Benjamin. And I accept your sincere offer of help. When can I expect your security force?"

Benjamin had risen, too. "I plan to interview these men myself; make certain they are of the proper sort. But I believe I can have a suitable team here within two days."

"Then I'll inform my mother and sisters so they won't be alarmed when strange men begin surrounding the house. Thank you for your kindness. I bid you good day." As Benjamin bent to kiss her hand she leaned closer. "And since I have no wish for you to spend the rest of your days in misery, perhaps you can join me for tea next week as we endeavor to rekindle our friendship. It is a good place to start."

"I . . . I shall look forward to it." He bowed then walked to the door and turned. "But please know . . . my affection for you needs no rekindling for it is as ardent as ever." With that he exited the room, leaving Charlotte overcome by this sudden turn of events.

Virginia tucked the crumpled coffin notice into the bodice of her soiled work dress and slipped out the kitchen door leading to the back yard. She was glad Mother and Charlotte were busy at the stove where pots boiled and plumes of steam dampened the rafters. She was also grateful that Kate was in the dining room setting the table, and that dinner was going to be late again tonight. Ever since the coffin notice, nothing seemed to be on schedule. But it meant that everyone would be too busy to concern themselves about her. And hadn't Mother told her to finish washing that last window in order to complete the chore she had been engaged in most of the day? It was all working to her advantage.

But it got dark earlier now, and the angle of the sun told her the breaker whistle would be blowing soon. There was no time to waste. This morning, with great fan-fare, Charlotte announced that the se-curity force Benjamin Gaylord had promised two days earlier would finally arrive tomorrow. That meant, after today, meeting Patrick O'Brien, unobserved, would no longer be possible.

She scurried past the small ladder, pail and rags positioned near the large hall window, and prayed her subterfuge would work. It was doubtful anyone would check on her while she was supposedly wash-ing the window, but if they did, hopefully they'd think she had taken a brief trip to the outhouse.

She walked cautiously along the thicket of trees ringing the cleared yard. After a brief pause to see that no one observed her, she scurried down the path toward the Mattson Colliery. Earlier, she had slipped into town hoping to get a message to Patrick through Michael O'Malley. But the grocer, Antonio Carbonetti, had told her Michael had not been to Sweet Air for days. So she would have to contact Patrick herself. And she needed to get there before the breaker whistle blew. She would also have to keep her meeting brief. Just a few min-utes. But that's all she needed, just a few minutes.

Virginia was certain the coffin notice was meant for her, and not Kate. And she was certain that Patrick O'Brien would know who sent it. She had not told her family of Patrick's claim concerning Mr. Blakely's killer. It would only bring the law down on him. No. She needed to give him time to work this out, but she also needed to tell him of this new threat—this danger to her and perhaps her family. As far as Virginia was concerned, the coffin notice meant the killer had no intention of turning himself in. That meant Patrick would have to, and he needed to do it before things got out of hand.

The deserted path, with its thick clump of rustling trees on either side, made her quicken her pace. Why was she so skittish? She had walked this path a thousand times. Had one coffin notice really reduced her to a trembling female? The kind of female she so disliked? Still . . . wasn't it on this path . . . yes, along this very path, right at the bend ahead, where Superintendent Foley was found nearly dead? She hugged her chest as she passed the bend, then laughed. If only Kate could see her now!

She just wished her errand was more pleasant. She so wanted to tell Patrick the exciting news; how this morning she had gotten a letter from his friend, Davin MacCabe at the *Monitor*; news she hadn't even told her family since she wanted him to be the first to hear. Patrick had been right all along. It *was* better to write for a paper than start one. She still couldn't believe her dream was really coming true. And she was grateful to Patrick for his part in it and wanted to tell him that.

But this news would have to wait. There would be no time to discuss Mr. MacCabe's offer to come work fulltime for him as a *salaried* reporter. Oh, what this could mean for them both! For their future! And she needed to ask Patrick what he thought of her moving to Tamaqua, to be closer to the newspaper office as Mr. MacCabe suggested. It was only sixteen miles from Higgins Patch, not the end of the earth. And her salary could mean leasing that doghole Patrick mentioned. But that discussion could take hours, and this unpleasant business of the coffin notice needed to be resolved first.

At last she saw Higgins Patch, and just beyond that, the dark hulking breaker. Only a handful of women milled about; some carrying crying babies, others gathering vegetables from their small gardens. Most of the women were inside heating bath water for their men and preparing supper.

She ignored the stares of the outside laborers as she entered the colliery and positioned herself near the giant pulley and head frame. Within minutes the breaker whistle sounded and the creaking of the pulley could be heard. When the large wooden cage finally broke the surface and its gate opened, more than a dozen men filed out, their faces blacked, their shoulders stooped.

It took another four trips before Patrick emerged. He was as grimy and weary looking as the others. Virginia almost wished he was coming home to her and the wash tub he so prized. And these thoughts reminded her of the conversation she and Mother had had after they bound Patrick's broken ribs; the only one they ever had concerning her shameless display of hugging and kissing the man Virginia was finally willing to admit she loved. Now, Virginia tried to dispel her mother's words, but they rang, as shrilly as any breaker whistle, in her ears. "*A miner's life is hard. And many young wives become old before their time.*" And then the blow: "*And you, Virginia, haven't been conditioned for such a life. How then will you be able to bear up under it? Think carefully. Don't let your emotions take you where you're not equipped to go.*"

What would Mother say if she knew Virginia's emotions had already taken her to a place she never thought possible; a place of danger and deception that involved murder and a cover up? But it was too late. Here she was. And there was no turning back.

"Patrick," Virginia called when he passed her. "Patrick!"

He glanced around, then seeing her, smiled broadly, his large white teeth flashing amid his blackened face. He broke from the other men and hurried over, the tin lunch pail swinging like a toy in his oversized hand.

"*Jenny!*" Dropping his pail, he wrapped her in his arms. "Oh, lass, how I've longed for the sight of you! But poor little Michael O'Malley is down with the bloody flux and I've had no means of askin' you to meet me at the church." With that, he kissed her. When Virginia pressed against him, she heard him moan.

"What's wrong? It is your ribs? Oh, Patrick, you haven't done what Mother said, and rested!"

"The Company don't pay men to rest, darlin'. And I'm a man on a mission. I'm determined to save every penny I can for that doghole I talked about gettin'. You'll be marryin' a man who's on his way to becomin' an independent miner. I plan on makin' you proud of me, lass."

"You won't be much of a miner if you puncture your lungs, and I've *not* agreed to marry you yet, so . . . ."

"Ah, how sweet that word 'yet' is. 'Tis the word before 'yes'. I see your heart, Jenny, and how much you love me. But don't worry over me so."

"Patrick, be serious. I haven't much time. I must get home. But before I say why I've come, tell me what can I do for Michael O'Malley? He must be terribly sick to miss work. Can I bring him healing herbs or perhaps a thin soup?"

"Poor wee one. I fear this has taken the stuffin' out of him. But there's nothin' for you to do. His mum is a good woman and has things well in hand. But 'tis kind of you to ask. Now . . . tell me, lass, why are you here?"

Virginia reached into her bodice and pulled out the crumpled coffin notice. "Is this the work of your friends?"

Patrick read the note, then crushed it in his hand. "When did you get this?"

"Three days ago. Do you know who sent it? Is it from one of your Mollies? I haven't told my family what you said about Mr. Blakely's killer. I wanted to honor your confidence, and I didn't want to cause you trouble. But if you know something, you must act before someone gets hurt."

The look on Patrick's face was frightening. It was hard and cold, and there was violence in it. "Come Jenny, I'll walk you home. It's gettin' dark."

"No. You can't. My family doesn't know I'm here, and how can I tell them without betraying you? But please take care of this."

"I will."

"Do you . . . do you know who sent it?"

"I *know*."

The way he said it made Virginia shudder. "Is it the man who killed Mr. Blakely?"

"I'll take care of it, Jenny. Go home now."

"Promise me you won't do anything foolish. Just turn this man over to the law before it's too late."

"Go home, Jenny, while you still got some light."

She nodded, then turned and headed for the path, all the while thinking she shouldn't leave him, not with that look in his eyes.

⌒

When the wind kicked up, Virginia wished she had taken her cloak. The days were still pleasant, but the nights were getting cold. And though the sun was barely setting, there was already a sharp chill in the air. Many were predicting another harsh winter. Judging by these early fall nights, it seemed a certainty. Would their new gaggle of geese make it through? They couldn't afford to lose any more. Mother had saved for months to replace those lost last winter. Virginia would have to make a good shelter for them in their basement. What would she use? She tried keeping her mind on the geese . . . on how she'd construct their shelter . . . on anything other than that look on Patrick's face. It still frightened her.

She hugged her chest trying to keep warm as her mind shifted from Patrick to her family. Had she been missed? Would she be able to convince anyone she had never left the yard; that all this time she had been washing her last window . . . *in the dark*?

Everything was shadows now. Higgins Patch glowed with lamps flickering in house windows. Inside, she knew men were bathing, and women were putting supper on the table. It made Virginia's thoughts return to Patrick and what he might do. Would he see his Molly friends and get their help? Or would he go on his own and force the killer to turn himself in? But what if the man refused, and they fought? What if someone got hurt? And if the police found out that Patrick had known about this man, what would happen? Would that make him an accomplice? Compromise him in some way? *Oh, stop!* Better to spend time thinking up a story for those back home. It was more necessary than ever to shield Patrick until he could resolve the matter.

She hurried as fast as she dared over the rutted path. Aside from the wind in the trees and the occasional shrieking of an owl, it was eerily quiet. She took a deep breath, relieved she was already half way home. Only that awful bend to pass, then it would be a straight run to her back yard. And when she got home, she'd carry the pail and rags into the house as if nothing was wrong. And if anyone questioned her she'd say . . . what? Well maybe she could say . . . ."

Suddenly, Virginia felt a rough hand cover her face, felt a large powerful body press against her, felt a sharp blade at her throat. "I'll cut you if you give me trouble," came a deep, gravelly voice Virginia didn't recognize. Then she felt herself being dragged off the path and into the woods.

Oh, God, help me!

She heard twigs snapping beneath her feet. Felt the branches of trees scrape her face and neck while the powerful body half dragged, half carried her deeper and deeper into the brush. She could hardly see through the darkness. And she could hardly breathe. She tried shaking off that large hand that smelled of kerosene, but his grip was too tight, and the only thing she accomplished was to nick herself on his blade. She felt her skin burn, felt blood trickle down the hollow of her neck. But if she didn't get air . . . soon . . . . Oh, she felt so dizzy. She must get air! She could hardly . . . breathe . . . must get hand . . . away . . . need air . . . can't breathe . . . .

CHAPTER 10

"Charlotte, *please* stop crying! I know you're upset. We all are." Kate was ready to scream. Her sister had been crying most of the night and all morning. How could anyone cry so much? Her eyes should be prunes by now. "We need clear heads. We need to *think*."

"That's not helpful," Mother said.

Kate averted her eyes as she settled in one of the damask-covered chairs. Yes . . . she was being unkind. Still . . . Charlotte wasn't the only one distraught over Virginia's disappearance. They were all beside themselves. No one had slept a wink, and they all still wore the same wrinkled clothing from yesterday. *Oh give me patience, Lord, and tenderness of heart.*

"It's not helpful, Kate, because tears and emotions cannot be turned off and on like an oil lamp. And we all have our own way of dealing with calamity. You need to remember that." Though her voice was calm, Mother's fingers traced and retraced the edge of the fireplace mantel. The room was chilly but no fire had been lit. Virginia was to ready the hearth this morning. Even now, the two andirons, still wrapped in muslin and brown paper, lay forgotten in the corner.

"I don't mean to be harsh, Mother, only . . . tears and hand wringing won't bring Virginia back. We need to expend our energies in *action*—scour the woods, the foot paths, the patches, the collieries, Sweet Air, and if necessary, Pottsville itself."

"I suppose there's no use in just sitting around. It's already noon. If Virginia was able to return . . . ." Mother's voice broke and she looked away. "What should we *do*, Kate? What *can* we do?"

"I think we should divide the neighborhood into sections, then each of us takes one. Surely, we'll find someone who has information concerning Virginia."

Mother nodded. "Yes . . . a good plan."

Without another word, Kate went to the desk, pulled paper from the drawer and began drawing a map.

Charlotte blotted her tears with her handkerchief. "I've sent one of the men with a note to Benjamin telling him about Virginia. I'm sure he'll enlist his new security force in the search, too." She straightened in the chair. "If only they had come yesterday! But I suppose it's foolish to think of that now. I still don't know how Virginia could disappear like that. She was right in back, finishing her last window. I don't understand. What could have happened?"

"We must consider the possibility that Virginia is hurt somewhere and unable to return home," Kate said, reluctantly, as she turned from the desk.

"Oh, don't say such a thing! There has to be another explanation!"

"It does make sense." Mother's fingers stopped roaming the edge of the mantel. "But it also raises more questions, too. Virginia seemed anxious to put the window washing behind her. Is it logical, then, that she'd choose instead to take a walk, not only leaving her chore unfinished, but knowing supper was nearly ready? And if she fell and injured herself, why didn't she call out? And why haven't we found her? Joshua has already checked the yard and surrounding woods, and there was no sign of her anywhere."

"Which means she's not nearby."

"What are you saying, Kate?" Mother's face whitened. "You're not suggesting the writer of that coffin notice has made good his threat?"

Charlotte began to sob.

Kate put down her pen. The truth was she had already contemplated all the possible scenarios, even the worst imaginable, but one look at Charlotte and Mother made Kate understand she needed to temper her response. Mother had been willing to skirt the edges, but even she was prepared to go only so far, and the thought of Virginia in the hands of some deranged writer of coffin notices was beyond Mother's reach. Still, the fact remained, Virginia had been missing since supper. And from last night to now was a long time where anything could happen.

"Joshua is a trained detective. He knows what to look for," Kate said slowly. "He said there were no signs of a struggle. I can't imagine Virginia going anywhere against her will without a struggle. Can you? And a struggle of any kind would have left some telltale signs: torn fabric, an overturned pail, perhaps some . . . blood."

Both Mother and Charlotte gasped.

"I think a more likely scenario is that Virginia left on an errand, or went to meet someone and became injured enroute. Let's proceed on that assumption." Kate returned to her mapmaking and silently prayed that God would give them the strength to scour the countryside. With no sleep and everyone's nerves on edge, they would need it. And just as she rose from the desk, the parlor door flew open and there stood Joshua and Benjamin, shoulder to shoulder, beneath the lintel.

"We met coming in," Joshua said, looking as harried and upset as Benjamin. He walked to the desk and stood near Kate while Benjamin went to the damask-covered chair where Charlotte sat. "I've just come from Main Street and found that yesterday morning Virginia was there looking for Michael O'Malley."

"She never went to Main Street yesterday," Mother said, shaking her head. "You must be mistaken."

"With all due respect, Mrs. Farrell, she did go. Mr. Carbonetti himself spoke to her and said she appeared agitated."

"Agitated? I know she was troubled by that awful note, but under the circumstances, she seemed rather calm to me. And why would she go without telling anyone?"

Kate saw the distressed look on Joshua's face, and sensed his reluctance to speak further. "Obviously, she didn't tell anyone, Mother, because she didn't want anyone to know. Perhaps if we find out why she wanted to see the O'Malley boy, it will give us a clue as to where she is now."

Kate handed her scribbled page to Joshua. "It's a crude map. If we all take a section we can cover the ground faster. Perhaps we'll find someone who saw Virginia last night."

"Yes, good thinking, Kate."

"My men can help, too." Benjamin reached for Charlotte's hand and held it as if cradling a robin's egg. "And so can I."

"Well, that's it then. We have a plan. Now let's execute it." Joshua quickly organized everyone into teams of two, which, counting Benjamin's six men, made five teams in all. "If it's all right with you, Benjamin, I'll instruct your men when we are finished here."

After Benjamin nodded his agreement, Joshua assigned the territories and outlined the systematic method they should employ. When done, Mother approached him.

"You've not paired me with anyone."

"No ma'am. It's best you stay home in case Virginia returns. If she does, it's up to you to notify the closest team in your area, and they in turn will notify the next team, and so on. You can see the need for a point man . . . ah, woman, right here."

Mother nodded but looked convinced, and Kate couldn't help wondering if Joshua was keeping her home because of what he feared they'd find.

As they were about to exit the parlor, Benjamin stepped forward. "I hope I haven't trespassed beyond appropriate bounds, and I hope no one objects, but when I learned what had happened, I took the liberty of notifying my solicitor and authorizing him to post a five-hundred dollar reward for any information leading to Virginia's successful recovery." He glanced at Charlotte. "People generally dislike getting involved, and a reward might be just the inducement to make them decide otherwise."

Instead of Charlotte uttering a polite "thank you" as Kate expected, she gave Benjamin a generous hug, amazing everyone, especially Benjamin, judging by the look on his face.

⌒

"Where are you going, Kate? That's the way to Main Street. I've already questioned everyone there. We're supposed to be covering Higgins Patch and the Mattson Colliery. Remember?"

"I'm taking a detour." Kate continued walking toward town. She was disappointed that Joshua had paired himself with her because if it was anyone else, she could bully her way through this without much of an explanation. Now, she'd have a fight on her hands, and she dreaded it.

"Kate . . . stop."

"I'm *going* to Main Street. You can go on to the patch if you want."

"Why? Why are you going?" Joshua barred her way. "*Please* don't tell me it's for the reason I'm thinking."

"And how am I to know *what* you are thinking? But if you must know, I'm going to have a talk with Martin Roach."

"Didn't you promise me you'd tell me first before doing anything rash?"

"That was before Virginia's disappearance. The rules have changed."

"Kate, you can't do this!" He shook her shoulders. "Stop and think! You're not a child. You can't go around doing whatever you like!"

"I must see Martin Roach, Joshua. If he hired someone to scare us, to make us stop our investigation of him, then he'll know where Virginia is."

"You're not making sense. If he did this, do you think he'd *tell* you? What are you trying to prove? That you can intimidate your way in and out of situations? You can't treat people like this, Kate. You can't always do everything your way." He sighed and shook his head. "All right, go. But I'll not go with you. I'll not watch you make a fool of yourself."

The look on Joshua's face showed his utter contempt for her plan, and though she tried to stop them, tears filled her eyes. "Oh, Joshua, don't you see? If it was Martin's thugs who kidnapped Virginia, they made a terrible mistake. *I'm* the one they were after. *I'm* the one who should have been taken. And if anything happens to Virginia, how am I to live with that? I couldn't do anything for Father, but maybe I can do something to help Virginia."

For a long time Joshua just stood looking at her. Finally, he drew her into his arms. "I know you want to help your sister and I know you feel guilty, thinking this is all your fault."

"It is. It is my fault. Oh, Joshua, I don't want to hate anyone. I'm tired of feeling angry and bitter. I don't care about revenge. It's already cost so much and brought my family nothing but misery. I want to be done with it. I don't want to hurt Martin Roach, anymore. I don't want to hurt anyone in Sweet Air. I nearly lost my family from all my browbeating and stirring things up. And I don't want to lose you. But the thing I want most right now is to find Virginia. To bring her home."

They held each other for a long time, then Kate prayed, right there in Joshua's arms, for God to forgive her and heal her heart of all bitterness, and when she finished, Joshua bent and kissed her.

"Come," he whispered, "we'll go see Martin Roach together."

Kate's heart plummeted when she entered the dry goods store and saw it crowded with shoppers. Her meeting with Martin Roach was sure to be unpleasant and she had hoped there would be few to observe it. But men, women, and even a few children hovered around counters and shelves, and filled the air with their chatter. Hester stood behind the counter, cutting green baize from a bolt and looking harried, while her husband was on the other side of the store demonstrating the wick mechanism of a prescut lamp for a customer.

When Martin Roach saw Kate, his mouth dropped, and soon everyone turned to look. When they did, Joshua stepped in front of Kate like a shield.

After ridding himself of the lamp, Martin headed for the door. "You're not welcome here! You best leave now!" He looked passed Joshua and directly at Kate. "Go on, now!" He made shooing motions with his hands, then tried forcing Kate out the door but Joshua stopped him.

"Keep calm, Mr. Roach. You're alarming your customers." Joshua gripped the shopkeeper's shoulder, holding him in place. Even in his rumpled clothes and disheveled hair, Joshua exuded a quiet authority. "We don't wish to make a scene. Is there somewhere we can talk? Our business is personal, nothing you'll want anyone to hear."

"I . . . suppose we could go to the stockroom. But she's not to come." Martin pointed at Kate. "She can wait outside. I won't have her in my shop!"

Kate ignored his outburst. What did it matter where she waited as long as Joshua learned of Virginia's whereabouts? That was the only thing that mattered now. But just as she was about to leave, Joshua gripped her arm and held her in place.

"She *will* be privy to our conversation. If need be, we'll conduct it right here." When Martin neither responded nor showed any sign of relenting, Joshua nodded. "As you wish. The purpose of my visit is to inform you that I've begun an official investigation and have sent a detailed letter to Mr. Franklin B. Gowen telling him . . . ."

"*Stop!*" Martin Roach threw up one hand, his face as red as a radish. "Just stop! It will be as you wish. We'll go to the stockroom. *All* of us. And talk there." He signaled, by a flick of his head, for them to follow him, then smiled, a frozen kind of smile, at all the customers he passed.

Kate trailed behind with Joshua, ignoring the startled looks or smirks or how people put their heads together and whispered. But before Kate reached the stockroom, Hester scooted from behind the counter and barred her way.

"You have some nerve coming here! You're not welcome! You better leave before . . . ."

"Hester, go attend to the customers!" Martin barked, retracing his steps, his frozen smile melting into a frown.

"But Martin, you said she was never to come here again and . . . ."

"I'll handle this. Now *go.*" When Hester didn't move, Martin pushed her in the direction of the counter. "I said, *go.* Leave this to me."

As Kate continued to follow Martin Roach, she couldn't help feeling sorry for Hester. She had nothing against her. The woman probably didn't even know about Martin's shady dealings. But Hester wouldn't be the first wife to suffer because of an errant husband. And it was out of Kate's hands now. Virginia's disappearance and Joshua's report to Franklin B. Gowen had seen to that.

Finally, Martin Roach stopped beside a small desk and wooden chair at the rear of the stockroom then turned to face Joshua. His face was fierce, with eyebrows raised and his bottom lip forming a thin line beneath his bushy mustache. All pretense of the former congeniality he had displayed for his customers had vanished.

"Now, what's all this about you contacting Mr. Gowen? What would a no-account like you have to say, anyway? Nothing that could possibly interest him. So any attempt to slander me will fail. I am, after all, a highly respected businessman who has helped Mr. Gowen and the railroad in the past, while you . . . ," Martin's lips curled in distain, "while you are just a country bumpkin no one is going to take seriously."

"I'm actually from Philadelphia, and in the employ of the Pinkerton Detective Agency."

"*What*? You're a . . . *Pinkerton*?" Martin Roach dropped into the nearby chair.

"I am. Mr. Pinkerton has been hired by Mr. Gowen to investigate certain issues concerning the railroad's mining operations. And he'll indeed be interested in anything I have to say. As a Pinkerton agent, I was able to gain access to your colliery contracts. In my report to Mr. Gowen I highlighted the discrepancies in seven of them, and advised him to initiate a full investigation into those remaining. I'm afraid, Mr. Roach, you've been found out."

Martin's mouth dropped, and though his lips moved as if trying to form words, nothing came out.

"It goes without saying, sir, that you are in a great deal of trouble. However, if you cooperate, tell us everything we want to know, perhaps I'll be willing to put in a good word for you."

Sweat poured down Martin's face as he nodded. "Tell me what you want."

"I want to know where your thugs have taken Virginia Farrell."

"My thugs . . . what . . . what are you talking about? What have I to do with Miss Virginia?"

"She's been abducted."

"*What*? So . . . that's why you were here earlier this morning asking questions . . . but I never dreamed . . . are you sure she's been kidnapped?"

"Quite certain."

"But . . . you don't think . . . you *can't* think that *I* had anything to do with it?"

"Didn't you? You knew Kate and I were investigating you. What better way of stopping our investigation? After all, you've done it before." When Martin attempted to rise from his chair, Joshua pushed down on his shoulder. "Don't deny it. We can produce a witness who will swear you hired two men to scare Roger Blakely into selling his colliery. We know it was to make it appear that Kate's father had resorted to violence."

Martin covered his ashen face with one hand. "Yes . . . but only because I wanted something on him, something I could use to stop him from . . . ."

"To stop him from what? Trying to check into your contracts like I did?"

Martin's head dropped to his chest as he nodded.

"And to use it as blackmail if he didn't?"

Again Martin nodded.

"And what were these thugs supposed to do to Mr. Blakely? Rough him up a bit; hurt him enough to scare him? So he, too, would stop looking into your activities? But your thugs got out of hand, didn't they? They went too far and ending up killing Mr. Blakely."

At this, Martin jumped to his feet in spite of Joshua's firm hand. "No, it didn't happen that way, I *swear*! They never did the job. Before they could, someone killed the old man." He glanced at Kate. "Like everyone else in town, I thought it was your father. All the evidence pointed to him, and there were no other suspects. I had nothing against him. I always liked him, Kate. But I thought he was guilty."

Kate felt Joshua's hand on her back as if steadying her. With his other hand he pushed Martin back down onto the chair.

"You've just admitted you hired thugs to hurt Mr. Blakely in order to keep your double dealings a secret. So why should we believe you didn't do it again, by having Virginia kidnapped? Or was Kate the real target, and your men botched the job?"

Martin Roach shook his head. "No, no. You must believe me! I know nothing about Virginia or what happened to her. And I never hired anyone to go after Kate."

Tears mingle with the perspiration on Martin's face and Kate wondered if they were tears of remorse or because he was now visualizing his world collapsing around him?

"Come on, Kate, we're finished here."

"Does this mean you believe me?" Martin straightened in his chair.

"Yes."

"And I cooperated, so you'll put in a good word, right?"

"You told us nothing."

"But I had nothing to tell!" Martin rose to his feet, his hands outstretched like an imploring child. "You'll speak to Mr. Gowen for me? Won't you?"

Without answering, Joshua led Kate past the tall shelves of merchandise, out the stockroom, through the store, then out the front door. "You did well, Kate," he said when their feet touched the sturdy planked sidewalk. And though his face was grave, the shimmer in his eyes told Kate he was pleased.

"So did you." She took his hand and squeezed it. "But talk about being reckless, you shouldn't have blown your cover like that. Oh, why did you do it, Joshua? You should have used another approach. This will not sit well with your superiors and may even compromise your standing with the agency."

"It might."

"If you lose your job I don't know what I'll . . . ." She sighed. "How can I ever thank you?"

"How about we discuss it for the next forty or fifty years?"

She slipped her arm through his, brushing her cheek against his shoulder. "Why not make it sixty or seventy?"

"I'd like that. But for now, we're back to where we started. It's obvious Martin doesn't know anything."

"So what are we to do?"

"Head for Higgins Patch and the Mattson Colliery as planned."

~

It didn't take Kate long to find someone in Higgins Patch who had seen Virginia.

"She was on her way to the Mattson, all right," said an elderly woman Kate had seen several times at the colliery but didn't know by name. "Yes, sir, headin' for the Mattson and lookin' like she was on a mission. Nearly dark, it was, too. But I saw that red hair of hers and how she walked as if someone was chasin' her, like a chicken before you're fixin' to make a pot of soup." The woman smiled a toothless grin as though amused by her own joke. "But that's all I can say. Don't know any more." She returned to weeding the small herb garden by her feet, indicating the conversation was over.

Kate thanked her, then she and Joshua headed for the colliery. But here, Kate wasn't as fortunate. She and Joshua questioned more than a dozen outside laborers before finding a young man who claimed to have seen her.

"A red head, right?" he asked with a mild brogue, his own tangled blond hair matting his forehead. "About so high?" One coal dust-covered hand hit the top of his shoulder. "And *very* pretty?"

Kate nodded. "Yes, yes, that sounds like her. But what was she *doing*?"

The young man grinned as if visualizing Virginia. "She came just before the breaker whistle blew. I noticed her right off. I'd never seen her before. I mean, you don't forget a girl like that. Didn't look like no miner's wife I'd ever seen, if you get my meanin'." He chuckled. "My friends all tell me I have a real eye for the ladies."

"Yes, but what was she *doing*?" Kate repeated.

The young man rubbed his upper arm as though massaging a muscle. "Well, I had just tipped one of them full cars onto the top of the breaker chute and was returnin' it to the shaft for reloadin' when I saw her standin' by the head frame, and I asked myself that very question. 'Now what would such a fine lookin' lass be doin' here all alone?' Then, after thinkin' a moment, I came to the unhappy conclusion she was waitin' for her man."

"Waiting for her man?"

"Sure. And wasn't I right, too? Soon as he come up from the shaft they were huggin' and kissin', and it wasn't a casual 'hello' kiss, you can be certain of that. And I thought to myself, what a lucky bloke. Then when the kissin' stopped, they said a few words, and she left."

"The man—was he Patrick O'Brien?" Kate asked.

"The very one. It's hard to believe Patrick could get a girl like that, but don't go tellin' him I said so. He's not someone you want to be insultin'."

Kate waved his remark aside. "You said she left, but you didn't say if she left alone."

"Oh, she left alone, all right. And it didn't please Patrick none. I could tell by the expression on his face." He grinned and leaned closer to Kate. "Don't suppose you're lookin' for a man, now, are you, lass?" When he glanced at Joshua and saw the frown on his face, his grin deepened and he shrugged. "No, suppose not. Well, I best be gettin' back to tippin' cars." He winked at Kate, then sauntered off.

"At least we know she was here." Kate turned to Joshua. "Now we need to talk to Patrick and find out *why*. And we need to find out where she was headed. The breaker whistle won't sound for hours. I only pray that all this waiting won't mean more danger for Virginia."

"We're not going to wait. I'll ask the superintendent to send someone for Patrick."

"Will he do that? Just on your say-so?"

"He will if I show him my credentials."

"Joshua, you can't! It will finish you for sure with Mr. Pinkerton."

"Let me worry about that, Kate. Right now, finding Virginia is what matters."

Kate's heart sank as she watched Joshua disappear into a small grimy looking building. So far, she had done a good job of nearly ruining the life of everyone she loved. Would she ruin his, too? She was still thinking about it when a man, wearing glasses, a white shirt and dark trousers held by suspenders, stepped into the wooden elevator. At once, the overhead pulley creaked as the cage was lowered into the shaft.

"Acting Superintendent Winston was most obliging and has sent his man into the mine," Joshua said, suddenly appearing beside her. "Now, let's hope Patrick has something useful to tell us."

It seemed to Kate that the cage was never going to return to the surface when at last the large circular sheaves with their grooved rims began to turn in the huge frame, pulling the thick heavy cable upward

in fits and starts as if straining with its load. Then came the bonnet—
the heavy sheet of metal that covered the top of the cage to protect
those inside from falling debris—followed by the cage itself. When
it stopped, out stepped two men: one covered in coal dust, the other,
spotless in his white shirt and suspenders. Both walked toward Kate
and Joshua without saying a word.

"Here he is, Mr. Adams," the tidy man said, adjusting his glasses.
"If you need anything else, let me know." Then he disappeared, leaving Patrick O'Brien standing in front of them, his large hands dangling like mitts by his side.

"Must be important for the Super to bring me up like this." He
glanced at Kate, then at Joshua Adams. "And your faces don't look
none too happy, neither. Best be comin' out with it and tell me what's
wrong."

"We understand Virginia came yesterday to see you, and we'd like
to know why," Kate answered.

"'Tis a private matter. If Jenny had wanted you to know, she'd
have told you. I'll not be sayin' a word about it."

Kate laid her hand on Patrick's dirty jacket. "She's missing,
Patrick. She never came home last night. We have people out looking for her now. *Please*, won't you tell us? It could help us find her
quicker."

"Jenny is *missin'*?" Patrick's hands balled into fists. "I shouldn't
have listened to her. She wouldn't let me see her home on account of
her not wantin' any of you to know she'd been here."

"But *why*? What was so bad that she felt the need to keep it from
us?"

For a long time Patrick remained silent, his head down as he
kicked the black grimy soil with the toe of his black grimy boot.
When he looked up, his countenance was so fierce it made Kate
step backward.

"She was protectin' me. She came to show me the coffin notice and asked if it was one of my Mollies who sent it."

While Joshua appeared surprised, Kate only shook her head. "I don't understand. She already told me you were part of the Molly Maguires. Why would she feel the need to protect you now?"

"She didn't want the law askin' me questions. She was . . . ." his voice broke, "she was always worryin' over me so." He looked past Kate and Joshua. "She went home that way." He jutted his chin in the direction of the usual trail; the very one they had traveled to get here. "Best you start there. Trace her steps and see what you find."

"Will you be coming? The more eyes we have the . . . ."

"No. You go on."

It was obvious by the way his lips were drawn tightly together, the way his body was planted so firm and straight, that for Patrick, the matter was settled and he wasn't going to change his mind. And by the look in his eyes, Kate saw that he was somewhere else, somewhere far away.

"I'm a Pinkerton agent, working for Mr. Gowen," Joshua said, stepping closer. "If you know anything about Virginia's disappearance, anything at all, and are withholding that information, it won't go well with you, I can promise you that!"

Patrick continued staring past them, but his eyelids fluttered just a bit. "If that's a threat, be savin' your breath, Mr. Adams. If anythin' happens to Jenny, it won't matter a bit what you do to me."

CHAPTER 11

Virginia brought her shivering arms up to her chest. Her bare shoulder was so numb she couldn't even feel it. She tried covering it with her bound hands hoping their warmth would relieve the ache. The trip here had been a blur. Even so, she had felt the dense brush snag her green linen dress, ripping it at the shoulder and elsewhere, and making what was left of her long sleeves hardly warm enough for the interior of a mine. And the line of squeezed timbers—bent like a regiment of old men—and the rusted and misaligned car rails told her that this mine was abandoned.

She held her breath when a rat darted across the rails, then pressed her back against the hard, rough wall when she saw another scurry by. Then another. Did they smell blood? Her wrists were bleeding from the coarse ropes; so were her ankles. She sighed with relief as the rats passed without stopping and disappeared behind the mound of coal and slag that looked like it had fallen from the roof.

At least it wasn't pitch black. Half a dozen oil lamps, placed along the tracks, lit several yards of the shaft. It also enabled her to see the roof, though she wished she couldn't, for a large crack, centered above her head, ran in both directions.

She had been struggling against her ropes ever since her captor buried himself beneath that filthy blanket. But no matter how hard she tried, she couldn't loosen them. All she had succeeded in doing was cutting herself deeper.

Now as she sat motionless against the wall all she could think about was the cold. It made even that disgusting blanket look inviting. And she was tired, too. So tired. Her lids felt like anvils. But she dare not sleep. Not now, when any minute *he* might wake up. She needed to stay alert, to keep her wits, so she could make her escape.

She tried ignoring the stench that floated from the body and blanket several feet away. It was a mix of body odor, dirt, whiskey and kerosene. The kerosene, especially, was distasteful, reminding her of the hands that had dragged her from the path to this shaft.

But what shaft? There were so many abandoned shafts in the Schuylkill Mountains. It would take weeks for rescuers to search them all. *But she couldn't think of that now.* She needed to keep up her courage. If only she wasn't so cold and tired. And in pain. Her whole body ached, including her back which had been pressed against this hard wall for what seemed an eternity. Still . . . she was grateful he had not gagged her. She supposed it was because he didn't care if she screamed or made a fuss. Who would hear?

Suddenly the blanket moved, writhing like an anaconda she had once seen at a circus—so big it could swallow a grown man. It would be easy for him to leave her; let the shaft swallow her, and the rats finish what was left. Earlier, when he was drinking, she thought he'd do just that. Now, any minute he'd be up. Would he start drinking that foul smelling liquor again? And act crazy?

She watched the blanket ripple. Who *was* he? What kind of man made his home in a dark underground hole? The signs of his makeshift abode were everywhere. Half a dozen large tins held kerosene for the lamps. The place reeked of them. And nearby, a cluster of amber-colored whiskey flasks formed a small pyramid. Next to it, amid the coal and slate chips, sat a dirty tin plate and fork, a can opener, several cans of tomatoes, and a can or two of some kind of meat spread. He could spend days here without having to return to the surface.

Oh, God help me.

Virginia worked the ropes again, pulling here, twisting there, then stopped. *What was the use?* Even if she managed to untie herself, how was she ever going to find her way to the surface? Mine tunnels could go on for miles, and often led to dead ends. If only she hadn't been nearly unconscious when she first came. Then she could have observed the markers and landscape showing the way out.

Was this to be her grave?

Suddenly, the dark, odious man threw off his blanket, then yawned a phlegmy-sounding yawn. When he sat up and rubbed his stubbled face, it sounded like sandpaper scraping wood. Another phlegmy yawn, then he routed around in his things before picking up one of the amber bottles, which he quickly uncorked and drank. She was so thirsty that even a mouthful of that cheap whiskey would have been welcome. She was hungry, too. When had she eaten last? She couldn't remember. And he had given her nothing. No food or water. Not even a blanket to keep her warm. She watched as he drained half the bottle in only a few gulps. The last time he drank this much he rambled incoherently for hours.

He wiped his mouth with the back of one hand, then tilted his head and the bottle, and drank the rest. When he finished, he tossed the bottle behind one of the sagging timbers. Virginia heard glass shatter as though it had landed on a pile of other bottles.

He rubbed his face once more, then glanced up. When he saw her, he blinked then rose and began pacing—his footfalls surprisingly steady between the ruined tracks.

"'Tis all your fault, you know. 'Twas your meddlin' that done it. Turned Patrick against me. And him just about my only friend."

Virginia held her breath. He had talked this way after draining his last bottle. He had cried, too, and pulled his hair, and raved like a madman.

"You shouldn't have done that. Turned Patrick against me. When it was me that done you all them good turns by takin' your articles to Tamaqua and that fella at the *Monitor*. Bet you didn't know that, did you?"

Virginia stared at him in horror. *Who was he?* Until now, she had been too terrified to speak. But that had to change if she hoped to learn why he had brought her here, then use it to her advantage. "Well . . . thank you Mr . . . Mr?"

"Patrick gave me two silver half-dimes every time I made the trip." He fumbled in the pockets of his dirty trousers and pulled out the coins. "See! I still got the last ones. He was good like that. Always tryin' to throw a little work my way."

She closed her eyes and tried to remember if Patrick had talked about any of his friends, and only one name came up; Powderkeg Kelly. "Yes . . . Patrick said he liked giving you jobs."

"He was . . . my only friend. And now you've gone and ruined it!" He turned and scowled at Virginia. "It's your fault you're here. Don't blame me. I didn't mean for none of this to happen. But what's a man to do when he's down on his luck? And me, the best blaster in Schuylkill."

It had to be Powderkeg Kelly. Virginia's heart dropped as she remembered Patrick's words: *some say he's crazy.* "Yes, Patrick told me you were skilled with blasting powder."

"He did?" Powderkeg wiped his eyes with the back of his blackened hand. "He was my best friend, you know."

"Patrick also told me how you helped him find the two men Mr. Roach hired." She tried to sound calm. "And how fearless you were." She needed to gain his confidence.

"Well you can't be no sissy if you handle explosives for a livin'. But that don't mean I like hurtin' people. Don't go thinkin' I wanted to tie you up like this! It don't give me no pleasure. You're a real lady, I can see that. And I don't mean you no harm."

"Then why don't you let me go, Mr. Kelly?" She'd have to tread carefully. Not push too hard. He was a tall, massive man, someone she could never overpower. Freedom would come only by employing her wits. "If you let me go, it will please Patrick."

"You just stop that now!" Powderkeg smashed his hand against one of the bowed timbers causing it to shudder. "You stop talkin' about Patrick! I don't want to hear no more about him. He was gonna turn me over to the law. And me, his best friend! Now why would he do that?"

Was this the man who killed Mr. Blakely? "Did you do something wrong?"

"I should never have asked Patrick to sell that gold for me."

"What gold?"

"But what was I to do? Me, being down on my luck?" He paced up and down between the tracks, his hand smacking the timber pillars as he passed, making them groan and creak.

Virginia trembled as she envisioned the entire roof caving. *Don't think of that now! Keep your wits!* Years ago, hadn't Father told her about a gold nugget Mr. Blakely used as a paperweight? Was that the gold Powderkeg was talking about? It had been the only thing missing from Mr. Blakely's office the night he was killed. Father had talked about how much Mr. Blakely prized that nugget, a worthless piece of fools-gold weighing nearly a pound; a nugget he had found as a young man panning during the California gold rush. She remembered Father talking about how Mr. Blakely kept it as a reminder of the price of greed since it cost the lives of his two best friends; friends who had been his mining partners and who had been killed by would-be claim jumpers thinking they had struck it rich. The incident made Mr. Blakely pull up stakes and head back to Pennsylvania. And Father had told her that as long as he could remember, Mr. Blakely had used that nugget as a paperweight.

"I should never have shown Patrick the gold." Powderkeg tore at his hair. "No. Shouldn't have done that."

"Are you . . . talking about Mr. Blakely's paperweight?"

"I liked Mr. Blakely. He was a good man. All I wanted was a job. I asked him nice like, too, but he said he couldn't use me on account of the drink. Said I would endanger the other men." Powderkeg thumped his chest. "I can handle my liquor. He shoulda known that. Besides, I don't drink much. He shoulda given me a chance."

"Mr. Blakely was a good man. I'm sure he would have used you if he could. Everyone knows what a good blaster you are. Mr. Blakely knew that too."

"I never meant him no hurt." He wiped his runny nose on the sleeve of his jacket. "Why did he have to leave that stack of money on his desk? And with that big chunk of gold sittin' right on top? A man down on his luck . . . well he . . . he might do anythin'. But I was only goin' to borrow it. 'Til I got back on my feet. I would have repaid every cent, don't think I wouldn't have, either!" Powderkeg beat his head with his balled fists. "I would have paid it back."

"You . . . took his money?" There had been no mention of missing money at the trial, and being so close to payday when collieries had an abundance of cash in their strongboxes, anything missing would have been noticed since everyone knew, based on the size of a given colliery and the number of men working it, how much payroll there should be. But Mr. Blakely's paymaster handled all that, not Mr. Blakely himself, and pay was dispensed in gold and silver pieces, not folding money since many immigrants didn't trust it. And during the trial it had come out that there was a stack of paper currency on Mr. Blakely's desk but no one had bothered trying to figure out why. If it wasn't for payroll was it for the investigation he and Father were conducting into Martin Roach's activities? Was that why Mr. Blakely wanted to see Father that night? To tell him he had found a contact at the railroad who could be bribed into letting them see Mr. Roach's contracts, and the money on his desk was the bribe? And Father, being a railroad man, was the one to handle it? Why else would he leave a stack of paper currency in the open like that? But it hardly seemed to matter now. What did matter was Powderkeg's role in it. "Did you . . . steal Mr. Blakely's money?" she repeated.

"His money? No . . . no money. Just that gold nugget . . . in my pocket, though it was the foldin' money I was after . . . being so light, and easy to carry and all . . . and so much of it, too. I'd seen a stack like that at a bank once. It would have kept me for a year, maybe two. But Mr. Blakely turned from the cabinet, the one he had been shovin' all his papers into, just as I was reachin' for it. I didn't mean him no harm. He was a good man. I never meant to do him hurt." Powderkeg wrung his hands as if remembering that day.

"Is that when you . . . killed him?" Virginia couldn't believe she had said that. What was she thinking? It was dangerous pushing him to the edge like this.

Powderkeg waved his hands in the air. "I told Mr. Blakely I just wanted to borrow the money. But he said he'd get the law after me if I didn't get out. He shoulda let me go. I was goin' too, 'til he started shoutin' somethin' about his paperweight. I told him he was daft. What would I be knowin' about any paperweight? He shoulda let me go."

Virginia was picturing what happened: the elderly Mr. Blakely holding Powderkeg's arm; refusing to let him go until he returned his prized paperweight; and Powderkeg not understanding that he meant the worthless gold nugget in his pocket. And then what? Mr. Blakely had been killed by his own knife. Had he pulled it on Powderkeg? They must have fought. Mr. Blakely was getting on in years and no match for a more powerful, younger man. It would be easy for

Powderkeg to wrestle the knife from him and then . . . . She suddenly felt sorry for her captor as she visualized the skirmish.

"I didn't mean to hurt him. The knife . . . he fell on it and . . . I ran."

"You must tell that to the police."

"No! No police. They wouldn't believe me anyways. They'd say I did it on purpose, and then they'd lock me up. And even if they did believe me, they'd still be mad about Superintendent Foley. But that was his fault. He shoulda left town like I told him."

"Are you the one who . . . hurt Mr. Foley?"

"He shouldn't have fired me. Now what am I supposed to do? A man needs to work. He goes crazy if he don't work."

"We'll go to the police and make them understand. We can tell them together."

"No! I said no police! Now stop tryin' to confuse me!" Powderkeg pointed a shaking finger at her. "I know what you're up to! But we're not goin' nowhere. Not to the police . . . nowhere. Not for another day or so, 'til it's safe. Then we're goin' far away, you and me. No one is gonna hunt me down while I got you. Not Patrick. Not anyone. I thought it all out, careful like. When I'm safe, I'll let you go. But no more talk about the law or I'll bind your mouth shut. See if I don't!"

Virginia closed her eyes. *Mr. Blakely was killed over a piece of fools-gold. And indirectly, Father, too.* Oh, the irony of it, after Mr. Blakely's two friends had been killed for it as well. Now, was she to die for the same reason? *Oh, God, don't let this happen!*

"It don't give me no pleasure stealin' you away like this and trus-sin' you up as if you was a turkey. Don't think I wanted to. But you only got yourself to blame. You shouldn't have turned Patrick against me. You only got yourself to blame."

Virginia slumped against the wall. Let him rant. She wouldn't say another word. She had already learned what she needed to. It was clear that Powderkeg wasn't going to turn himself in for killing Mr. Blakely or for the Foley beating, or allow Patrick to do it, either. It was also clear he was planning to make his escape, perhaps to another state, and use her as a hostage in order to keep everyone away. Maybe even as a shield if things got rough. But he wasn't going to hurt her. Not yet. Not while she was still useful. She'd bide her time, and once out of the mine, make her escape.

"Jenny!"

Virginia jerked upright, scraping her back against the wall and causing pain to shoot up her spine. She must have been dozing . . . and dreaming, because she thought she heard someone call her name. And there was only one person who ever called her "Jenny." How her heart ached for him now. And how she wished she had told him, just once, that she loved him. What a wretched thing pride was.

She looked around. Why was it so dark? Oh . . . just three kerosene lamps were lit. What happened to the others? Had Powderkeg let them go out? He must be drinking again. And what was that scuffling noise? She craned her neck in the direction of the sound but saw nothing. Too many shadows. The three lamps illuminated only a few yards. Beyond that was nothing but a black void. Surely Powderkeg had not left her here? No . . . wait . . . there he was . . . coming out of the shadows and waving his arms like a wild man. And . . . what was that in his hand? A knife? Too dark to tell, but it flashed whenever he moved. And he was shouting something, too.

"Stay back! Stay back or I'll cut you!"

He must be stark raving mad, fighting shadows like that. She had heard of this happening to people who drank heavily, how they saw snakes and other visions that terrified them. She drew her arms and legs tighter to her body as he continued to flail at the shadows. What next? Would he turn his knife on her?

"Jenny! Jenny!"

There was that voice again. She must be going mad, too; imagining Patrick calling her like this.

"Jenny, where are you!"

No, that was no imaginary voice! "Over here, Patrick! I'm over here!" she shouted. But where was he? Why couldn't she see him? "Is . . . that really you?" she added, feeling the need to make certain her mind was still anchored to reality.

"Jenny, I've come for you. Be ready."

Be ready? But how? She struggled against the ropes, pulling this way and that. No use. Then she stretched out her legs and raised her skirt to expose her ankles. If he had a knife he could cut the rope. Even if there was no time to do her wrists, she could still run. But the ankles, they were the key.

She peered through the shadows and watched as, inch by inch, Powderkeg was driven backward. When Patrick finally entered the field of lamp light, her heart leapt.

"Be careful, Patrick," she said, her voice a whisper. He had a knife, too, and she began praying when she saw it was still clean while Powderkeg's was covered in blood.

"Stay back. Don't come no further or I'll cut you again!" Powderkeg growled.

Steel met steel as Patrick continued driving him backward. But when he finally saw Virginia, sitting on the ground between two timber pillars, he let his guard down for an instant, enough time for Powderkeg to strike again. From where she sat, it looked like the blade went deep into his heavy shirtsleeve. Virginia held her breath. Maybe it only penetrated cloth. But when Powderkeg pulled out his knife, she saw that the sleeve was wet and that Patrick's arm dangled, like a dead cod, against his side. Mercifully, he still had his fighting arm, which he used with such ferocity it made her gasp. "Be careful, Patrick, be careful," she mumbled.

She didn't want to watch but was powerless to stop. The two men were like wild beasts clashing as they thrust and parried, darted and weaved, shoved and pushed and crashed into each other and the timbers, making the whole tunnel shudder.

Patrick was the next to draw blood. His knife went into Powderkeg's side, just below his ribs. But instead of stopping him, Powderkeg became more enraged; and growling like a bear, he swung his knife so hard that when it connected with Patrick's, it knocked Patrick's from his hand and sent it flying several feet away.

Now Patrick was unarmed.

Virginia's silent prayers intensified while she watched in horror as Powderkeg moved in for the kill. But just as Powderkeg was upon him, Patrick stepped aside making the crazed man lunge into open space and lose his balance. Then Patrick picked up a large piece of fallen slate, and while Powderkeg was still trying to regain his footing, Patrick, using his good arm, came down hard with the rock on Powderkeg's head, sending the crazed man to the ground. At once, Patrick bent over the body, pulled the knife from Powderkeg's hand and rushed to where Virginia sat.

Without a word he cut the rope around her ankles. Then he worked to free her wrists. His knife was nearly through the rope when suddenly Powderkeg was upon him. And with one ferocious, almost maniacal movement, he raised his boot and kicked Patrick full force in his chest, sending him sprawling to the ground. Patrick groaned and writhed with pain, but managed to hold onto the knife. And when Powderkeg flew at him, it was only a second or two before the crazed man was dead.

But Patrick remained on his back, limp as death, too. Virginia tore at her nearly severed bonds, deeply cutting her wrists as she struggled to free herself. And after she did, she crawled to where Patrick lay.

"Patrick! *Patrick!*"

He groaned as she checked him for wounds, running her hands down his arms, torso and legs, and finding only the gash in his upper left arm, and another across his cheek. And that worried her.

"Patrick." She was on her knees beside him, her face close to his. "I think your insides are damaged. I must go for help."

Patrick opened his eyes. "Come, darlin', help me up. I must get you free of this tunnel. You'll never find the way out on your own."

"No. You can't. You're hurt. Badly hurt. Inside. It could be your ribs . . . your lungs. Just tell me the way and I'll go for help."

"'Tis no use, lass. If you do that we'll both die here. You must get me up. I'll take you out. Then you can go for help."

"First, let me bind your arm before you bleed out." Virginia leaned sideways where Powderkeg lay and nearly heaved as she pulled the knife from his heart. Then she began cutting the edge of her skirt. She willed herself to be calm as she wound the strip of fabric tightly around Patrick's gash, and knotted the ends. Then she rose and went to where the three remaining flickering lanterns were positioned along the track, and picked up each one to determine which contained the most kerosene. They were all woefully low, but there was no time to trim or refill a lamp now, so she chose one and carried it to the pillar nearest Patrick, placed it on the ground, and returned to where Patrick still laid. He was such a large, powerful man. How was she ever going to get him to his feet?

Oh, God, give me strength.

"I'm going to sit you up," she said, kneeling by his head and drawing his shoulders up over her lap. "After I do, I'll drag you to that nearby timber and prop you against it. Then I'll try to raise you. But you need to help me by pulling yourself up with your good arm."

He groaned with every move, but slowly, slowly she was able to get him to the post. But if he hadn't used his feet to help propel himself backward, she doubted she could have done it. But it cost him. The look on his face and the constant grinding of his teeth told her just how much. But getting him to stand was even more difficult. Virginia put both hands under his left arm, while he held the timber post with his other, and helped shinny himself up. She pulled and pulled with all her might, causing fresh blood from his wound to soil the newly applied bandage. And more than once, Virginia feared Patrick would pass out from the pain. When he finally got to his feet and leaned against the pole, Virginia picked up the lamp. With lamp in one hand and the other bracing Patrick's back, and with Patrick's arm around her shoulders and hardly able to stand, they began the long trek to the surface.

Patrick was right. There was no way she would ever have found her way out of the maze of tunnels that twisted and turned in every direction. Even Patrick often lost his bearings, though Virginia suspected it was due more to his pain than anything else.

They stopped often to rest. It was difficult for Patrick to walk for long. But those times when they stopped, Virginia noticed how his breathing was becoming more labored and caused him to grimace with pain. There were times she was sure he was going to pass out, for he'd close his eyes and weave. And just when she'd think he was about to go down, he'd rally, as if something deep inside kept urging him forward. She marveled at his determination, but doubted he could keep this up much longer. They just had to reach the surface soon.

Finally, there was light, way up ahead, a small light, like the flame of a candle that seemed to flicker and move as they wound their way through the dank tunnel. *Oh, God, help us make it!* They were nearly at the opening when their lamp went out, causing them to stumble over the last few yards. Virginia knew these final yards were utter agony for Patrick for he could barely keep from crying out with pain every time his foot found a broken track or pile of rubble which caused him to misstep and jar his body.

And then . . . freedom . . . with sunshine streaming on their faces, the sound of birds chirping, the smell of pine filling the air. Virginia couldn't keep from laughing and praising God. But as she gave thanks, Patrick collapsed in her arms.

With what strength she had left, she lowered him to the ground. They appeared to be in an old clearing, for it had few trees while the surrounding area was so thick with yellow and white pines, maples and hickories and even birches, she could barely see through them. And though the mine was so old the dirt road leading to it was covered with underbrush, Virginia could still see signs of a trail. It was the trail she would follow.

"I must go for help now," Virginia said, kneeling beside him, her hands caressing his blood-and-dirt streaked face, her lips kissing his bruised forehead.

"No, lass, 'tis no use. I'm only grateful I found you. I went to them all. Powderkeg's hidin' places. I knew you'd be in one of them."

Virginia looked up at the sky. The position of the sun told her it was late afternoon. "There's no time to waste. We've not much daylight left. I'll need every bit to bring help back here to you."

When he grabbed her arm and prevented her from rising, it surprised her. But it also gave her hope. He would make it. He was still strong.

"Listen," he said, his voice raspy, "when it's time, keep the sun to the right of you, and head south. This is the old Cargill mine, just north of the Mattson. You'll be fine, Jenny. People are lookin' for you, even now. You'll . . . be all right."

"Then I must go."

Patrick shook his head, still holding her arm, but loosely now. "Not yet. Stay. It's not . . . time." He seemed to be barely breathing.

Tears streamed down Virginia's face. "You must let me go before it's too late. You're badly hurt, Patrick. Your lungs might be punctured. You may need a surgeon. There's no time to waste."

"For me, it has run out, lass." His hand dropped to his side. "I feel as though I'm . . . slippin' away . . . ."

She kissed his lips as she stifled a sob. "No! Don't say that. I love you, Patrick. Do you hear? I love you!"

His lips formed what looked like a partial smile. "I know, darlin'. Your heart has always been easy for me to read . . . like the primer my friend Davin MacCabe used when teachin' me the . . . . a-b . . . but it's . . . nice hearin' you say it." He closed his eyes. "I shoulda listen to you, Jenny . . . about the law. If I had, this wouldn't have happened . . . forgive me."

"Stop. Don't talk anymore. Save your strength. And there's nothing to forgive." Tears dripped from Virginia's cheeks as she continued kneeling by his head, his motionless body sprawled over a mass of dried hepatica leaves that covered the small clearing like a blanket. She stroked his hair as she watched his color drain. "Did you know your friend, Davin MacCabe, offered me a job? As a *reporter* for the *Monitor*. An honest to goodness *reporter*! With pay. Oh, Patrick, think what this means! Now we can get that doghole you wanted, and a lot sooner than you expected, too. I wanted to talk to you about it, but there just hasn't been time. I wanted to know what you thought about me moving to Tamaqua like Mr. MacCabe suggested. It's only about sixteen miles away, you know. Or should I . . . ."

"Davin is a good . . . man. He'll do right by you. I'm proud . . . did I tell you that? Proud of what . . . you're tryin' . . . to do . . . for coal . . . con . . . ."

Virginia sobbed. "Oh, please don't leave me Patrick. How am I to live in this world without you?"

"If anyone's love could keep them here . . . it would be mine . . . but . . . listen . . . . Jesus is callin'. You're strong, Jenny . . . you'll be fine . . . I love . . . you . . . ." His eyes rolled toward the back of his head as his lids closed.

"Patrick!"

"Forgive me, Jesus . . . save me . . . I'm . . . yours . . . ."

And those were Patrick's last words, though Virginia tried to rouse him with her shaking. And when she didn't have the strength to shake him any longer, and when she was certain he really was gone, she lay down beside him, and with her arm around his chest, sobbed uncontrollably.

~

"Kate, look at the sky. It's getting late, and that dress of yours won't keep out the frigid night air. You'll not be good to Virginia or anyone else if you wind up catching your death of cold. Go home while it's still light. I'll follow the trail until dark, then find some shelter for the night. I promise that at first light I'll begin the search again."

Through the trees, Kate saw just enough sky to know the sun was dropping. "I'm not leaving. We'll see this through together."

"And have your mother and sister worry all night? That would be cruel." Joshua frowned as he put his arm around her. "And I don't want to have to worry about you, either."

Kate removed a twig that had become embedded in her hair, ignoring the fact that most of her hair was hanging unfettered. The trek through this part of the mountain was dense with trees and underbrush, and had left their mark. But this was where the trail had led them. Hard to find at first, it was Joshua who spotted the broken branch containing strands of red hair. It led them to a path where they soon saw other broken branches and trampled vegetation. But their overall progress had been slow, and they lost the trail half a dozen times causing them to backtrack. The real breakthrough came when she found a piece of fabric on the branch of a spoonwood; fabric from the dress Virginia wore the night she disappeared. It made them continue following their present trail, a trail that defied logic because it wound north, across the back of Higgins Patch, and deep into woods that, for miles, led nowhere.

"You must go," Joshua repeated.

Kate nodded, heavy hearted and not wanting to give up the search. But Joshua was right. She shouldn't worry Mother and Charlotte. And what could she do in the dark? "If I thought for a second we were close, you'd have to use blasting powder to get me off this mountain."

"And don't I know it." He held her for a minute. "It should be easy enough to follow the trail back. But be careful."

"I still don't understand why anyone would come this way. It doesn't make sense, Joshua. There's nothing around here for miles. Nothing but trees and brush and . . . the *old Cargill mine*." Kate grabbed Joshua's arm. "That's it! The Cargill mine! It closed down before I was born. But Mother told me all about it. Her father was superintendent there. The colliery, what's left of it, is further north, on the other side of the mountain, but I forgot that one of the shafts open, here, on the backside."

"I'll find it, Kate, and check it out. But you go on home."

"Oh *please*, Joshua, not now! Let me go with you. With all this brush it will take two pair of eyes to find it."

Joshua looked up at the sky again. "Is it far?"

"I can't know for sure, but I don't think so. I remember Mother saying it was just north of the Mattson Colliery, and if we continue following the trail, we should find it. It's the only place that makes sense."

"You thought the old abandoned saw mill could be it, too."

Kate nodded in understanding. They had wasted an hour chasing that speculation.

"If you go with me now, and the mine isn't close by, it will mean you'll have to spend the night out here."

"I know. But Virginia could be so near! Should I worry about my comfort or my family's if it means losing the chance of finding her? And you, yourself, said we only have a little daylight left. It will take a lot less time if both of us are looking for the trail."

Joshua furrowed his brow. "All right. But let's hurry. We've no time to waste."

⌒

The brush seemed to be getting thicker. It pulled Kate's hair, snagged her sleeves, tore her hem, but she wasn't about to give up now, because it was this very thickness that made the trail easy to follow with the many broken twigs and branches, as well as the matted vegetation on the ground, all showing them the way. And they had not gone far when suddenly, through the tangled brush, Kate saw a small clearing.

"Look, Joshua, over there. See how the landscape changes? Only a few mature trees, and plenty of low brush. It must have been cleared years ago. Maybe it's the entrance to the mine shaft."

Joshua nodded. "Yes, but stay behind me. No telling what we'll find."

So with Kate following Joshua, they maneuvered the remaining distance to the clearing.

"It is the mine!"

"Quiet," Joshua said as he held Kate back with one arm and pointed with the other.

At first she couldn't see them in their dirty clothes that blended in with the dried hepatica leaves covering the ground. But then she noticed the two bodies lying side by side, and so still it made her breath catch. The bodies were those of a man and woman, their faces obscured. The man was on his back with only his chin visible, while the woman's face was buried in his shoulder. But what Kate could clearly see was that the woman had flaming red hair.

"*Oh, Joshua.*"

At once, Joshua pulled out a gleaming revolver that Kate didn't even know he carried. "Stay here."

And while Kate lingered along the edge of the clearing, Joshua crept closer to the pair on the ground. Any minute, Kate expected someone to jump from the bushes, but when she saw Joshua return the gun to his inner coat pocket, she ran over.

"Virginia! *Virginia!*" Kate knelt by her sister. "Are they . . . *dead*?" She looked at Joshua as he bent over the pair.

"Yes . . . Patrick is. I'm not sure about Virginia."

With trembling hands, Kate gathered Virginia up in her arms. "Virginia? Oh, please be alive!" She stroked her sister's hair. Oh, how scraped and bruised Virginia was! And her dress nearly shredded and so filthy from coal dust. Her hand traveled down Virginia's bare shoulder. It was cold to the touch. Kate bent and kissed it, and when she did, she heard Virginia moan. And, oh what a wonderful sound it was! At once, Kate began shaking her sister. "Virginia! Wake up! Wake up!" And she would have gone on shaking her like this if Joshua hadn't stopped her.

"Can't you see she's unconscious?"

Kate began laughing. "Yes, and unconscious means she's alive! Oh, Joshua, she's alive!"

"Come, let me have her." He pulled Virginia toward him. "I'll carry her home. But we'll have to hurry if we want to make it before dark." And then in one swoop, he picked her up in his arms."

"You're exhausted, Joshua. How are you ever going to manage?"

"I'll manage," he said. "Now stay close."

Kate looked at the prone body of Patrick O'Brien. "I . . . hate leaving him here like this."

"I promise at first light I'll come back, with help, to get him. But quickly, now, we must go."

Kate sighed as she glanced once more at Patrick before following Joshua. "I wonder what happened?"

"Virginia will tell you soon enough."

Kate's heart soared with joy at the thought of being able to speak with Virginia. Oh, what a good God she served! He had enabled them to find Virginia in time. And yes, Kate and Virginia would sit together and talk, and Virginia would tell her all that had happened. But one thing Kate didn't need to be told, one thing she already knew was that somehow, someway, Patrick O'Brien had saved her sister's life.

CHAPTER 12

———— ⌒ ————

"You should have let me die," Virginia said, as Kate tried to insert another spoonful of broth between her dry, cracked lips. "You should have left me on that mountain."

"Don't talk nonsense." Kate readjusted her spot on Virginia's bed and hoped she sounded as if she hadn't taken Virginia seriously—not for one instant—while inside, her heart was troubled. Virginia was a fighter. It wasn't like her to say such things.

"We were so worried." Charlotte sat on the other side of the bed stroking Virginia's hair. "And we're so happy you're home with us now."

Virginia responded by turning away.

"Come now. Mother made this broth for you and infused it with all manner of good things." Kate held the spoon in midair. "You must eat in order to regain your strength. You're as weak as a kitten.

"Alright, be stubborn," Kate said, when Virginia refused to open her mouth. "But as you know, I can be stubborn, too." With that she forced the spoon between Virginia's lips. Most of the liquid dribbled into Virginia's mouth, but some rolled down her chin. Kate brought another spoonful to Virginia's mouth, emptied it forcibly, then another and another. Her stubbornness paid off, for soon Virginia willingly took the broth, her eyes brightening with each spoonful.

"Just tell me . . . ."

"No. No talking until you have finished. All of it! Then I'll tell you anything you want to know." But Kate already knew what Virginia's first question would be. And what was she going to say? How was she going to tell her sister they had left Patrick O'Brien behind?

They had been home for hours and Kate had been thinking about this very thing. It had taken all this time for Virginia to revive. And while Mother had been busy preparing the broth, Kate and Charlotte had stripped Virginia of her filthy rags, washed her hair, and bathed her body with lavender soap, then dressed her in one of her prettiest nightgowns. But Virginia's clean skin enabled them to see how deep the cuts were around her wrists and ankles; to see how very bruised she was. And seeing it all made both Charlotte and Kate weep. Kate had cried the entire time she removed twigs from her own hair, removed her own tattered dress and bathed her own tired, sore body. But she managed to compose herself before Virginia awoke; while Charlotte still kept a lace handkerchief on her lap for easy access.

"Now," Kate said, as she slipped the last drop of soup into Virginia's mouth. "What is it you wanted to know?"

"Patrick? Did you bring Patrick back?"

"No, my darling. We were barely able to get you home before dark. It was just the two of us, Joshua and I, who found you. Joshua carried you all the way. We couldn't bring Patrick down the mountain, too. But Joshua promised he and others would go at first light and get him."

Virginia tried to rise, but she was so weak it was easy for Kate to restrain her. "You can't leave him up there all night! Alone! You just can't! Make Joshua go now!"

Kate pointed to the window over which they had yet to draw the drapes. "It's pitch black outside. No one could navigate that mountain in the dark. It would be too dangerous. But first thing, first thing in the morning, they'll go for him."

Virginia began to weep.

"Please don't cry, Virginia," Charlotte said, blotting her own tears with her handkerchief. "Benjamin will go with Joshua tomorrow. And they'll take good care of him."

Kate blinked back tears, too, as she brought Virginia's hand to her lips and kissed it. "He saved your life, didn't he?"

Virginia nodded.

"When you're ready, you can tell us about it. We'll be here." Kate tucked Virginia's hand beneath the clean white sheet. "I just wanted you to understand that we know what a fine and grand thing Patrick did for you."

"I . . . think I'd like to talk about it . . . now. Right now. I'd like you, both of you," she turned to Charlotte, "to understand how wonderful Patrick is . . . was."

And then, with Charlotte sitting on one side and Kate the other, Virginia told them everything that had happened; about the abduction and Powderkeg Kelly; about how Patrick came to rescue her, the fight, his injuries, and how knowing he was badly hurt and shouldn't move, threw away his chance of survival by enduring great pain and bringing her out of the mine to freedom.

"He shouldn't have come for me," Virginia said, when her story ended. "*Why* did he have to come?"

"Because he loved you, Virginia. Because he *loved* you," Kate whispered, still awed by the great love Patrick obviously had had for her sister.

"But how can I live my life knowing it cost Patrick his?"

"By making it count." Kate readjusted the sheets. And as she did, Virginia appeared so grief-stricken, so utterly sorrowful it made Kate scoop her up in her arms, and in spite of her resolve, cry like a baby.

"I'm not sure that would be proper." Charlotte frowned at Benjamin as he stood by the sputtering logs in the back-parlor fireplace.

"Why not? It's money I never expected to see again. Why shouldn't I give away the five hundred dollar reward? Two hundred to that elderly woman at Higgins Patch and another two hundred to the young man at the Mattson Colliery. After all, their information did help Kate and Joshua find Virginia."

"Yes." Charlotte smoothed the folds of her day dress as she sat in one of the damask-covered chairs. "But it's the hundred dollars for the funeral that I'm worried about. I . . . I'm not sure Virginia would approve."

Benjamin chuckled. "I'm afraid it's too late. When Joshua and I brought Patrick's body to his boardinghouse, I gave the woman of the house a hundred dollars in coins, and told her I wanted Patrick to have a first class funeral; though I'm sure it won't cost even a fraction of that, but the rest she is welcome to keep for her trouble."

"Well . . . Virginia has been worried about the funeral. You should have heard her last night. She said she'd never let any medical school have him. She went on and on about it, too, until Kate told her how Joshua had been paying rent, and why he was, then promised Virginia that Patrick would have a grand wake and funeral, even if she had to sew a dozen quilts to repay Mother any of Joshua's rent money it might cost. But now that you've . . . well . . . it's wonderful, really . . . but what will people say? It's indecent for a lady to accept such a lavish sum from a man, even if it's not for herself."

"Not if it's from her *fiancé* as part of her wedding gift."

Charlotte caught her breath. "Oh, Benjamin . . . how clever and good you are! And yes . . . I do believe you're right. And I'm happy, so very happy that you phrased it that way because I do love you, too. I love you so dearly."

Grinning, Benjamin came over and sat in the chair beside her. "You might as well get used to my gifts, Charlotte."

"Then . . . would I sound too . . . too terribly ungrateful if I asked for just one more?"

Benjamin's smile deepened. "No, indeed. It is my pleasure to give you all I can."

"Well, there is a woman who needs a train ticket West and perhaps a little traveling money. A sick woman who has fallen on hard times and . . . ."

"Someone from the Women's Home?"

Charlotte nodded.

"Yes, I've heard of your visits there and I must say it pleases me, for it shows a tender heart. And what man would not prize such a heart in his wife? But say no more. When she is well enough to travel I shall arrange everything." Benjamin let out a contented sigh. "I must admit I'm enjoying this. I look forward to spoiling you as my wife."

Charlotte hesitated, then reached out and took his hand. "Dear, dear Benjamin, you'll not find a more grateful wife on which to dispense your good pleasure, I assure you."

With her arm entwined in Joshua's, Kate walked toward the small grey wooden house wondering how they were going to get through this. It would take God's strength, for sure. Her dark wool skirt swirling in the wind, her free hand clutched her cape. Already, the throng was so thick she could barely see the door, though the large black ribbon nailed near the top was clearly visible. A sea of both men and women filled the small yard and spilled out across the dirt footpath like water overflowing its banks. She was pleased to see a small band of musicians playing perky Irish tunes, though it created an odd contrast to the wailing of the professional keeners that could be heard coming from inside the house.

She hoped it pleased Virginia, too. It was obvious that the landlady had done her best to provide a first class wake, though, at Virginia's insistence, it would last only one day. Two large wooden tables, covered with white Irish lace cloths, had been set up outside, one containing bread spread with real butter—Mother made sure of that—along with platters of assorted cheeses and sliced meats, while the other table—stationed near three giant wooden barrels of beer—held pewter mugs along with tea pots and cups.

Still, Kate worried about Virginia who walked just ahead, holding the arm of Davin MacCabe. She was dressed in a black linen day-dress, her beautiful red hair gathered at the nape of her neck. MacCabe had not left Virginia's side since coming from Tamaqua in response to the telegram Virginia had asked Kate to send. As one of Patrick's oldest friends, Virginia felt he should be informed. And Kate had thought so, too. And since his coming, he had proven to be a strong pillar. Even so, Mother and Charlotte, who each held one of Benjamin's arms, looked ready to act as brace should the need arise.

Kate watched the crowd swallow Virginia and the ever present MacCabe. Virginia belonged to them now. These people, these miners and their wives, were her people, and they greeted her with deference and with sincere condolences as if she had actually been Patrick O'Brien's wife.

"It's a grand wake," Kate said, bending closer to Joshua. "It's sure to please Virginia, though I worry she'll overdo. She's still not strong, you know."

"She's stronger than you think. And she'll be fine. But I suppose my saying so won't stop you from worrying. I wonder, would you worry like that about your husband?"

Kate laughed. "I don't know. I suppose if he carried a gun, for instance, and chased criminals for a living, I believe I'd worry a great deal."

"Ah . . . but what if your husband was a school teacher? A plain, rather boring, schoolteacher? And the most dangerous encounter he'd have would be with a cussing miner's son? I suppose you wouldn't have much to worry about then, would you?"

Kate pulled him to a stop. "Oh, Joshua, you got fired! I knew it! I just knew it was going to happen. Oh, that ungrateful Mr. Pinkerton! Letting his best agent go. And it's all my fault. If I'd only . . . ."

Joshua placed his fingers over her lips. "Mr. Pinkerton didn't fire me, Kate. He put me on probation for blowing my cover and compromising my assignment. And though he was furious, he said he understood why I did it. And he *did* say I was his best agent. In fact, he told me I reminded him of Timothy Webster, his famous operative who was executed as a spy during the Civil War. He thought highly of Mr. Webster, so when I handed him my resignation, he couldn't believe it. And when he found out I was leaving to teach school, well . . . he cursed a blue streak. But in the end, we shook hands and parted as friends.

"But before I submitted my resignation, I had a talk with Mr. Gowen. He was in a good mood—all awash with gratitude for my investigation and subsequent information concerning Martin Roach— so I figured there would be no better time to ask him to add another room to the Higgins Patch school house so the upper and lower grades could be separated, and to install two new large coal stoves to keep the children warm, and finally, to add me to the teaching staff; all to which he agreed."

"What . . . what brought this about?" Kate said, unable to believe her ears.

"Virginia's article. The one about how most miner's children never stay in school long enough to reach their tenth birthday, and how the boys, especially, think going to school is a disgrace and that only "sissies" did so if they could be working at the mine. It made me want to change things, made me want to make a little history right here in coal country as well as teach it. And I already have, for I believe Higgins is the only patch in the vicinity that can boast of having two teachers. Now what do you think of that?"

Kate slid her arms around him. "I love you Joshua Adams. But is that your sole reason for wanting to stay?"

"Well . . . after you accepted my rather trepid proposal outside Martin Roach's store, I realized I was tired of a detective's life. I want to settle down, Kate, and if I stayed with Pinkerton I'd be all over the country, going from one case to another. And he'd never let me take you along. And I fear I'd miss you so much I wouldn't be able to concentrate on my job. And constant separation wouldn't be much of a life for either of us. And once we had a family, well . . . a son needs his father, and so does a daughter because . . . ."

Without letting him finish, Kate kissed him on the lips, right there on the dirt path.

Virginia was overwhelmed by the love that poured from all those around her. She thanked each mourner, shook every hand, even the men's, who seemed glad to shake hers, too. It gave her strength. She was sure, now, that she could make it through the day, even though she still felt weak and her body ached and her heart felt like someone had ripped it open with a knife. She was glad that her long-sleeve dress covered those awful cuts around her wrists so no one could see them. As it was, the attention of far too many people lingered on her scratched face and neck, and elicited sympathy she didn't want, for she wished everyone's attention to be on Patrick, and to honor him this day.

As she moved through the crowd, Davin MacCabe moved with her. He was like a guarding angel, taking her arm when he saw her falter; smiling and nodding when she seemed to need encouragement. He had not left her side since coming from Tamaqua this morning to their house. He had held her arm all the way to Higgins Patch, and talked of Patrick and the old days when they were boys. And though he seemed as stunned and grief stricken as she, he had tried to make her laugh and to bring Patrick back, for a moment at least, to both of them by his stories. And once, Davin actually did make her smile when he told her how Patrick came to his rescue when they were seven, after two local bullies had cornered Davin and were ready to beat him to a pulp. And how Davin ended up returning home without a scratch, while Patrick got his nose bloodied, one eye blackened, and a whipping from his mother for fighting and tearing his new shirt.

Now, the strain of greeting everyone left Virginia exhausted. She needed to regain her strength, at least her inner strength, before going inside to where Patrick lay. So when she spotted an area near the rear of the house, where few people had gathered, she headed there and Davin followed. Here, in this quiet space she would work up her nerve before seeing Patrick. How would he look? How would she react when she saw him? Her heart raced at the thought.

She glanced at the man standing quietly beside her. How would he fare? Davin appeared to be the sort who could handle himself well enough—as tall as Patrick and as well built. And yet . . . there was something soft about him, too. Something kind and tender about his eyes, about the way they smiled, the way they looked at a person as though with thoughtfulness and insight. And though outwardly Davin appeared in control, stoical even, Virginia was sure that when the time came for them to go inside, he would weep, too.

"I'll be goin' back to Tamaqua tonight," he said, breaking the silence. "And though I hesitate mentionin' this, I need to know your plans. Have you considered my offer?"

"Yes, Mr. MacCabe, and I'm going to take the position."

He chuckled. "I've read and published so many of your articles I think it only fittin' that you call me Davin. I feel I know you, Virginia. Not just from your articles but from Patrick, too. He spoke of you often. And I know he'd want us to be friends."

Virginia nodded. "He said you were a good man."

"Did he now? Well, maybe that's because he never worked for me. I *am* fair-minded, but I'll work you hard. And I won't pamper you because you're a woman, either, and I'd be disappointed if you'd expect me to."

"I think . . . hard work is what I need right now. It might help."

"No, lass, nothin' is gonna help. Not for a very long time. But if all Patrick said about you is true, you'll be fine. And though you might not believe it now, you will find joy in livin' again."

Virginia stared at him and shrugged. Right now, life without Patrick seemed a joyless proposition. "Patrick tells me . . . told me that Mr. Gowen was trying to bust the union. I haven't seen any articles in the *Monitor* about that. Would you want me to investigate? See what he's doing to lay the foundation? I could . . . ."

"Will you be movin' to Tamaqua? There's a respectable boardin' house near the paper. Clean, and cheap, too. I could book you a room . . . that is, if you were thinkin' of movin'."

"I've only spoken to Kate about it. Not Mother or Charlotte, but yes, I've decided to go. It will be too hard staying here, near Higgins Patch, near . . . ."

"I know, lass. I know. But while I'd like to give you all the time in the world to mend, and to convince your family that this is right for you, I can only give you two weeks. With all that's goin' on, I need you at the paper. I'll make the arrangements at the boardin' house. And once you come, be ready to work. You can start with that article you proposed. Now . . . shall we go and see Patrick?"

Virginia closed her eyes and took a deep breath. She hardly knew Davin, but for some reason his presence comforted her. When she opened her eyes he was looking at her so intently, it startled her. "Yes," she said, threading her arm through his. "I'm ready." And together they walked toward the front door.

⌣

Kate stood alone on the footpath. The wake was over, the food table and beer kegs empty, the keeners hoarse, the band played out. Joshua was off to one side talking with Benjamin and Charlotte, leaving her free to watch the pallbearers—a group of six muscular men—ready themselves. They would be the ones carrying the casket to the nearby cemetery. As her mind replayed how Virginia had sobbed uncontrollably when the casket was closed then nailed shut, she was grateful that the strong arms of Davin MacCabe would be there to steady her sister during the burial.

Kate gathered her cloak around her as the chilly air made visible puffs out of her breath. The smell of smoking pork permeated the patch. It was autumn, the time when pigs were butchered and the flitches or sides hung in chimneys to cure. And at home, Mother had already started putting up the heavier bed and parlor curtains. To Kate, it spoke of routine and rhythm. It told her life would go on, even for Virginia. And there would be joy again in the Farrell house. By the look of Charlotte and Benjamin, she was sure their wedding wasn't far off. And neither was hers, though she and Joshua hadn't set a date. But she was sure Joshua felt as she did, and wanted to wait only long enough to plan a modest wedding. And modest it would be, for a teacher's salary hardly left extra money for frills.

But Virginia was the Farrell Kate worried about most. Virginia had told her of Davin MacCabe's offer. *A woman reporter*! It was still hard to believe. And it was sure to cause a stir. But Kate had the feeling Virginia would always be causing a stir. Virginia was breaking a barrier here in coal country, and why not? It was the 1870s; the time of breaking barriers in the newspaper world. Hadn't it seen the birth of several black newspapers? Something unthinkable just a few years ago. But would Virginia move to Tamaqua? Knowing her, Kate had to say, "yes", though Mother would hardly be pleased. But like all of them, Virginia had to follow her own path.

Kate thought of that now as she watched the six large pallbearers enter the house, and minutes later, exit, with the wooden casket resting on their shoulders. Virginia followed close behind, with Davin on one side and little Michael O'Malley on the other. The child looked poorly and Kate wondered at his fate. Would Virginia be able to improve his life by working at the *Monitor*? She hoped so. Though God had woven all their lives together, He now seemed to be taking them on separate paths. But the one consolation was that *He* was in control. Kate could rest in that, now.

"I think Mrs. O'Brien would be pleased with Patrick's wake," Mother said, coming up alongside Kate. "Though no wake is ever welcome. But what guarantees do any of us have in this life? Still, it grieves me to see Virginia so distraught. But she's young . . . and strong. In time, her heart will mend." She threaded her arm through Kate's. "And you? Has your heart healed? Are you happy now that your father has been cleared? They say that poor man they took from the old Cargill mine, the one they call Powder . . . Powderkeg, was deranged. God surely weeps over him, too, Kate, don't you think? And Mr. Roach? He's ruined and going to jail, for a very long time. But darling, what has all this brought *you*?"

Kate sighed. "I don't feel the vindication I thought I would. But I'm grateful to God for bringing out the truth, and relieved, too, that it's all over. And I feel as though I'm finally able to grieve the loss of Father. Grieve without bitterness, and that's no small thing. I'm going to be all right, Mother. I know that now. We're all going to be all right."

"But was it worth the sorrow, do you think?"

Kate watched Virginia weep as she followed the casket down the path. "I can't speak for my sisters, but I have a feeling they would agree with me that 'yes,' it was worth it, though for different reasons. But for me it was worth it because I learned something wonderful. I learned that love is stronger than hate."

The End

adze: similar to an ax and used for shaping and trimming wood

Allan Pinkerton: famous for creating Pinkerton's National Detective Agency, the first detective agency in America and for many years America's only reliable police force. In 1873, Pinkerton was hired by the Philadelphia and Reading Railroad to investigate Molly Maguire activity in Pennsylvania's anthracite area.

anthracite coal: a hard coal; best for heating and one that gives off little smoke

Anthracite Monitor: A union paper owned by individual members of the WBA for twenty dollars a share. Published in Tamaqua, Schuylkill County.

AOH-Ancient Order of Hibernians: A respectable international Irish fraternal society whose chapters in the Pennsylvania anthracite district seems to have been infiltrated by the Molly Maguires in the 1870s. Pinkerton's inside man, James McParlan, eventually infiltrated this group himself, and was able to compile a list of those he believed were Molly Maguires. It was largely due to his efforts and testimony that nine Molly Maguires were executed in the yard of Pottsville Prison between 1877 and 1879.

barouche: an enclosed four-wheel horse drawn carriage, containing two facing double seats

Benjamin Banner: Editor, for forty-four years, of the Pottsville paper, *Miners' Journal*, and the man who perhaps did more to vilify the Molly Maguires than anyone else during that period.

Blakely Colliery: fictitious colliery

breaker: part of every colliery, it was a huge structure comprised of high walls and a large, noisy room full of iron chutes that ran from the height of the breaker to the floor and carried coal, already crushed by the crushing machine, in order for the slate, rock and other refuse to be separated out.

breaker boys: young boys who straddled the chutes while picking out the debris from the coal

breasts: the area of the mine where coal is being removed

broderie anglaise: whitework embroidery which creates eyelets, usually on fine white linen or cotton

butty: a miner's helper who carried his tools and assisted him

cambric: cheap thin cotton fabric

coffin notice: a threatening notice sent by the Molly Maguires to those they wished to intimidate. It usually had a picture of a coffin or other threatening visual aids such as a knife or skull.

colliery: the complete mine which included not only the mine but all supporting facilities

culm: the coal refuse picked out of the chutes

culm banks: huge piles of refuse found in every colliery and often where the children and wives of mine laborers picked out bits of coal for their daily needs. A hazardous task since the pile could shift and bury the pickers.

Farrell family: fictitious family

Five Points: a notorious crime ridden slum in New York City in 1800s.

flux: a stomach disorder marked by diarrhea

Frank B. Gowen: President of Philadelphia and Reading Railroad, under whose control the railroad dominated transportation and almost all coal mining operations in the lower anthracite region of Pennsylvania in the 1870s. During this time the Philadelphia and Reading became one of the richest companies in the world. The violent backlash made Gowen hire Allan Pinkerton to infiltrate the infamous Molly Maguires. It was Pinkerton's operative, James McParlan, the "inside man" who was finally able to bring down this group. But Frank Gowen's story does not end well. After the railroad went into receivership in 1880 he was fired and subsequently committed suicide.

full coal: loading five or six four-ton coal cars per day

gangway: a tunnel, the main highway inside a mine used to haul coal from the various chambers

garret: an attic

Gaylord family: fictitious family

green goose: a young goose

John P. McCartney: called Prince of Counterfeiters, famous counterfeiter who eluded the law for years. One of Allen Pinkerton's cases

John Pott: Pottsville was named after him.

Joshua Adams: fictitious character

Higgins Patch: a fictitious patch, but one that closely resembles the many patches or small villages owned by the company operating the nearby colliery

Irish Sheet Iron Gang: Irish gang

Irish Speaker: spoke Gaelic, the Celtic language used in Ireland and Scotland

laggings: wood, often tree branches, used between the shoring timber in a mine to give added support

Lamballe bonnet: small, similar to a pill-box but more oval, secured by strings under the hair at back of head and also with a ribbon tied under the chin in a large bow

Mattson Colliery: fictitious colliery

miner's asthma: later called "black lung;" the lung disease miners get from working in the mines and breathing in coal dust

Modocs: a Welsh gang

moiré: a fabric with shiny finish and wavy pattern

Molly Maguires: a "so-called" secret organization of Irish immigrants who were either miners, mine laborers or had once been, and who used violence to settle disputes or perceived injustices, as well as in efforts to make things better for the miners and laborers.

Morgan Powell: a Welsh mine superintendent assassinated by the Molly Maguires for favoring the Welsh over the Irish

nib: the sharpened end of a quill pen

Patrick Burns: foreman of the Silver Creek Colliery, killed by the Mollies

Pennsylvania Bureau of Industrial Statistics. In 1873 the Bureau put out a "Report on Labor" which praised the WBA for their peaceful work in bettering labor relations in the anthracite region while warning of the possible danger posed by the rapid accumulation of collieries by the Reading Railroad.

Pottsville: In 1870s largest city in Schuylkill Country; its county seat; surrounded by numerous deep anthracite mines

Schuylkill County: lower Pennsylvania anthracite region that lay in the diocese of Philadelphia

shalloon: a twilled woolen fabric

Sherman Colliery: located on Pottsville's Sharp Mountain

Sweet Air: fictitious town

Timothy Webster: English born, came to America when he was twelve. One of Allan Pinkerton's best operatives who was hanged as a spy in Richmond, Virginia during the Civil War.

WBA: Workingmen's Benevolent Association; A trade union that sought better pay and working conditions for coal miners, and a major obstacle to the Reading Railroad and Franklin B. Gowen's plan for obtaining a mining monopoly in the lower anthracite district of Pennsylvania

Whitework: an embroidery technique where fabric and stitching are the same color, usually white linen

Widows Row: housing set aside by the more generous collieries for the widows of miners. The only obligation the widows had was the stipulation they take in boarders, those who worked in the colliery. It was a win-win situation because the widows got free housing and the collieries drew in more workers for the mine.

AUTHOR'S NOTE

When researching for *The Daughters of Jim Farrell* I fell in love with Pennsylvania and those hardy and wonderful men and women who lived and worked in mining country. But my research also reinforced my belief that man is incapable of governing himself without God.

At the time of the story, two opposing forces met and clashed in this area. In 1871, under the leadership of Franklin B. Gowen, the Philadelphia and Reading Railroad began devouring the lower anthracite district of Pennsylvania. By 1872 the railroad owned 98 collieries and 80,000 acres of coal land, changing coal country forever. By 1875 only 36 collieries remained in the control of independent operators. Having a lock on the coal mines, working conditions worsened, causing the mine workers to organize the WBA or Workingmen's Benevolent Association, a trade union that sought better pay and working conditions for coal miners. This takeover by the railroad also saw the resurgence of a group who employed violence and worked outside the law, a group that became known as the Molly Maguires.

There's no historical evidence that the WBA ever used violence or intimidation tactics. Unfortunately, as time progressed, some of the tactics of the Molly Maguires infiltrated into the practices of subsequent labor movements. The callous indifference of corporations toward their workers, and their obsession with profits often at the expense of everything else in times past, and to a much lesser degree in the present, as well as organized labor's willingness to trample individual rights, their willingness to use violence, intimidation, force, and sometimes outright dishonesty, and to promote mediocrity at the expense of excellence, is a reminder that unless God builds the house they labor in vain (Psalm 127:1)

The Daughters of Jim Farrell is also a story about forgiveness. God often uses trials to show us our true character and our need for His cleansing touch. We are all sinners in need of forgiveness and a Savior. True peace is found only in Jesus Christ. If you don't know Him, won't you change that now by confessing to Him that you are a sinner, then ask Him into your life? It will change you forever.

Blessings to all,
Sylvia Bambola
Website: http://www.sylviabambola.com
Email: sylviabambola45@gmail.com

QUESTIONS FOR READING
GROUPS / CLUBS

• In Chapter 3 Joshua Adams reveals the underlying philosophy of Allen Pinkerton. Pinkerton believed that lying and deception were necessary in his trade, and that the end justified the means. Does the end ever justify the means? And if it does in one case, why not in another? Or are God's laws absolute? Patrick O'Brien also has the philosophy of the end justifying the means. Is there any difference between the two of them? Is there any difference between anyone who holds this philosophy?

• In Chapter 4 Virginia is surprised to learn Patrick O'Brien can both read and write, having formed a hasty and unfavorable opinion of him. How common is that? How often do we judge someone by the way he/she speaks? Or dresses? Or where they live? Is it fair? But on the other hand, shouldn't we use discernment to make judgments that keep us from dangerous alliances or situations? And what's the difference?

• In Chapter 6 Kate accuses Benjamin Gaylord of caring about his reputation at the expense of others. Then Charlotte accuses Kate of the very same thing. Are we often blind to our own faults, yet quick to see the faults of others, especially when those faults mirror our own? How can we prevent that? David asked God to search his heart for any wicked ways. Do we really need God to show us our heart or can we know it ourselves? What does the Bible say?

- Do we sometimes make excuses for those we love, like Virginia does in Chapter 7 for Patrick? Do we sometimes excuse someone for their bad behavior or bad choices, coming up with what we think are good reasons? And generally what are the results? Good or bad?

- In Chapter 8 Kate, on incomplete evidence, rushes to judgment, and in her mind condemns Martin Roach of murder. Though she is partially right about his being a scoundrel, she was quick to conclude he was also a murderer. How easy is it to condemn someone, especially someone we don't like? What does the Bible say about this?

- How important are manners? Though at times Charlotte may appear silly and excessively concerned with protocol, doesn't her preoccupation with them suggest some level of consideration for others? What happens to a society when manners become less important or disappear altogether?

- In Chapters 8 and 9 Virginia acts recklessly by not disclosing that Patrick knows the identity of Mr. Blakely's killer. Does love sometimes make a woman reckless? Is this why it is so important for a woman to be discerning when it comes to choosing a man, a husband? How often has the dangerous lifestyle of a man brought down a woman? Or pulled her into unwise or unwanted situations? Can you name some in the Bible, or in your life?

- Is anyone really free to love another as long as he/she is ruled by bitterness and unforgiveness? Why or why not?

- The fools gold paperweight symbolizes all the vain and foolish efforts of man to acquire wealth apart from God, as well as the effects of greed upon a life. How has striving for riches affected your life or the lives of those you know and love?